Love and D

E.L Shorth

Copyright © 2022 E.L Shorthouse All rights reserved

The characters and events portrayed in this book are fictitious. Any similarity to places, real persons, living or dead, is coincidental and not intended by the author.

No part of this book may be reproduced, or stored in a retrieval system, or transmitted in any form or by any means, electronic, mechanical, photocopying, recording, or otherwise, without express written permission of the publisher.

ISBN Print: 9798515004590

ISBN eBook: B09967H6Q5

Cover design by - Star Child's Book Design and Pre-Mades

Editor: Lin Lasky - Book Dragon Edits

Formatter: Mary Meredith - On Pointe Digital Services

Contents

Dedication	V
Authors Note	VI
1. Chapter One	1
2. Chapter Two	5
3. Chapter Three	9
4. Chapter Four	14
5. Chapter Five	19
6. Chapter Six	23
7. Chapter Seven	28
8. Chapter Eight	33
9. Chapter Nine	37
10. Chapter Ten	42
11. Chapter Eleven	46
12. Chapter Twelve	51
13. Chapter Thirteen	56
14. Chapter Fourteen	60
15. Chapter Fifteen	63
16. Chapter Sixteen	68
17. Chapter Seventeen	73
18. Chapter Eighteen	77
19. Chapter Nineteen	82

20. Chapter Twenty	86
21. Chapter Twenty-One	90
22. Chapter Twenty-Two	95
23. Chapter Twenty-Three	100
24. Chapter Twenty-Four	104
25. Chapter Twenty-Five	108
26. Chapter Twenty-Six	113
27. Chapter Twenty-Seven	117
28. Chapter Twenty-Eight	122
29. Chapter Twenty-Nine	126
30. Chapter Thirty	130
31. Chapter Thirty-One	134
32. Chapter Thirty-Two	138
33. Chapter Thirty-Three	142
34. Chapter Thirty-Four	146
35. Chapter Thirty-Five	150
36. Chapter Thirty-Six	154
37. Chapter Thirty-Seven	158
38. Chapter Thirty-Eight	163
About Author	167
Also By	168

I would like to dedicate this book to everyone who reads it or has read my other books. To everyone has worked so hard to get this book complete because it hasn't been easy. Thank you to every single person in my life for the support on my writing journey.

Author's Note

Love and Darkness is book one of two. Love and Light with be released later in the year. Yes, the book is shorter than my other books, but book two will be longer.

Chapter One

KAYLA

I head into Burns Law Firm to collect my best friend for lunch, she works here as a corporate lawyer. The firm works with some of the biggest businesses in the state of New York. I am very proud of her, Elaine has worked so hard her entire life to get to where she is, and trust me, it wasn't easy for her, but she did it. Her drive, confidence, and tenacity are inspiring.

I say hello to the receptionist who knows me since I am here at least twice a week. I usually chat with him for a little while, but he is on the phone and looks busy. I head towards the elevator as Elaine works on the fifth-floor. I am not walking up all those stairs. I don't have the energy this morning, I'm exhausted after working night shift at the hospital.

I step into the elevator and hit the fifth-floor button. Just as the doors begin to close, a foot wedges between the doors, and someone slips in next to me.

"Didn't you hear me call out asking you to hold the doors?"

The sound of a man's annoyed voice makes me look up. I see a man who is at least six feet tall or more, glaring at me. He's handsome, with an angular jaw covered in a dark stubble, slicked back black hair, and plump lips, but is ruining his looks with the way he's frowning.

"No, and there is no need to be rude about it."

"Excuse me?" he snarls.

I roll my eyes and move further back into the elevator, turning away from him and rest against the wall. I am not even going to engage with the douche.

"Has no one ever told you it is rude to ignore someone who has asked you a question?"

"I don't need to answer to you for anything. I don't even know you." I am not in the mood for him.

"And? Weren't you taught manners as a child?" he snaps.

Seriously, what is this guy's problem? I look up to find him standing closer to me than he needs to be. It was then his eyes get my attention. They are gorgeous, a deep brown color. I am a sucker for a nice pair of eyes. I lose my train of thought for a moment and then snap myself out of it when I remember he is an arrogant douche.

"Yes, but it goes both ways. You were the one that came in here all annoyed and rude because I didn't hear you call out to me."

"Or you purposely ignored me, angel."

"Do not call me that. I didn't hear you, okay. You can accept it or not, it's your choice."

"You could always make it up to me?" he says with a smirk. Why is he smirking at me?

"No thanks. I have nothing to make up for."

"Maybe not, but I think you should let me take you for a drink."

Is this man high or something? What part of this conversation makes him think I would join him for anything? Are we having the same conversation? Nothing I have said to him has hinted I am interested in him.

"Not if you were the last man on earth. I have a boyfriend." This is a lie. I am single, but he didn't need to know it.

"If you say so, your loss, sweetheart," he says with a laugh.

Sweetheart? God, I hate it when someone calls me that! I roll my eyes again and put my attention on anything that isn't him. I swear this is the slowest elevator ride I have ever been in. I want it to end and get away from him! Although I do have to admit he smells good, his scent is intoxicating. Overall, he is a good-looking man. It's a shame about his attitude and arrogance though.

The second the elevator comes to a stop and the doors open, I dart out. I look over my shoulder and see he's getting off on this floor also.

"Hey, Rae. Is Elaine free, or in a meeting?"

"Hello, Kayla. No, she is free. Her last appointment didn't show. You can head through," she says with a smile.

Rae is Elaine's assistant and has been since she started here two years ago. I quickly chat with Rae before heading toward Elaine's office, not even glancing back to see where Mr. Arrogant has gone. I knock on the door before I peek my head in, just in case she is on a call or something.

"Come in," she says with a smile, visibly happy to see me.

"Hey, how has your day been?" I ask with a smile.

"Busy, and not bad. Well, I'm slightly annoyed because my last client didn't show up, or even get in touch to tell me he wasn't coming," she sighs, and shakes her head, "but I am used to it with him."

"He sounds like an asshole," I say with a giggle.

"And you would be right," she agrees with a laugh. "How was your shift last night?"

"Hectic, but I am used to it, working in the ED and all."

I have been a nurse for a couple of years. I like my job because I love helping people, but sometimes it isn't the easiest job in the world.

"After lunch, you go straight home and get some sleep, okay?" She says firmly.

"Yeah. I will because I'm back on tonight, but thankfully after tomorrow I'm off for a couple of days."

"You will be ready for them, that's for sure."

I nod, and Elaine signs out of her computer and grabs everything she needs for us to head out. Just as we reach the door, someone comes in. I look up, and see it is none other than the guy from the elevator.

"You are late, Mr. Maddox. You were supposed to be here an hour ago," Elaine spoke sharply to him. Was he one of her clients?

"I know, I am sorry. I'm here now," he said.

His voice is deep and manly, the type of voice that sends a shiver down your spine and straight to your vagina.

"And? I am going out for lunch. If you want me to see you, come back in an hour."

"I don't have a damn hour to waste," he responds, sounding annoyed. So far it seems to be his usual state I think to myself.

"Well, if you were here when you were supposed to be, then we wouldn't be having an issue right now, would we? I am not giving up my lunch break for you."

"Fine, we can have a meeting over tea."

There is a hint of a smirk resting on his lips when he says it. Elaine looks at him and raises her brow.

"We have been through this before, Mr. Maddox, that will never happen. So, you can either come back in an hour, or come see me first thing tomorrow."

He groans and runs his fingers through his dark hair.

"I will come back in an hour. I am moving into a new place tomorrow so won't have time to stop by," he said. "I will give you my new address."

"Okay. I will see you back here in an hour."

He nods, mumbling goodbye and heads toward the door. He stops and turns to face us before walking out. His attention falls squarely on me.

"My offer still stands, angel, if you want to go for that drink," he says saucily with a wink. "Your friend has my number if you want it."

"As I told you in the elevator, not if you were the last man on earth," I snap.

He let out a loud laugh and finally leaves. The man doesn't give up easily, that is for sure, but there's no chance I will meet him for a drink. I shake my head and face Elaine because I can feel her watching me. She stands there with her hand on her hip and a 'what the fuck' look on her face.

"I met him in the elevator. He was rude and arrogant, then tried to hit on me."

"And you said no? Why? Yes, he is a jackass, but he is hot," she says, she looks incredulous.

"I don't care. He is an asshole," I groan. "And what if you were single, would you have said yes to tea with him?"

"No, because he is my client."

"Yeah, I am not going there. I have had enough idiot men in my life. I do not wish to have another one."

"I understand, but you need to get laid, babe. It has been too long."

"Yes, that is true, but I sure as hell will not be fucking him."

"Okay, if you change your mind, let me know, and I will give you his number since he gave me permission to," she smirks, looking happy with herself.

I flip her off as I laugh, and begin to walk away. I hear her chuckle from behind and she quickly catches up with me. We discuss where to go for lunch as we make our way to the elevator.

"Do you want to go out this weekend since we are both off?" she asks.

"I like that plan. We haven't been out in a while, and we both deserve a night to let loose," I can't help but grin at the idea of a night out.

"Sorted. Saturday night?" she suggests.

"That works for me."

We will invite our other friends to make the most of it. We don't get to see each other much due to our jobs, we all work in sectors that have long assed hours, and by the time we all finish work all we want to do is go to bed, and it shouldn't be that way. We are still in our mid-twenties, we should be out more, enjoying life, but it is easier said than done. Elaine and I are the only ones who see each other the most out of our group of friends.

We head out of the building and just as we exit we hear, "Hello again, ladies." I know who it is straight away.

"Can we help you, Mr. Maddox?" Elaine asked.

"Come on. I have been your client for a year now. I am sure you can call me Luca," he says with a smile.

"Can I help you, Luca?"

"You can't, but your friend can."

"What do you want, Luca? I am not interested in you, and I have a boyfriend, so leave me alone," I reply firmly.

"I don't believe you, but okay. I am sure I will see you around, sweetness," he winks. He swaggers off after that.

"He thinks you have a boyfriend?" Elaine laughs, looking at me shocked.

"I thought it would make him back off, but obviously not."

"You are lucky he doesn't get to see you more because he isn't a man who gives up easily."

"It seems I have had a lucky escape then," I giggle.

Thank God I don't need to see him again, unless I run into him when I visit Elaine. Hopefully, it will not happen. I don't know how she puts up with him.

"I am so hungry," Elaine states as we arrive at the restaurant.

"Me too," I agree.

I haven't eaten yet today. When I got home from work, I had a shower and got ready for lunch, I didn't have time to eat. I will not tell her that. She will give me trouble for not eating. I am the nurse, yet she is always getting onto me about my health. I am the same with her. I need this, our friendship, it gives us both a chance to rant about everything that happens at in our personal lives or work because the line of work we are in we don't always have such good days, it was a support system for us. My lunches with Elaine always made me feel better.

Chapter Two

LUCA

I'm heading over to my new apartment after my appointment with Elaine. I don't officially move in until tomorrow, but I nearly have all of my things there, so I decide to head over and start to put things away. My meeting with her was interesting. It was supposed to do with my business interests, but I spent most of my time trying to get information on her friend. I didn't get much, only her first name, and she let it slip that Kayla doesn't have a boyfriend. She lied about it, the little minx. It got to the point where Elaine got pissed off at me, and we finally got down to why I was there.

Kayla piqued my interest the moment my eyes fell on her. She is gorgeous, and that body of hers is incredible! She is at least a few inches shorter than my six-foot frame, maybe around five feet seven but I am no expert. She isn't my usual type, I usually prefer blondes, and she's a brunette. Plus, the way she got all snarly and feisty with me was sexy. I don't have many people in my life who stand up to me like that, or answer me back. Elaine and Kayla are some of the few who do.

I arrive at my new building and head inside. The place has ten floors, I am on the third-floor. It was an upgrade from my last home. My previous building was nice, but I had been there for a while. This building is more luxurious. I have more money now, so I can afford a place like this. I like how the building is secure, because you can't trust people. I even have a doorman called Archie.

"Good afternoon, sir," he smiles as I approach his desk.

"Good afternoon."

"We weren't expecting you back until tomorrow," he replies.

"I know, but I thought I would come and make a start."

"Yes, why not. Enjoy your day, sir."

"You too," I respond.

I decide to use the stairs rather than the elevator. There are only a few flights. I'm a fit guy and taking the lift would be laziness. I take the key from my pocket as I reach my floor. I walk along to my apartment and put my key into the door to unlock it, but as I place my hand on the handle—

"You must be my new neighbor," I hear from behind me.

It's a female voice, and I recognise it, but I can't quite put my finger on where I know it from. I am not the kind to get to know my neighbors. I tend not to have too many people in my life, and that is my choice. I groan to myself, put a smile on my lips and turn around. The moment I do, my smile turns into a smirk.

"We meet again, Kayla."

"You? What the hell are you doing here?" she huffs.

With a wink I say, "I am your new neighbor, angel."

"You have got to be joking!" she groans and flings her hands in the air.

"Nope," I say smugly.

However, I am curious about what she does for a living if she can afford a place like this?

"Could this day get any worse?!"

She didn't speak to me after that, instead, she just opened her door and rushed inside. I laugh as I make my way into my place. This is perfect! With her right across from me, I am going to have a lot of fun. I'm not looking for anything serious, just a little fun. I don't do dating or relationships. I do one-night stands and casual flings.

I push Kayla to the back of my mind, for now I have a lot to do. I start in my bedroom and then work my way through the apartment. The kitchen and living room are open plan. I have two bedrooms, two bathrooms, an office, a balcony, and a great view. It is understandable why they were so expensive to buy, they are high-end. I could have bought a house, but what would have been the point? There is only ever going to be me living in it. I will never get married and don't plan on having kids, so buying a house would be pointless. I would be a shit husband and father—the same way my father was.

I got a lot done, but then I was fed up with it. I need something to occupy myself because when I do nothing—that is when my dark thoughts happen, and I don't want them. Then I have an idea. I think I may need some sugar, which I do have, but Kayla doesn't need to know that. I exit my place and go across the hallway to hers. I knock loudly on the door. I am sure when she sees through the peephole it is me, she might not be happy, I doubt she will even answer the door.

I hear her footsteps get closer, and then they stop. Kayla is on the other side of the door. I know right now she can see me. I'm surprised when I hear her opening the door. She came into view, and I can't help but look her over. She only has a tee and a pair of boxers on. Damn, those legs of hers are gorgeous, never-ending. I wouldn't mind those wrapped around me. I feel my length twitch at the thought of it.

"What do you want, Luca? I am trying to get some sleep before work tonight."

"I am looking for sugar. Do you have any?" I ask innocently.

"You came here for sugar?" She has her arms crossed over her chest and arches an eyebrow as she says it. I think she seems suspicious of me when she spoke.

"Yes. Why do you think I came over?"

"I don't know, but yes, I do have sugar," she answers. "Come in."

I nod, and she stands to the side to let me in. I walk in and look around. The place is identical to mine, size and layout wise.

"Brown, white, or sweeteners?" she asks, going to the kitchen.

"White. Have you stayed here long?"

"About two years. It was my aunt's place, but she moved away and gave it to me." At least that answers one of my questions about her earlier.

"That was nice of her."

"Yes. I could never afford a place like this otherwise."

Kayla reaches up to the top shelf of the cabinet, and as she does the tee she has on crawls up, giving me a nice view of her ass, which her boxers cover unfortunately. I run my eyes over her ass and thighs. Fuck! She is sexy. I lick my lips and groan to myself.

"See, if you don't stop perving on me, you will be wearing this sugar, Luca."

"I am sorry, I couldn't help myself. You have a nice ass."

I hear her mumbling under her breath before she gets back entirely on her feet. She swings around and glares at me.

"What? I am only complimenting you," I shrug.

Kayla rolls her eyes and finds something to put the sugar into for me. She grabs a cup and fills it up.

"Here you go. Now can you please leave? I need to get some sleep."

"What work do you do?" I question curiously.

"I'm a nurse."

"So, you enjoy helping people then?"

"Yes."

I couldn't do a job like that. My bedside manner is terrible, and I don't do well dealing with people. Yes, I'm in business, I have meetings and whatnot, but I don't need to be nice to them. They don't expect me to be nice to them. As long as we get the work done, that is all that matters.

"Long-assed shifts then?"

"Yes. I work anywhere between twelve- and fourteen-hour shifts. It depends," she replies.

I know how she felt in a way. I work long days too, but somehow, I think her work would be more challenging than mine. She'd constantly be on her feet. My days are usually ten hours, though.

"Do you find time for a social life?" I ask.

"Not as much as I would like."

"You need to find a better balance, angel."

"No offense, but that is none of your business."

I hold my hands up and drop the topic of conversation. Kayla walks me to the front door.

"If you want some company, or a way to de-stress, you know where I am," I say. "I am good at helping women out that way."

I am not the best person. I am not good at much, except for two things—business and sex.

"I am sure I will be fine."

"Okay, but my offer stands if you change your mind."

"Goodbye, Luca."

"Goodbye, for now, sweetness."

I flash my best smile at her before she closes the door. I sigh and head into my place. I check the time. It's only three o'clock. The very few people I do have in my life are all still at work, and it's too early to go to a bar. I set the sugar down and instead grab a glass and bottle of scotch, and pour myself a double and down it. I pour another, then go over to my piano. I set the glass and myself down, lift the lid, and start to play. Music helps soothe me and keeps the dark thoughts at bay.

I close my eyes and let my fingers do the work. I let the sound of the music take over me. I learned to play when I was twelve, and since then playing has always been an escape for me. I get lost in my own little world, losing track of time. I change the song I was playing without realizing it, and the second I notice, I stop. I slam down the top, grab my drink and gulp it down.

"Fuck!" I hiss and throw the glass at the wall.

It shatters on my floor. I need to get out of this house. I grab everything I need and head out. I will clean the mess up later. I start walking around with no destination in mind. The sounds surrounding me are a good distraction. I pass a few bars and am tempted to go in, but change my mind. That will not do me any good. I just need to make it until about seven o'clock, and then I can visit someone who will make me feel better and forget about everything else. We have an arrangement. She and I help each other out when we need it. All we know is each other's first name and age, nothing more.

Maybe coffee would be best for me right now. If I was in a coffee shop, then there is less chance of me going to a bar. I stop at the closest place and order myself a large black coffee, and find a seat away from everyone else.

I sit there thinking and come up with a plan. I am sure Kayla won't want to cook a proper meal before she goes off to work. And she needs to eat a good, substantial meal. I assume she will start between seven or eight o'clock so I can pick tea up for us both and stop by her place about six.

I only hope she doesn't close the door in my face. I would need to get something simple because I am not sure what she eats. Everyone loves pasta, right? Pasta with a side salad, tasty and healthy. It may not entirely be for her benefit, but partly for mine, also. It will save me from eating alone yet again. I hate feeling lonely, but I don't want anyone in my life. It is a no-win situation for me.

I give myself a shake and get back to drinking my coffee. I can stay here for an hour or two. That will help pass some time. I sigh to myself and run my fingers through my hair. It's just another day, and I will get through this one like every other one before and any that come after it.

Chapter Three

KAYLA

I'm in my kitchen, trying to decide what I want to do for tea. I'm looking for something quick and easy; I'm in no mood to cook. I have everything ready to take to work with me, so that was out of the way at least, and this way I won't need to be rush around. I open the fridge and went to reach for the leftover pasta from yesterday, but I don't get a chance because someone knocked on my front door.

I wasn't expecting anyone, but I have a feeling who it might be. I sigh, closing the fridge I go to answer the door. I look through the peephole, and standing on the other side is Luca, right enough. He has what looks like takeout food in his hands. I mumble to myself and take a deep breath before answering it.

"Hi," I say as I open the door.

"Hey, angel, have you eaten yet?"

Why does he keep calling me that? I shake my head; Luca takes it as an invitation to come right in.

"Haven't you got better things to do than have tea with me?" I question him as I close the door.

"Nope! Do you like Chinese? I hope you do because it's what I have brought with me."

"I do, yes. Thank you."

Yes, he was a complete ass when I first met him; maybe that is who he is, but it was sweet how he brought me food. I got us some plates while he laid the food out. He has way too much food for only two people.

"I wasn't sure what you liked, so I mixed it up a little and hoped you might like at least one of these dishes," he says with a rueful chuckle, as he passes a hand through his hair.

"I like most Chinese dishes," I say with a smile, hoping to ease him.

"I will remember that for next time," he grins.

Next time? What makes him think this will be happening again? Does he believe we are making a habit of this? I don't reply to him. When I turn back around that is when I notice his hand is wrapped in a bandage, and there is a little blood seeping through it.

"What did you do to your hand?"

"I accidentally smashed a glass. I cut myself when I was cleaning it up," he shrugs and runs his fingers through his dark hair.

He didn't do an outstanding job of patching it up. If he doesn't clean it properly there's a risk it could become infected.

"Let me look at it."

"It's fine. It is only a cut. I am sure I will survive."

"I wasn't asking, Luca."

I make sure my voice is firm. Luca cocks his brow at me. I demand he follows me, which he does. I lead us to my main bathroom, where I keep my first aid kit.

"Sit," I state.

"Are you always this bossy?" he questions.

I don't think he's used to someone telling him what to do.

"Luca, sit your ass down, now. Don't make me ask you again."

He holds his hands up, eventually doing what I ask. He sits on the edge of my bath, and I kneel in front of him.

"Give me your hand."

He does what I ask. I remove the bandage from around his hand and take a look at it. At first glance, it doesn't look like he hurt himself by picking glass up. Instead, it seems like he broke a glass in his hand.

"So, do you want to tell me what really happened to your hand?"

"I told you what happened."

He sounds nervous when he replies. I look up at him, and he turns away from me. He is lying, but I sense he doesn't want to talk about it. I left it at that. It isn't my place to push. A silence falls between us while I see to his hand. I have to take shards of glass out with a pair of tweezers; he doesn't even flinch, it's like he doesn't feel it. I clean it up with antiseptic wipes, put a little cream on it, before I wrap it up properly in a bandage.

"All done. Keep an eye on, okay?"

"Yes, nurse," he says with a smirk. I roll my eyes at him and he laughs. I put everything away.

"We should eat before it gets cold. I need to leave soon for work."

"Thank you for taking care of me," he says with a smile.

"No, bother."

We head back through to the kitchen. We plate the food up and take it over to the sofa and eat there.

"What time do you finish?" he asks.

"Eight in the morning. I am off this weekend, which I am thankful for. It has been a busy week."

"Any plans?"

He sure asks a lot of questions. I inform him of my plans with Elaine.

"What about your boyfriend? Where is he?"

"Um, work..." I feel my entire face heat, something which tends to happen when I lie. I am a terrible liar! It is a good thing, most of the time, but not always.

"You are a terrible liar. I know you don't have a boyfriend. Elaine let it slip out."

Thanks, Elaine!

"Oh. Okay, I am sorry I lied to you. I wanted you to stop hitting on me."

"Which was pointless because as you saw it didn't stop me," he replied smugly.

With a snicker I say, "Yes, I picked up on that."

He smiles brightly at me and turns back to eating his food. I do the same. With nothing else said between us. I begin thinking, I don't know if I should worry about his wound because it looks like it was self-inflicted. There is no point enquiring about it to him because he will get defensive and shut down.

"How do you get to work?" His question pulls me out of my thoughts, and my attention falls back on him.

"I walk. It only takes me fifteen minutes from here."

"No. I don't like it. I will walk you there. You shouldn't be walking alone, especially not at night."

"I will be fine. I do it all the time."

"I don't care! I am walking you to the hospital. End of discussion."

There is an authority to his tone. I don't need him to do walk me. I can take care of myself. I can try to argue with him on it, but it will be pointless, he won't listen.

"Fine!" I huff.

"Don't huff at me, gorgeous. I am only looking out for you."

I roll my eyes at him. I stand to take my plate to the kitchen, Luca following only seconds later.

"Do you want to take this food with you?"

"No. You can put it in your fridge or the trash."

I wasn't wasting all of this food. I will put it in my fridge and eat some of it tomorrow. I put it into containers and take them over to the fridge, as I place them in, Luca suddenly comes up behind me. He's closer than he needs to be.

My breath hitches, and I shudder as I feel his warm breath against the skin of the back of my neck.

"I knew you were attracted to me," he whispers seductively. "Here is the rest of the food."

He reaches over me to put the things in. His body brushes against mine. I bite down on my lips to stop a moan from falling from them. Yes, the man irks me, but it is hard not to be attracted to him. Elaine is right. I need to get laid! Maybe it will help me get my senses back.

Luca lets out a small chuckle and steps back. I take a moment to pull myself together before I close the fridge and swing around to face him. I find him resting against the counter, with a stupid sly look on his face.

"I should get going to work."

"Yes, you don't want to be late," he replies.

"I just need to grab my bag."

"And a coat. It's cold outside," he pipes in.

I put my coat on and grab my bag. I hope he has changed his mind about walking me to work. We head out of my apartment. I want him to go across to his place, but he doesn't. It would seem he hasn't changed his mind.

"You honestly don't need to do this, Luca."

"I know, but I want to," he smiles. "Plus, I am going to see a friend in that direction."

At least he has another reason to go in this direction.

"Okay." I respond simply.

"Have you lived here long, in New York City, I mean?" he questions.

"Since I was eighteen, so about six years. You?"

"Since I was sixteen, so, about fourteen years."

Luca randomly asks me questions on the way, basic ones. But when I ask him the same questions, he avoids them and turns the conversation back to me. It feels like no time has passed until we arrive at the hospital. He walks me to the entrance.

"Thank you for walking me here, and for tea."

"You are welcome, angel. Thanks for fixing my hand," he replies, then kisses my cheek.

"Goodnight, Luca."

"Goodnight, Kayla."

He flashes a charming smile at me before he walks away. I watch after him and sigh before making my way inside.

"Damn, who is that fine specimen that walked you here?" My colleague Lesley-Ann asked.

"My new neighbor."

"Since when do new neighbors walk people to work?" she asks with a huge smirk. I assume she doesn't believe me; I wouldn't believe me if I was her either.

"He insisted." I giggle. "And nothing is happening between us before you say anything."

"You should get on that. The man is gorgeous."

"I know he is, but he is an ass. I don't want to get involved with him."

"Hey, you don't need to like him to fuck him," she says then laughs loudly.

I shake my head, then laugh with her, and we head towards the locker room to get ready for our shift. Hopefully, tonight won't be as hectic as last night.

I am completely done in as I leave the hospital. Last night was crazy! I am glad I have my days off now.

"Good morning, sunshine."

The sound of his voice makes me look up.

"Luca, what are you doing here?"

I wasn't expecting him to be here, yet here he is standing against a car.

"I was on my way to work and thought I would bring you coffee." He offers me a cup as he speaks, which I gladly take.

"Um, thanks."

"Can I give you a lift home?" he asks. "I don't usually have my car for work, but I have a meeting outside of the city today."

Not many people drive in New York City for various reasons. The fact that he has his car with him surprises me. With traffic and parking spaces not being the best, most people walk, take cabs, or use the subway.

"I can walk, thanks. I don't want you running late because of me."

Luca insists. I follow him into his car, and he drives us back. We make small talk on the way. I'm not sure if I should be worried about why he is being nice, especially after the way he was when we first met. Maybe he has some plan, or my first impression of him was wrong. Who knows?

"Stop by after you finish work so I can take a look at your hand." I tell him when we pull up outside the apartment building.

"Sweetness, if you want to see me all you have to do is ask. You don't need excuses."

And there he is! The man I dealt with yesterday.

"Goodbye, Luca."

I quickly climb out of his car and make my way inside. My plans for this morning are to shower, have breakfast, and then sleep for a few hours. After that, I need to go food and clothes shopping for an outfit for tomorrow night.

I am ready for a night out with my girls.

Chapter Four

LUCA

I have never been so glad to get out of a damn meeting in my entire life. Most of them are incompetent idiots! Thankfully I only need to deal with them every three months. I wish my workday is already done, but sadly it isn't the case. I have to drive back into the city and go to my office. Thank God I have two days off after this. I could hire more people to work for me, which would mean I'd work less, but it'd be laziness. At least when I do it myself, I know it gets done right. I have worked my ass off to get to where I am. I am not allowing anyone to ruin it.

I rush to my car before anyone could stop me and ask another stupid, pointless question. If I had to spend another second with them, I'd have lost my mind. I rest back on my seat and sigh. I need a breather. I check my phone because I haven't had a look at it since this morning before the meeting. It lasted nearly three hours.

I have emails and calls regarding work. A text from a friend just checking in, and lastly, a message from my 'lady friend' thanking me for last night. I will deal with them later.

I set my phone aside, close my eyes and let out a loud breath. I am shattered. I slept for maybe an hour last night. I got lost in my thoughts of Kayla. I know she didn't believe the story I told her about my hand. The truth is I did it to myself. I broke a glass in my hand on purpose, just so I could feel something after I got back from having my coffee, I needed something stronger. She is a nurse after all, I am sure she could tell what happened.

While I thought about Kayla an idea came into my mind. Opening my eyes, I pick up my phone and call Elaine's office. It didn't take long for her assistant to answer and put me through to her.

"Hello, Luca. How can I help you?" she answers, her voice sounding surprised I'm calling.

"Hey. What are the chances of you giving me Kayla's phone number?" I ask hopefully.

"No chance at all," she laughs. "What are your intentions with my best friend?"

"Aww, come on! I know she wants me. I want her also, so why beat around the bush?"

"Not the point. Kayla isn't like that. If she wanted to give you her number, she would."

"Fine! You deny your best friend the pleasure of incredible sex," I say with a laugh. "I will get her number on my own, which should be easy since we are neighbors."

"What? Since when?"

"My new apartment is right across from hers."

With a sardonic chuckle she says, "Oh, well, this could be interesting."

I chat with Elaine for a few minutes, then give her my new address before we hang up. It was worth a try. I will get Kayla's number from her personally later. I start the car and go on my way. I only have six hours to go, maybe less if I decide to work from home for a couple of hours; I do that when I have had enough of dealing with people. My patience with humans is on the lower scale.

I need a coffee before I go to my office. It didn't take too long to get back into the city. I stop by a coffee shop close to my office. I have been here a lot over the years. I may have fucked one or two of the workers. Thankfully things aren't weird with either of them. I find a parking space and make my way inside. The place isn't busy, and I am soon being served.

"Hey, Luca." Ebony smirks.

"Hey, sweet cheeks. Can I get my usual, please?"

"Coming right up, handsome."

As she makes the coffee, Mona comes over to say hello.

"Are you ever going to call me?" She asks with a pout.

"That will be a no," Ebony answers for me, laughing as she comes back over.

"I know," Mona spoke.

I like how they don't expect anything from me. I am always clear with my intentions before jumping into bed with anyone. It makes things less dramatic for everyone involved. The three of us flirt back and forth as I pay and take my coffee.

When I turn around, I am met with Kayla standing there and shaking her head at me. She is staring at me intensely with her baby blues.

"Hey, angel," I say with a wink.

"Don't call me that," she snaps at me.

Kayla seems annoyed with me! Her brows are furrowed and she is tapping her foot on the ground.

"If I didn't know any better, I would say you are annoyed at me."

"You are such an arrogant, male hoe."

I laugh loudly. People have called me that multiple times and much worse.

"Are you jealous? Would you prefer if all of my attention is on you?"

Kayla rolls her eyes, shakes her head, and barges past me to give her order. I think I may have made her mad. I wait for her to get her order so I can walk her out. Kayla has other ideas. She walks by me and heads straight for the door. I say goodbye to the girls before going after her.

"Kayla, wait up." I call after her.

Surprisingly she stops and turns.

"I got shit to do. What do you want, Luca?"

"Why are you mad at me?"

"I am not mad," she says with a nonchalant shrug.

"You seem it."

"I am not mad or jealous, okay? Now, I need to go. I will see you later."

"If you insist," I respond. "I will be there about six o'clock."

She nods and says goodbye, and we go our separate ways. I smirk as I go back to my car. I'm still convinced she is jealous, and it's the reason why she's pissed off at me. I will annoy her later about this. It will give me something to look forward to.

I'm getting ready to head over to Kayla's place. I got home an hour ago, but I had a shower and quickly reply to some emails. I dress in joggers and a tee. I'm not going any further than Kayla's apartment, so there's no point in putting proper clothes on. I chose to leave my phone at home because I didn't want to take it with me. If anyone wants me, they can wait until later. I grab a bottle of wine before I leave and head over to her place. It only takes her a moment to answer my knock. She is dressed in sweats, her hair is pulled back, and there's no make-up in sight, yet she looks gorgeous.

"Hey, gorgeous."

"Hello, again. Come in," she says with a smile.

She steps aside to let me I walk in. I hand her the bottle of wine.

"Thank you. I will get us glasses after I see to your hand," she says firmly.

"Yes, boss." I can't help but laugh.

She glares at me but eventually laughs too. Kayla demands I sit on the sofa while she gets her first aid kit.

"How is your hand?" she asks when she came back.

"It is fine. It's not painful at all." It hurt when I did it, but now I wasn't feeling anything.

"Give me your hand."

I give it to her, and she gets to work. Her hands are soft and warm, they feel nice on my skin. I watch her closely. The look on her face as she concentrates is cute, her tongue is slightly out and her nose wriggles.

"All done," she finally announces.

She looks up at me, her face is only inches from mine. I want so badly to kiss her, but she might slap me; I will eventually kiss her, but it all has to do with timing. Instead, I lean in and stroke a few stray hairs away from her face. Kayla's eyes connect with mine, and I hear her breathing speed up.

"Wine—" she cuts off abruptly, "I should go get us some wine," she says more firmly.

"Hmm, if you like," I whisper.

I can sense a part of her didn't want to pull away. In the end the opposite facet of hers wins, and she pulls back. She stands quickly and disappears to get us wine. At least she isn't throwing me out after checking my hand.

Kayla takes longer than needed to get us wine. I have a feeling she's composing herself after our moment. It's evident she's trying to fight her attraction to me. Elaine said Kayla isn't into the kind of thing I want. She finally re-joins me.

"Here you go," she says as she smiles and passes me a glass. I thank her as she sits next to me.

"Did you get what you needed when you were out today?"

"Yes. Groceries and an outfit for tomorrow night."

"An outfit? What did you get? Can I see?" I'm curious about the way she dresses when she goes out.

"I bought a dress, and no, you can't see it," she laughingly says.

"It was worth a shot." I shrug and have a sip of my wine.

I feel a little strange sitting here with a woman just talking and drinking. I am usually naked and fucking them, not doing this. I don't even know what to say to her. I'm not much of a talker.

"What business are you in?"

"Mainly real estate, that is how I started. Over the last couple of years I have ventured out of that and have shared ownership in a couple of big advertising companies and online sites, only to name a few," I answer, "but, I don't want to bore you."

"Oh, wow, that is a lot. What sort of real estate?" I don't mind discussing my work because it isn't as personal as other things.

"Apartment complexes, condos, clubs, and so forth."

"Do you own this building?" she asks curiously.

"No, just my place. I wanted to buy somewhere to live that has nothing to do with my business."

Kayla questions me about work, and after some time I'm fed up talking about it. "Can we change the subject?"

"Sure," she says.

With a grin I ask, "Good. Let's talk about you and what type of man you usually go for." Yes, this is a more exciting topic to discuss.

"Um, in what way?"

"Looks to start us off."

"I am a sucker for a man with nice eyes and a smile. Brown eyes are my favorite," she blushes.

I have brown eyes!

"Personality-wise?"

"A man who can make me laugh. A man who is sweet and passionate in every aspect."

Hmm, part of what she said could describe, well—me—minus the sweet factor, because I am nowhere close to sweet. This doesn't mean I will not change her mind, though, and bring her to the wild side.

"I could ask you the same thing, but something tells me the type of women you go for varies," she says giggling.

That is true, but it would strictly be Kayla if I have to choose a specific type.

"It does vary, but if I had to describe it, then you are my type." Kayla looks like she didn't believe a word I was saying to her.

"Bullshit! A man of your standards goes for women who are close to perfection. Women who are not me."

"Kayla, you are beautiful. You could be the definition of perfection." I'm not lying. She is as close to perfect as one can be, well, in my eyes. Kayla is the kind of woman I should stay far away from because I will ruin her. I would drag her down, but knowing I shouldn't go after her just makes me want to do it more.

"Nonsense."

She shakes her head, downing the last of her drink. "Drink up. I will get us another one," she adds.

I do as she asks and hand her my empty glass. I don't believe she wants to talk about this anymore, so I will drop it, but not permanently.

Chapter Five

KAYLA

Patting my tummy I smile in contentment, nothing like left over Chinese the next night. Adding good company and two bottles of red wine, I have a happy buzz.

"Pass the vodka, angel." I pass it to him thinking he's been really nice to be around tonight.

"I am curious, Luca, why are you spending your night with me? Is there no woman craving your attention?"

"There's always women craving my attention," he says with a smirk. "Yet the one I seem to be craving right now doesn't want me."

"I am sure she has a reason for it." I have a feeling he is referring to me, but I don't want to say anything in case he is talking about someone else.

"And would you like to share the reason with me, angel?"

"Because I am not that sort of girl," I respond.

"I don't believe it's the only reason."

It wasn't the only reason, but it's the suitable one. Plus, I don't have the energy to fight the trouble which would come with him. I honestly believe the moment I give into him I will lose all of my senses. This is the last thing I want or need.

"Humor me. What other reasons do you think?" I want to know what his thoughts are on this.

"I believe you fear the attraction between us. You worry I will break you out of your comfort zone, and discover sides of yourself you never knew existed."

"You think very highly of yourself if you think you can do all of that to me." I reply and raise brow.

"Do you disagree with what I am saying?"

"No comment," I shrug. What a terrible way to respond because we all know what it means when someone says that. He is more accurate than I like, but I am not giving him any leverage because I refuse to go there.

"I will take that as a yes," he says, laughing gleefully. "You will break, eventually. I don't know when or how, but you will."

"If you insist."

"I do, but until then I will back off."

I don't think I believe him, but I will act as if I do. He reaches over, resting his hand on my knee, making circles with his fingers.

"This doesn't look like you are backing off, Luca."

"I know one thing, sweetness. I always get what I want. And when I get what I want, I don't like to share," he said. "So, when I finally get you under me, I will be the only man you will want or need."

"I don't know how you expect that to happen because I enjoy going on dates, and you only want sex. So, if I do give into you, then you wouldn't be the only one I would need because you would only be taking care of me sexually. I want more than that."

"Yes, that is true. I only want sex because I don't do more than that. I don't want anyone close enough to me to see my fucked-up ways, and trust me, that is better for everyone," he whispers.

I'm surprised by his words because he isn't one for getting personal. "Fucked-up ways?" I have to ask. I see him tense up when I ask the question.

"Forget I mentioned it. Do you want another drink? Do you want to go out for a drink? Or you can come to mine. I have plenty to drink there."

He keeps rambling on and I know it is because he wants me to forget the things he's said. I sit here in silence while he continues. He isn't even stopping to take a breath. He needs to stop before he passes out.

I reach over, and rest my hand on his knee as I look at him.

"And breathe, Luca," I say gently.

He looks back at me, and I notice a sadness in his eyes which wasn't there moments ago. I believe there is more to his story than I could imagine. Luca stops talking and takes a couple of breaths.

"Thank you," he tells me with smile. "But I do need an answer to my drink question, or we can go to your bedroom and do more exciting things."

I sense he mentions my bedroom as some sort of defensive mechanism so I wouldn't bring up the way he was only moments ago.

"No, Luca, we can't go to my bedroom," I reply and pull my hand away from him.

"It was worth a try. Do you have any more drinks that aren't vodka? I don't like what vodka does to me if I drink too much of it."

"No, I don't have anything else."

"Do you want to come to mine? I have wine and scotch."

I won't be drinking much more because if I do, I might not make my night out tomorrow. One more won't do any harm, plus I don't want him to go away and be alone. I'm not sure why, but my gut tells me leaving him by himself right now isn't a good idea.

"Yes, we can do that. I will only have one more, two at a push, since I am going out tomorrow," I say to him.

He nods, and we put the plates and glasses into the sink before heading over to his place.

"There are some things lying around, so be careful," he warns as we enter.

I look around, the place is beautiful. It's the same as mine, well, the layout is, but everything else is different. Some of the furniture he owns is something I can only dream of.

"This place is incredible," I gush while I look around.

I notice he doesn't have any personal effects. There are no photos or anything like that in sight. Maybe he hasn't unpacked them yet.

"Thanks," he says, shrugging. "It is only things."

"I guess."

"Scotch or wine?" he asks.

"Wine, please. I don't drink scotch for a good reason," I say with a laugh.

"Hmm, I think I need to know the story behind this," he says, smirking at me.

Luca got us some wine, and motions for me to join him on the sofa insisting I tell him the story.

"I have many, but they have a lot of factors in common. Those of which are dancing on tables or bars, hooking up with men I wouldn't usually, putting detergent in a fountain dressed as a unicorn, and nearly stripping and going skinny dipping."

I had done a lot of that while I was in college, except for the latter one—which was only last year—the whole nearly stripping thing.

"Are you sure you don't want a scotch or two? I want to experience your fun side."

"Are you trying to say I am boring?" I say with a pout.

"I am still working that out."

"I am offended," I huff. "I am a fun person who enjoys the good things in life."

"You may need to prove it to me," he says, trying to challenge me.

"And I will! Do you have something in mind?"

I like to enjoy myself, but it takes me time to come out of my shell. I need a lot of coaxing. I am sure his definition of fun is different from mine.

"I will think of something," he says with a chuckle. "Although you can finish that stripping for me if you like."

"Sorry to disappoint you, but you will never see me naked," I reply slyly.

"You shouldn't tell me shit like that because it will make me work harder to get it," he smirks. "And trust me, angel, I can have you naked in my bed within minutes if I try hard enough."

"Yeah, right. It takes a lot for me to get into bed with someone," I tell him with a laugh. "And a good start is usually a date or two."

"Come on now, are you trying to tell me you wouldn't love to have a man just take complete control and fuck you senseless? No attachment, no expectations, just pure, passionate, wild sex?"

I do admit it does sound good. I have never had a man take control of me in that way. I have thought about it, fantasied about it, but never had the confidence to tell a man to do that or been with a man who wanted to do that.

"I would say by the way you have disappeared into your own little world and from the look on your face this is a thought that excites you."

The sound of his voice brings me out of my thoughts.

"Hmm?" I query.

"A man has never done that for you, has he?" he asks, and I shake my head. "Well, you are missing out. Any woman I have been with loves it."

"I am sure it will happen one day," I say with a shrug.

"Give me a shout if you want that day to happen sooner rather than later."

"I will keep you in mind," I tell him with a giggle.

We need to change the subject; all this sex talk is getting to me since it has been a while since I have had any.

"We shall leave the conversation there for now."

"Thank you."

I keep my reply short and sweet because he doesn't need to know how long it has been since I've been laid. I am sure he would try and use it to his advantage.

"When was the last time you had a boyfriend?"

"Um, over a year ago," I say. "Have you had a girlfriend? Or has it always been only sexual for you?"

"One, and no. I don't want to talk about it." The last words came out in more of a snarl. I guess this is a touchy subject. I turn away from him and take a sip of wine.

"Kayla, I am sorry. I didn't mean to talk to you like that."

"It is fine. You have nothing to be sorry for."

Maybe the one girl has something to do with the way he is now, but it is none of my business.

"I should put some music on, lighten the mood," he says with a smile.

"Yes."

It is better than sitting in silence or having a conversation turn stilted between us. I will be going home soon anyway. It is an excellent way to pass the time.

Chapter Six

Luca

It takes me a moment to realize I am in my bed. How the hell did I get here? The last thing I remember I was sitting on the sofa, drinking and flirting with Kayla. The way my head is spinning suggests I had way too much to drink. Slowly sitting up I search for my phone to check the time. I find it on my bedside table, it's not in the usual place where I keep it. The time is four in the morning. I don't know how long I have been out. Usually when I am wasted I can sleep for roughly four hours if I am lucky, rather than only a couple I have most nights.

Did Kayla put me to bed? When did she leave? I hope I didn't act like too much of a jackass and scare her off. I climb out of bed to get myself a bottle of water. I go into the kitchen, and that is when I see her. She is asleep on my sofa; Kayla is still here.

She is curled up, and sound asleep, but she doesn't have anything covering her. It is cold now. She might be feeling it. I think for a second, trying to remember where I put the blankets, they were put in the spare room. I quietly go to fetch one, making sure not to wake her. Finally, I find what I am looking for and head back. I crouch down in front of the sofa and place it over her. I brush the hair away from her eyes. I sigh. She is so beautiful. I don't understand why she is still single. She seems to be a genuine, sweet, and caring person. Any man would be lucky to have her. If I had relationships or marriage in mind, Kayla would be the type I would want that with. Whoever ends up making her his, I hope he knows what he has.

Kayla stirs, and I pull back. I don't need her seeing me like this. Thankfully she doesn't wake and instead shifts into a different position. I think the best thing for me to do is go back to my bedroom.

I take a drink of water before climbing back into bed. I probably won't go back to sleep. I reach into my drawer and take a photo out I keep there. It's one of the few photos I do own.

"I miss you, Leah," I whimper, looking at her face. I shake my head, run my fingers into my hair and quickly put the photo away. I need to stop looking at it, it isn't helping me any, but I can't stop because it would feel like I had forgotten when I haven't. I lay there staring at the ceiling for a while. I close my eyes and hope sleep will come. It didn't work. I hiss in frustration because I know it isn't going to happen.

There isn't much to do at this time of the morning. I decide to switch the TV on, with the volume low and found some shit to watch. I could watch porn, which I do, but I won't, not with Kayla in the house. I will do this for an hour, then sneak out for a run, maybe pick breakfast up for us, well, if she is still here. I am not sure why she stayed when her apartment was right across the landing.

I get lost in the show until I hear a knock on my bedroom door.

"Luca, can I come in?"

"Yes." I hope I wasn't the cause of her waking up. She stayed near the door.

"Why are you awake? Are you okay?"

"I don't sleep well at night. I am okay."

I smile, and ask her to, "Come sit," patting the spot next to me. Kayla considers it but finally nods and comes over.

"How did I get to bed? Why did you stay?" I question her as soon as she settles.

"I put you to bed. You were highly drunk, staggering around," she tells me, "and I stayed because I want to make sure you were okay. You seemed sad."

Sad? God, I hope I didn't blurt out my secrets of the past. No one knows everything about my past, and I prefer it that way.

"Did I say why I was sad?"

"No, when I asked, you changed the subject. I felt like you didn't want to talk about it, so I didn't push."

She seemed concerned about me, which I don't understand. How can she feel that way for someone she doesn't even know? It is just another thing which shows she is a decent human being.

"Was I a dick about it?" I ask, hesitantly, not sure if I want to hear the answer.

"No. Do you want to talk about it?" she said softly.

"I don't. It is nothing personal."

"I get it," she says with a sweet smile.

Silence fell between us after that. Our attention turns to the screen.

"Maybe I should go back to my place."

The next thing I would say were words I haven't said to someone in a long time. I don't know if it is a good idea to say them, but here goes.

"Stay, please?" I stammer out.

"If you want me to," she replies. "I will go back to the sofa. You try and get some sleep."

"I mean in here, with me."

Kayla looks at me, in surprise. Trust me, I am more surprised than her about this. I get lonely a lot, and I usually use sex to stop the feeling, but that isn't what I want right now. Even if sex is what I want, it won't happen with Kayla. I just want to have someone next to me.

"Do you promise to behave?" she asks me firmly with a raised brow.

"I promise," I laugh.

"Okay, then turn the TV off, and we can get some more sleep."

"Yes, boss. You keep your hands to yourself. I know how tempted you will be," I say to her with a smirk.

"Oh, I will try my best." Her voice is dripping with sarcasm when she spoke. I chuckle, shaking my head I switch the TV off as she asked.

Kayla and I slip under the covers. I don't know if having her next to me will help me go back to sleep. We say our goodnights and turn in opposite directions. It is strange to share a bed with someone again just to go to sleep. I sigh, close my eyes, and hope sleep will take over.

I'm spooning Kayla. What a way to wake up. She is curled tightly into me, somehow, she seems to fit perfectly. I don't know my thoughts on that.

I slowly part from her and check the time. It is nine in the morning. I don't remember the last time I slept this late. Maybe to another person this is a normal time, but not for me. I am usually up between five and six o'clock. I climb out of bed, grab my running clothes, and head to the bathroom to change. A run is what I need to help clear my head. I will cut my run short this morning. I don't want to leave Kayla alone for too long. I feel refreshed for a change. It is amazing what a decent night's sleep can do, even if it was broken. My energy levels feel high also.

I double-check Kayla is still asleep before leaving. A part of me hopes she will be gone when I get back. However, there is another part of me which wants her to be in my bed. Everything in my head is confused.

I put my AirPods in and go for my run. I block everything around me out. I run for half an hour, dodging around people and objects with a light heart. I'm feeling better for it. I stop by a café to grab food and coffee for us both. If she has left I can just take it across to her.

I arrive back at my apartment, and put everything in the kitchen before I check my room. Kayla is still here and is sitting up when I enter.

"Hmm. Why are you all sweaty and flushed?"

"I went for a run," I tell her with a shrug.

Kayla didn't say anything. Why? Because she was too busy checking me out. I grin to myself while she does.

"I am going to have a shower. There's breakfast and coffee in the kitchen."

I fist the bottom of my tee in my hands and bring it over my head. A small moan escapes from Kayla's lips. I kick my trainers off and finally remove my shorts. I'm only in my boxers. Kayla's eyes are glued on me watching my every move.

"Like what you see, angel?"

Her eyes finally meet mine; her face is flushed. I think I may have excited her. I don't know what changed from yesterday. She is being obvious about her attraction to me, rather than masking it the way she has been.

"Sorry," she whispers.

"I don't mind."

I hook my fingers in the waistband of my boxers, going to take them off too. I have nothing to hide. I like my body, scars and all. I worked hard for it, and it is probably the only thing I sort of like about myself.

"No, you can keep them on." Her voice is soft, yet a little hesitant. Kayla giggles and covers her eyes with her hand.

"I will save these goodies for another time. I can't show you everything at once," I said before continuing, "I need to leave something to your imagination."

I laugh loudly before leaving the room to have a shower. I feel Kayla checking my ass out while I do. I switch the shower on and step into it, deciding to make it a quick one. I step out, wrap a towel around my waist, then dry my hair off with another one. Kayla isn't where I left her, she must have gotten up. I dry myself off and put a pair of joggers on.

Kayla is plating breakfast up when I arrive in the kitchen. She glances up for a moment, and then quickly turns her attention away from me.

"You could have put a shirt on," she said under her breath. I don't think I was supposed to hear her.

"Why? Is my half-naked torso distracting you, sweetness?"

"I didn't say anything," she responds innocently.

"I have said it before, you are a terrible liar." She rolls her eyes at me while I sit myself at the breakfast bar. She joins me, and slides a plate over.

"What are your plans for the day?" she asks between bites.

"Um, to get you into my bed." I pop a forkful into my mouth after I spoke.

"I meant in your real life, not in your dreams," she said teasingly.

"Mean!" I huff.

Kayla gives me a sly look and puts a strawberry into her mouth. She licks her lips slowly. I begin to imagine how her tongue would feel in my mouth, or along my length. My cock twitches at the thought. My mind is going back to the place it felt safest, the sexual place. I need to snap out of it.

"Luca, come back to me." The sound of her laugh brings my attention back to her.

"Sorry, my mind drifted."

We get back to eating breakfast, neither of us speaking. After we are done, we clean our mess up.

"I should go home. I need to have a shower and change."

"Okay. I have shit to do, anyway."

I have nothing to do, but I don't want to seem pathetic. Plus, I've spent enough time with her over the last couple of days. I need to put a space between us.

"See you around," she smiles.

I walk her to the front door.

"I think you should give me a kiss." I may as well try my luck.

"Nice try, but nope," she said with a laugh.

"Enjoy your night with your girls. If you want some "company" tonight, give me a knock."

"Thanks for the offer."

Kayla kisses my cheek before she saunters over to her place. I watch her leave, groaning. I need to get her below, above or in front of me. I need to up my game.

I will get her, eventually. I always get what I want. And right now, she is at the top of my list, a mark on my to-do list if you like. I can't let things get the way they did this morning again. I can't deal with that!

Chapter Seven

Kayla

I've enjoyed my weekend so far. Today is my last day off, and I plan on having a day at home alone. I had fun with the girls last night. Thankfully I'm not hungover, which surprises me because I've drank two nights in a row. It's been a while since I've done that.

As for Luca, I haven't seen or spoken to him since I left his place yesterday morning. I'm not going to lie, I nearly knocked on his door last night when I came home, but I came to my senses. I would have regretted it this morning if I did. I was drunk and horny, but I got over it. Jumping into bed with Luca would have been a bad idea! No matter how badly I wanted him last night.

I'm lying on my sofa reading a book. A part of me wants to go make sure Luca is okay. I'm worried about him. The way he was when I saw him drunk the other night broke my heart. I don't think I have ever seen such sadness in another person's eyes before. It is evident he is fighting his own battles and demons.

I set my book aside, get to my feet and head to the front door. I pause to think for a moment, asking myself if going to see him is such a good idea? After fighting with myself I decide to see him. It only needs to be for a minute so I know he's alright. I make my way across the hall to his place. I take a deep breath before I knock loudly. He doesn't answer, so I knock again. If he doesn't respond this time, I will leave it. I don't even know if he is home.

I turn to walk away but as I do I hear his door open.

"Hey, angel," he chirps.

"Hello," I reply as I turn to face him.

He looks like crap. His hair is a mess, and his eyes are heavy. It looks like he hasn't slept a wink.

"What's up?" He asks.

"I just wanted to make sure you were okay. That's all."

"I am fine. Why wouldn't I be?"

I don't want to answer him with the wrong words because I know if I do, he will back away and probably slam the door in my face.

"No reason," I shrug.

He steps aside and gestures for me to come in. Once I enter I hear him shut the door. Luca comes up behind me and rests his hand on the small of my back, he leans in so close his breath tickles my ear. I believe he is doing this to get to me, to see how I will respond to having him in my personal space.

"How was your night, sweetness?" He abruptly pulls away and appears in front of me.

"Did you get lucky? Were you drunk?" He seems sort of hyper. I can't help but wonder if he is on something, or if it could be down to him not sleeping.

"Yes, it was a good night. I was quite drunk, but no, I didn't get lucky."

"Did you want to get lucky?" He smirks before he steps into me.

"No, thank you," I say with a giggle. I can't believe his audacity.

"You suck," he says with a pout.

He puts distance between us and starts to pace. I glance around; there is no sign of drugs. He then begins to ramble on, half of which isn't making any sense.

"Luca, are you on something?" I blurt out.

"What? That is none of your fucking business, Kayla," he snaps.

"Sorry, but you seem extremely hyper and jittery," I reply softly.

He looks at me, shakes his head and storms off to his bedroom. Maybe I shouldn't have mentioned it. I sigh, run my fingers through my hair and leave, going back to my place. I may be barking up the wrong tree, but there is something not right with him.

I switch the kettle on to make myself a coffee. I get myself a snack, carrot sticks and hummus, yum! I get lost in my thoughts while I prepare everything. I feel bad for just blurting it out like that. I will go and apologize to him later. It isn't my place to say anything.

I take my place back on the sofa to continue to read my book. I push everything to the back of my mind and get lost in my novel. I don't know how much time has passed, but I get pulled away from it with a knock on my door. I groan, but put my book aside to answer it. I look through the peephole and am surprised to see Luca on the other side. Maybe he has come to shout at me. There is one way to find out, isn't there? I open the door to him.

"Hi," he said nervously while rubbing the back of his neck.

"Hi."

"Can I come in, please?" I nod, stepping aside so he can enter.

"I am sorry I snapped at you, Kayla."

"It is okay. It isn't my place to ask, Luca. I am sorry too."

He takes a spot on my sofa and leans into it. I get him a cup of tea before I join him.

"You were right," he whispers.

"You are on something?"

"Yes, coke. I had a bad night, and I took more than I should have."

"Do you use it a lot?" I pry.

"Not all the time, but on the odd occasion. It's a bad habit I picked up a few years ago." I can hear in his voice he is ashamed of it.

"Why?"

"For many different reasons. I know it doesn't help, not in the long run, but at the time, it does. I don't want to discuss the reasons before you ask."

"I understand you don't want to talk about these things, but if you change your mind, Luca, you know where I am," I reply gently.

He gives me a grateful nod. I sense he doesn't want to talk about it anymore. I think him telling me what he did wasn't an easy thing for him to do. I appreciate his honesty.

"Didn't anyone pique your interest last night?" he asks, looking at me.

There were a few guys who hit on me, but I wasn't interested in them. Also, Luca was on my mind, so that wasn't helping things.

"Nah, not really."

"Or were you too busy thinking of me?" he asks.

"No," I protest.

I chose to leave the part out about me nearly knocking on his door last night. The man doesn't need an ego boost.

"I don't believe you, angel."

I roll my eyes at him before swiftly changing the topic of conversation. I know he will be coming down soon from the drugs. I can see him getting tired.

"What are you reading, some soppy romance book?" He screws up his face as he waits for me to answer.

"No, it is a crime book. But what is wrong with romance novels?" I love reading a good romantic story.

"Because they suck! They build up too many expectations of what love should be when in reality it is just another thing that hurts you." I assume by his answer he has had his heart broken.

"The only way love hurts is when you are with the wrong person. It doesn't need to hurt, and if you are with the right person it shouldn't hurt."

"It doesn't matter if you are with the right or wrong person, it still ends up breaking you in the end. I'd rather not have it in my life at all," he responded. "Love is for the weak."

"Life would be lonely without it."

"I do just fine without," he shrugged.

No, I may not have love in my life in a romantic way, but I still have love with my friends and family. I have a feeling he doesn't have anyone in his life. I can't imagine not having anyone.

"That makes me sad hearing you say that, Luca."

"Don't be. I am fine," he replied. "Can we change the subject now, please?"

I nod and do as he asks. His energy levels seem to be subsiding. I don't think he will be able to stay awake for much longer.

Luca has crashed out on my sofa a couple of hours ago. I left him to sleep and threw a blanket over him. I've been keeping as quiet as I can because I don't want to wake him. He's going to feel like shit when he finally wakes.

I decide to make us some tea. I'm scouring the fridge to find something to cook. Hmm, a chicken stir-fry sounds good, something simple and tasty. I start the preparation. I enjoy cooking when I have the time. I usually have my music playing when I do, but I know it would disturb Luca. I soon get lost in what I'm doing, going into my own little world.

"Can I help?" I look up and see Luca coming towards me.

"No, I got it. Do you like chicken stir-fry?" I asked.

"I do, but you don't need to make me tea."

"I know, but I want to. How are you feeling?"

"Like crap, but I have no one to blame but myself." I tell him to get a bottle of water from my fridge, he needs to keep hydrated. Luca sits down at the counter. I feel him watching me.

"You are staring. Do I have something on my face?"

"No, you don't have anything on your face," he says with a laugh. "I'm admiring you."

"Admiring me? Why?" I ask with a chuckle.

"Because I want to. You are so naturally beautiful," he says with a smile.

His compliment sounds genuine. "Thank you," I say. I'm not able to stop blushing.

"You always seem to be smiling, well unless you are annoyed with me," he says, barking out a laugh. "How can you always be doing that with all the bad in this world? With the job you do."

"Because you need to see the good in the world, it isn't all bad. Yes, I see a lot of horrible things at the hospital, but I see a lot of good also."

"I wish I could view the world through your eyes," he says with a sigh. His laughter from earlier had disappeared.

"You could if you try," I say.

"I appreciate your enthusiasm, but that won't happen." Hmm, maybe I can change that. I need to come up with a plan. Someone needs to show him the good in the world because he clearly hasn't seen much of that.

"That smells good," he says, taking a deep breath in and releasing it.

I know he wants to stop talking about what we were so I let him change the subject; nothing will be gained by pushing the issue. I finish up cooking tea and plate it up for us.

"Thanks, beautiful," he says with a wink.

We sit on the couch to eat. "Do you want to watch a movie?" I ask.

He nods, so I find us a movie to watch. We become silent as we get busy eating and watch what was on.

I can't remember the last time I spent this much time with a guy in the way I have done with Luca these previous few days.

"You cook well. It has been a while since I have had a home-cooked meal."

"You can't beat it," I grin.

I would offer to cook for him again, but it may freak him out, or give him the wrong idea. The man needs someone in his life, even if it is only a friend. I am sure he has plenty of sexual partners, I'm sure he won't be lacking three, but it is a different type of connection. With the way his walls are so high, he obviously doesn't let anyone close.

I don't know how long he will stay tonight, but that is okay. It means I can keep an eye on him, and neither of us needs to be alone.

Chapter Eight

LUCA

Kayla suggested we move from the living room to her bedroom because I'm not feeling too good. She's taking care of me since I got here. It's simple little things, like making sure I wasn't hungry, or I was drinking enough, and warm enough. It is sweet of her; I just don't understand why she wants to do this. She barely even knows me. Or, maybe it is because I'm not used to it.

I roll onto my side to face her, and she does the same. Kayla gives me a soft smile. I reach over to brush the hair away from her face.

"Why are you single? You are like the perfect woman." I just blurt it out.

She laughs off what I said. "I don't think so."

"Yes, you are. You are beautiful inside and out. You have a heart of gold. You care for people and work your ass off."

What the hell is happening right now? Why am I being so nice? I don't do nice. Yes, every word I spoke is accurate, but I shouldn't be the one saying it. I blame the drugs and the lack of sleep; they are messing with my head.

"That is sweet, Luca, but it isn't true." Kayla turns away from me. I guess she doesn't believe it.

"You still didn't answer my question. Why are you still single?"

"I've never had much luck with men. The last one I was with I was engaged to, I believed he was the one I would spend the rest of my life with."

She was engaged. Then why the hell didn't the guy marry her?

"What happened?"

"Turned out he didn't feel the same. I found out he was having an affair. Thankfully we hadn't set a date for the wedding," she replied and turned to face me again.

What type of a man would cheat on her? Not a real man, that is for sure. I will be the first to admit I am an asshole, and I don't treat women the way I should, but I could never stray. If I was in a relationship with someone like her, I wouldn't find it in me to cheat on her. No, I will never be in a relationship again, but if I did get into one by some miracle, I wouldn't mess the woman over like that.

"He obviously didn't realize what he had."

"His loss," she says with a shrug.

"Yes, his loss," I agree.

Silence came between us, although we didn't break eye contact. I reach over again, only this time I stroke her cheek with my thumb.

"Thank you for taking care of me, not only tonight but the other night too. You didn't have to. I don't deserve it," I said.

"It is my nature to care. Everyone deserves to be taken care of, Luca. Even if they don't want it."

I was going soft tonight. If it was anyone else but Kayla I was talking to, I'd turn back into jackass mode right about now, but I can't, not with Kayla, not after everything she has done. I think the sensible thing for me to do is to leave.

I sigh, putting distance between us.

"I think I should leave," I whisper.

"Why?" Kayla asked, confused.

"It's for the best."

"Stay? Please?"

The way she is looking at me is freaking me out! The look in her eyes was doing something to me. If she keeps looking at me like this, I will give in to her and stay. That isn't a great idea! Kayla searches my face and waits for me to respond.

"W... why?" I stammer out, "you don't need me in your life, angel,"

Kayla crawls across the bed to kneel in front of me.

"Why do you want to leave?"

"Because you are making me soft, Kayla," I blurt out.

I watch as a look of surprise comes over her face. I didn't mean to say it out loud. Unfortunately, I can't take it back now.

"Luca, if you want to go, then go," she says, shaking her head.

Is she mad at me for wanting to leave? I groan in frustration as I run my fingers through my hair. I don't know what to do now. Should I stay, or should I go? Neither of us speak for the next few minutes. Instead, we stare at each other intensely. I briefly see Kayla's eyes dart from mine down to my lips and then back up. Is she thinking about kissing me at this moment? I lick my lips, the thought of her lips on mine consumes my mind.

"I don't want to, Kayla, I need to," I breathe out.

"Yet here you are still." Sarcasm is dripping from her voice.

"Don't get smart with me," I growl.

"Or what?" She replies in the same manner.

Is she trying to push me on purpose? Because it is working.

"Kayla, don't."

She stands up, moves away from the bed, then she turns around and comes back to me. She is only inches from me. I realize her breathing is heavy, and so is mine. How have we gone from laying in her bed talking to this in a matter of minutes? I am confused!

"Why are you still here if you are so desperate to get away from me?"

"Desperate to get away from you? You have no fucking clue what I want to do to you, Kayla," I exclaim.

Yip! The nice guy act has vanished, and now all I can think about is what I want to do to her if she would let me. I was back to thinking about sex! Kayla doesn't respond with words, rather, she looks at me with dark eyes and flushed cheeks.

The right thing for me to do would be to turn around and walk out, but I'm not good at doing the right thing. I'm going to do something that will make things harder, not easier.

I stand up, she steps back out of the way. I reach for her and grab her hips, bringing her roughly against me, and press my lips to hers. The second our lips touch she whimpers, causing me to groan. Kayla's fingers snake into my hair, and my grip on her body becomes tighter. I am a little taken back by how good this kiss feels. Yes, it is a passionate kiss, but a wave of calmness takes over me too. The sort of calmness I haven't felt in years.

I turn us around and push her against the wall. I trap her between the wall and my body, the kiss getting more heated by the second. I slide one hand into her hair, entangling her strands in my fingers. She gasps against my lips and fists my tee in her hand. Fuck! Her lips are incredible. I let my free hand run down the side of her body, over her thigh. I hook my hand under her leg and bring it around my hip, allowing my body to get closer to hers. Kayla doesn't protest; she continues to kiss me.

I can feel my heart pound in my chest, my pulse is racing, and I feel my length stir in my joggers. No, this kiss shouldn't be doing this to me, well, my excitement I can cope with, but the effect it is having on the rest of my body, I don't like that. I need to stop.

I abruptly back away from her.

"I am sorry, I can't do this."

I don't give her a chance to say or do anything which could change my mind. I rush from her apartment and into mine, slamming the door behind me as I rest myself against it. I need a moment to catch my breath. A kiss hasn't made me feel that way since Leah. No other woman is supposed to make me feel the way she did! It is wrong!

I slide down to the floor and lean back against the door. I bury my face in my hands.

"Fuck!" I hiss.

I sat there for I don't know how long.

"I'm sorry, Leah," I whisper.

I need to get out of this house. I need a distraction. I quickly change out of my joggers into a pair of jeans. I grab my wallet and house keys, put them in my pocket and head out the door.

I walk for ten minutes until I come across a bar. I go in and take a seat at the bar. I order a double scotch and two shots of tequila, downing one after another. I order the same again, and then look around. I see a sexy blonde sitting at the other end of the bar, checking me out. She smirks the second I look at her.

She motions for me to join her. "Hey handsome, you look lonely and sad," she says when I join her.

"So do you," I reply. "Can I get you a drink, gorgeous?"

"Sure," she smiles.

I place an order for her drink. Yes, she would do just fine for tonight. It's exactly what I need. I have to stop thinking and feeling, even if only for a few hours. I need to get Kayla out of my head. After what I did, I wouldn't blame her if she never wanted to see me again. I wouldn't want to see myself, either.

Chapter Nine

KAYLA

In the days since he ran away, I'm still confused by why he left abruptly. To say I feel rejected is an understatement. I gave him some time and went over to see if we could talk, but he was either ignoring me or had gone out.

I've tried to forget about it, but that hasn't worked so far. I hate how I'm such an overthinker, it has made life more complicated than it needs to be. It shouldn't bother me so much. I've no one else to blame but myself. I knew what he was like from the second I met him. I should have stuck with my first instincts and stayed away from him, well, the best I could with him living straight across the hall from me.

Today I plan to forget about all of it. I'm having a girly day with Elaine. I explained everything that happened when we chatted last night on the phone, and she decided to take the day off to make me feel better. Our plan is: breakfast, shopping, lunch with cocktails, and ending the day at my place with takeaway, wine, and movies. I'm looking forward to it because it will be a great distraction.

I gather my things and head out. When I finished my shift this morning I came home and went to bed for two hours. With only two hours sleep I got up to prepare for my day. I will be fine, coffee will give me the fuel I need.

I shut my front door to lock it. I find myself fighting with it because it's stiffened. I need to get a new one. It can be a pain in the ass as it happens to me from time to time. As I continue my fight, I hear Luca's door open behind me. No, this can't be happening! I don't want to see him! I hope he wouldn't notice me, but something tells me it is only wishful thinking.

Suddenly, I hear a female giggle and then say with a purr, "Mmm, thanks for last night and this morning."

"You are welcome, sweetness. I had fun," he replies.

I swear this is like some sick joke. Why couldn't they have come out once I'm gone? I roll my eyes while they speak to one another, the conversation is one I don't need or want to hear. I finally manage to lock the door. I turn and soon wish I didn't. I'm met with the sight of them making out. Eww, I don't need to see this.

"Call me, Dylan," she said.

Dylan? Who the fuck is Dylan? I guess he gave her a fake name. How mature of him.

"Sure thing," he replies.

She walks away, and Luca swats her ass. Luca looks up and finally notices I stand across from him. The look on his face changes when he does. He looks ashamed, but why would he be? He must do this sort of thing all the time I assume.

"Um, h... hello," he stutters.

"So, it was me after all? Cause, you sure as hell didn't seem to have a problem with her, and you don't even know her. If you do, I am sure she would know your real name," I bark out.

I didn't mean to say what I did out loud, but seeing him all over some woman who he didn't even give his proper name to pissed me off.

"What?" he asks me, he's surprised.

"Nothing, forget it, Dylan," I hiss.

"Is that what you believe, Kayla? I left because I didn't want you?"

He sounds hurt I would even suggest it. What does he expect me to think?

"Luca, I don't even care. Do as you please. It's none of my business."

"I'm sorry. I shouldn't have left the way I did," he says, then sighs.

"Whatever, forget it. I have," I tell him as I shrug.

I'm not sure if I'm overreacting to this entire thing. Maybe I am, but I'm still mad right now, and I have a right to be. I am sure once the anger stops all will be fine.

"Please, don't be like that, angel," he begs. "Can we at least talk?"

"I have things to do. Goodbye, Luca."

I walk away and ignore him as he calls my name. He is not ruining my day. I hear him slam his apartment door. I sigh as I make my way out of the building. I'm to meet Elaine at our favorite restaurant, who make the most delicious pancakes. It's only ten minutes away from my apartment.

I arrive at my destination in no time. I look around and spot Elaine. She smiles and stands when she sees me coming. We greet each other with a hug. We both take a seat and place our orders.

"How are you doing?" she asked.

"I'm okay. I ran into him on my way out."

"Oh, how did that go?"

I told her what had happened and about the girl.

"Male hoe! Are you going to talk to him?"

"Yes, he seems to be," I reply. "I will talk to him but only when I am ready."

"Yes, make him squirm for a while," she says with a laugh.

"Oh, I will," I laughed. "But enough about him."

I don't want to spend our girl's day talking about Luca. Elaine nods, and we change the subject. I am sure he will be brought up again at some point today.

"What are we going shopping for?" I ask.

"Whatever we like," she smirks.

I could do with some new clothes and underwear. I don't tend to buy myself things often, but on the odd occasion I like to treat myself.

"I need to go to a lingerie shop. Dane's birthday is next week, and you know how I love to dress up for my man," she exclaims confidently.

"Yes, I do."

Dane and Elaine have been together for about a year. They are the perfect match. I get a little jealous sometimes, not over them because I am happy for them, but for the kind of relationship they share. I want something like that.

"Talking about men—my offer still stands to set you up with someone."

"No, thank you. I will stick to being single for now."

"Fine, fine," she says with a laugh.

I will get back into dating eventually, but unfortunately my scars are still healing from my last relationship.

Elaine and I have arrived back at my place after a fun-filled day. We probably overspent, but it seemed like a good idea at the time. We drop our bags on the floor and sink into the sofa. We are exhausted.

"I needed this today, thank you," I tell her with a smile.

"Me too! I had fun," she beams. Elaine and I always had a good time no matter what we were doing

"Now, go try the dress on since you wouldn't at the store," she suggests.

I wasn't a big fan of trying clothes on. I didn't need the dress, but I liked it, so I got it. It was the perfect little black dress for all occasions.

"Okay."

I can't help but smile as I grab all of my bags and take them to my bedroom. I set them down on my bed and start to put everything away. I may as well do it while I'm here. I lay the dress on the bed and strip down.

I slip the dress over my head and look at myself in the mirror. It's a perfect fit and clings to me in all the right places. It's strapless and the hem stops mid-thigh. I smile to myself. Every woman should own an LBD. I put some heels on to see what it looks like, and altogether it looks good.

I make my way back to the living room. The closer I get I can hear Elaine talking to someone; maybe she's on the phone. It turns out she isn't on the phone after all.

"What are you doing here?" I ask him. I'm so annoyed.

Luca is standing in the middle of the living room. Why would Elaine let him in? He turns his attention to me, and the second his eyes fall on me, they go wide. He looks me up and down, a small groan escapes from his lips, and then he runs his tongue along them.

"Wow," he breathes out.

Elaine looks at me with a smirk.

"Damn girl, you look good," Elaine says.

I don't respond to her, instead, I glare at her for letting him in.

"Why are you here, Luca?"

"To talk," he answers.

Elaine excuses herself and goes to my bedroom. I'm left here with Luca. I will kick her ass for this later. God knows what he said to her that convinced her let him in.

"I don't want to talk," I state with a firm voice.

He is still letting his eyes roam over my body.

"And stop perving on me, okay? You had your chance. You blew it." My words may have come out smugger than I intended.

"Low blow, Kayla." he sighs.

"No, it's the truth. If I was ready to talk to you, I would have done so."

He shouldn't be getting under my skin like this. I am not normally a bitchy or sarcastic person, but that is the way I seem to be right now with him.

"Kayla, please, let me make it up to you," he begs.

"Why? Are you bored with your random women and decided you wanted a new challenge?" I snarl. What is wrong with me? This is not me!

"No, of course not," he groans. "I know you think I'm a complete asshole, and maybe I am, but I don't mean to be."

"Your life, your choice," I respond.

"I really am sorry, Kayla. What happened has nothing to do with you, I promise. It was all to do with me." There's a sadness in his eyes while he talks, his voice sounded strained. Things would be so much easier if I knew more of his story, but I know that isn't going to happen.

"Let me take you out for coffee tomorrow, Kayla? No expectations, just us talking things through."

He flashes puppy dog eyes at me and wets his lips. I let out a small giggle.

"Fine, coffee," I huff.

"Thank you. I will let you get back to your girl's night," he smiles and kisses my cheek.

"Okay. I will see you tomorrow, not too early though."

"Ten in the morning?" he suggests, and I nod.

He smiles brightly at me before walking to the front door. He put his hand on the handle, stops, and turns to me. "And by the way, you look damn good in that dress, angel."

With that, he walks out of the apartment. I groan in frustration and run my fingers through my hair. I don't know if agreeing to coffee is a good idea, but we should talk, especially since we stay in the same building.

I stroll to my bedroom so I can take the dress off. Elaine is lying on my bed.

"Everything okay?"

"I am mad at you," I say with a pout.

"I am sorry. I couldn't help it. He looked so sad when he showed up. The look in his eyes got to me," she replied.

"Yes, I know that look," I tell her with a rueful laugh. "We are going for coffee tomorrow."

"It's a start. Maybe the two of you can be friends."

"Maybe," I say, shrugging.

I have no clue what tomorrow will bring, but I am curious to find out. I remove my dress and change into my pjs.

"Can I ask you something without you getting mad at me?" Elaine asks.

"Sure."

"Do you like him? I know he annoys the hell out of you, and what he did the other night was a dick move, but I don't think I've asked if you like him?"

"Honestly, Elaine, I don't know. I'm still trying to work it out."

I don't know what I am feeling for Luca, but something is there. If it were nothing, then I wouldn't have kissed him the other night, and he wouldn't be irking me so much.

"I am sure you will work it out, just be careful, okay?"

"I will be, I promise. My guard is still up after what happened after the last time I let myself fall for someone."

"I get that, but you will get over it in time. You will find a good man, one that will treat you right," she said, smiling.

"Thank you. I hope so." I'm a true believer of everything happens for a reason.

Chapter Ten

LUCA

I've been awake since five o'clock and now I'm bored and frustrated. I went to the gym, showered, got dressed, and had breakfast. It's only nine o'clock and I wish I'd told Kayla nine rather than ten, but I know she has been working and will probably be tired.

I'm just thankful she's willing to give me another chance after what I did. I hated myself for doing it, and I'm still angry at myself. I shouldn't have run away like that. I've been feeling guilty since it happened. The way I have dealt with the guilt the past few days probably isn't the best. I've had three different women in bed since it happened. Sex stops me from thinking or feeling too much. The last thing I want is for Kayla to catch one of them coming out of my place.

I felt ashamed when I realized Kayla was standing there yesterday morning. The way she looked at me made me feel disgusted with myself. I've a feeling she's not only pissed at me but possibly jealous too.

I think it's evident by now I'm a screw up, and big-time screw ups are a normal setting for me, and usually I don't try to fix them or even apologize. I told myself maybe I could treat Kayla the same, but that didn't work. I have been anxious the last few days, trying to build the courage up to tell her I was sorry. That's unusual behavior for me, but knowing I had upset her—I rejected her—even without meaning to; it was fucking with my head. I need to fix it, and I hope today I can do that.

Kayla probably doesn't want anything to do with me now in a dating, or sexual way, but I hope we can at least be friends. As strange as it sounds my gut is telling me she is supposed to be in my life, no matter if I like it or not.

I begin pacing my apartment. I look around to see if I can find something to do, but there isn't anything. It is too early to play my piano. I don't think my neighbors would be happy.

I stop pacing when I hear my phone ding. It is a text message. I pick my phone up from the counter to check it and see it's from Kayla.

Hey, I'm sorry, but I don't have the energy to go out for coffee this morning. I feel terrible. I don't know if I am coming down with something X

As I read it, I wonder if it's true, or if she's just saying it because she changed her mind about seeing me? I hope it isn't the case. I sigh and start to reply but then change my mind. There is an easier way to find out, so I decide to go across to her place. If she's telling the truth, maybe I can take care of her and ensure she has everything she needs.

I've decided to get my second-in-command to handle the workload today just so I could see Kayla. Yes, the people I'm supposed to meet with are probably upset, but I don't care. It is my business. I can do as I please.

I exit my place and go to Kayla's. I knock, but not too hard, just enough for her to hear it. I wait longer than I usually need to. I realize if she isn't well then it would take her longer to answer. Finally, I hear the door getting unlocked.

When the door opens Kayla stands there in her dressing gown; she looks tired and pale. She wasn't lying. I can tell by looking at her that she is sick. I should have known better; she doesn't come across as a lair.

"Luca, didn't you get my text?" she asks, confused.

"Yes. It's why I came over to check on you."

"You didn't have to do that, but thank you." Kayla manages a small smile, but even that looks like it's hard for her.

"I know, but I want to. I'm here to take care of you."

"I'm sure you have better things to do," she says with a sigh.

"Nope! Can I come in?"

Kayla gives me a slight nod and steps aside. I walk in and close the door behind me.

"Do you want a cup of lemon tea?" I offer.

"That would be nice. I tried to eat, but I didn't manage."

"You go sit, angel, and I will get it," I tell her.

Kayla heads to her sofa, and curling up she brings her knees to her chest to hug them tight. I think the best place for her right now would be bed. I will suggest it to her after I have made her some tea. I got her tea and made myself a coffee.

"Maybe you should go to bed, Kayla," I say when I hand her a mug.

"No, I'm okay here for now. I will go lay down once I've had this."

I wasn't going to fight her on it because I'm sure it's the last thing she needs. Instead, I take the spot next to her.

"What is wrong?"

"I'm in for the flu, I believe," she sighs. "Which means I have to call work and take sick leave, and probably have to stay off work for the rest of the week."

"Do you have what you need? Paracetamol, cold and flu capsules, and whatnot?"

"Yeah, I always make sure my medicine cabinet is stocked."

She takes a small sip of her tea, before resting her head on my shoulder. So, um, what do I do? Do I wrap my arm around her, stroke her hair, or do nothing?

"Sorry, is it okay?" she asks and looks up at me.

"Yes, of course," I say with a smile.

I brush her hair away from her face. "Will you please let me take care of you today?" I ask her.

"Honestly, you don't have to. I will be fine."

"I insist." In the end, she gave me a nod. She fell silent as she sipped on her tea. I didn't say anything either. I caress her arm, and she cuddles in closer.

"I think I need to go lay down," she whispers. "I feel dizzy."

"Okay, let's get you to bed." I get up first, and offer her my hand to help her to her feet. She stumbles slightly, but I manage to catch her. I slip my arm around her and help guide her to the bedroom. I make sure she got into bed and bring the covers over her.

"Can I get you anything, sweetness?"

"No, I am alright for now. I need to sleep, though," she replies.

"You get some rest. I will clean up and go get some stuff to make soup; hopefully you will be able to eat it."

Kayla thanks me and smiles tiredly and before she lay down. I go to leave, but as I reach the door she says, "Will you lay with me for a bit?" she whispers.

I don't answer at first. I'm not sure it's a good idea.

"It's fine, Luca, if you don't want to."

I sigh, take a deep breath, and turn to her saying, "Okay."

I slip my shoes and hoodie off before I climb into bed. I lay down next to her, and she rolls over, and curls into my side. I freeze at first, until she rests my hand on her chest, and I hear her breathing, then I feel my entire body relax.

"Thank you," she says, giving me a kiss on my cheek.

I pull the covers over us, and it doesn't take her long to fall asleep. I sigh and watch her while she is sleeping. Even though she isn't well, she still looks beautiful. I reach for her and stroke her cheek, only with light touches because I don't want to wake her.

"I am sorry I hurt you, Kayla. I didn't mean to. You scare the hell out of me. You deserve better."

Maybe I should try to get some sleep too since I didn't sleep well last night. The only time I had Kayla sleeping next to me I slept better than usual. I am still confused by all of this between us. I don't know if it's a good or bad thing. I have a lot to work out in my head. Finally, I close my eyes and pray sleep would quickly take over.

I slept for two hours before I get up. I let Kayla sleep while I ran to the store to get things to make vegetable soup. It's in the pot, cooking away. I have cleaned up the little mess in her apartment. I take a bottle of water from the fridge and go to the bedroom. As I enter, Kayla is just sitting up in bed.

"Hey, how are you feeling?"

"Like crap. How long was I out?" she asked.

"Four hours. The soup is cooking. It won't be long."

"When did you get up?"

"A couple of hours ago."

I hand her the water, and she takes two flu capsules with it. I grab a spot next to her on the bed.

"Do you think you will manage some soup?" I hope she will because she needs to eat something.

"I will try, but not too much. And then I think a bubble bath is in order." She giggles.

"You get yourself organized, and I will run your bath. Anything particular you want in it?" I question her.

"Yes, there is a lavender bubble bath in there," she says with a smile. "But you don't need to run me a bath. I can do that."

"Nonsense, I will get it. I told you I would look after you today, and that is what I am going to do."

I keep my voice firm when I say it.

"Yes, sir."

I chuckle as I go to get her bath ready for her. I find the stuff she was talking about and put it in. I haven't looked after someone like this in years. I honestly didn't think I still had this caring side to me.

By the time I arrive back, Kayla has made it to the sofa. She has a fluffy blanket around herself.

"The soup smells good. What kind is it?"

"Vegetable soup," I reply.

"Yum."

It's something simple, which hopefully she can manage. I know there is a possibility she will not be feeling good for the next few days, maybe longer, but no matter how many days, I will try my best to look after her.

I don't want her to be alone, but not only that, I want to see if the caring side I once had is still there, deep inside, and if it is something which can last. I want to show Kayla I am not a total soulless bastard, even if it's the impression I probably gave her.

"Thank you for staying and taking care of me, Luca."

"I got you, angel." I smile at her. Well, I hope I do anyway!

Chapter Eleven

Kayla

I'm finally feeling better after a week in bed with the flu. I was going stir-crazy in my apartment. I'm not used to lying around and not doing anything. I'm not due back to work until tomorrow so my plan for today is to get out of the house.

If it wasn't for Elaine coming by on the alternate days where Luca wasn't here, I probably would have been worse. Luca has been amazing this last week. He has cooked most of my meals, got me everything I need from the shops, kept my house clean, and stayed with me a few nights. He has been a sweetheart for sure, which surprised me. I don't mean he is a bad guy, an asshole sometimes, but he's not a terrible person. I half expected him to disappear after a day or two, but he proved me wrong. Even when he was at work, he'd check in with me. I don't know if he was feeling guilty about what happened the night he ran away after our kiss. If that was the case, he has sure made up for it over the last week.

I firmly believe he has many sides I am yet to see because he seems to hide behind the worst side of himself. But who knows, maybe in time his other sides will begin to surface around me. I have decided for today I will treat him to lunch, and we can have some fun. I don't know what kind of fun but something.

Luca has no idea I have plans for us, so I only hope he hasn't made other plans. I know he wasn't working today; he mentioned it last night. It is only nine o'clock, so hopefully it's too early for him to have made other plans already.

I make sure I have everything in my handbag before I go across to his place. Hmm, what do I do if he has company? I will work it out if it comes to that. I knock loudly to make sure he hears me. He will probably be awake because I know he doesn't sleep very well. I hear him coming to the door, and when he opens it, he's wearing a towel around his waist. His hair is wet, and the water is running down his chest.

Oh no! I am not ready to see him like this again. Once was enough to make me nearly jump his bones. I have not long gotten over how amazing the kiss we shared was, now this.

No, don't look, Kayla, don't do it!

I repeat the words in my head, but it doesn't work because my eyes soon trace over his body, his well-toned, muscular, and tattooed body. I thought I could handle it, my attraction to him, especially after the kiss we shared and the not so good outcome of it. I believe because we shared my bed more than once this week, it hasn't helped since he has been so close to me, holding me.

"Morning, angel."

The sound of his voice makes my eyes dart up to his face. He has a smirk resting on his lips. He caught me checking him out.

"Um, morning," I smile nervously, feeling my cheeks heat. He doesn't need another excuse to be arrogant!

"I wasn't expecting you this morning. I thought you might have had enough of me this last week. It's a nice surprise. Come in, beautiful." Luca steps aside and lets me in.

"I have come to steal you away today," I say with a grin. "Unless you have plans?"

"No plans. And what are we doing?"

"I think breakfast to start with, then maybe go somewhere."

"And where will that be?"

I thought about it and came up with a few ideas in my head.

"Have you ever been to Prospect Park?"

"I can't say I have. I'm not the type to go to those places," he says, shrugging his shoulders. I think I'm drooling.

I had been once, a long time ago, and from what I remember it's beautiful. The scenery's stunning, plenty to do to pass the day and everyone seems happy. There's a lot to see, and places to sit and eat.

"Well, today, you are going to be that type," I reply firmly.

"Yes, ma'am," he tells me with a laugh.

"Good. Now please put some clothes on. You are distracting me." I soon regret the last words that came out of my mouth. Why did I need to say it?

"Happy to be a distraction for you, sweetness," he saucily replies with a wink.

I roll my eyes, and shake my head, then hurry him along. We can go for breakfast close by, then come back here, get his car, and drive over there. It's a twenty-minute drive. There are parking spaces outside, but I am sure I heard you can't take a car into the place, which makes sense since the amount of people walking around. I don't mind walking, plus there will be plenty to look at anyway.

"And don't take forever," I call after him, laughing.

"Yeah, yeah," he called back.

I sit down and look around. I realize he still hasn't got any personal belongings up, and he has stayed here for a couple of weeks now. I don't know, maybe he doesn't have any. My eyes fall on the piano. It's beautiful. I had admired it the last time I was here. I wonder if he plays, or if he has it for the sake of having one. I have to ask him because I'm curious.

I make my way over to it, running my fingers along the surface. I wouldn't lift the lid because it isn't mine to touch. I always wished I could play the piano, or another musical instrument, but it turns out I don't have a single musical bone in my body. I have always been more academic rather than creative.

"Do you play?"

His voice causes me to jump since I didn't hear him come back into the room. I look over my shoulder at him.

"No. You?"

"I do. I've been playing for years," he says. "Maybe I can teach you."

"Good luck with that. I don't have a single musical bone in my entire body," I tell him. "But I would like to hear you play some time."

"I am a great teacher," he responds with confidence. "And maybe I will play for you one day."

I sense a sadness in him when he talked about playing for me. It makes me wonder why, but I don't want to ask him since he isn't precisely the open-book type.

"You would end up killing me," I say with a giggle. I don't do well when people try to teach me things and tell me what to do. Maybe telling him he would kill me is a little dramatic.

"We could always make it a game—a fun, sexy game," he smirks.

"I'm not getting naked for you or with you, Luca," I tell him chuckling with delight at our banter.

"If you insist."

The look on his face told me he didn't believe a word I said to him.

"Are you ready to go?" I wanted to change the subject before he said anything more about it. Luca nods, checks he has everything before we head out. I tell him about my plan for our day. He seems fine with it.

I'm so excited to show him Prospect Park, and to see it for myself once again. I feel Luca hasn't seen much of New York, which is a shame because there's a lot to see and do. Maybe I can help him experience all of that.

"I'm glad you're feeling better," he states.

"Me too! Thank you for taking care of me," I say, smiling.

"No bother," he says with a shrug.

I plan on eventually asking him why he ran that night, but not today, today I want us to enjoy ourselves.

Luca and I chat easily as we exit the building and walk. We come to a crossing, and the moment we do I feet his hand on the small of my back. He isn't just placing it there he has grabbed my jumper.

"Luca, why are you doing that? I am not going to cross until I am supposed to," I question him, confused. I am not going to run across the road.

"I know, but you need to be careful near roads," he said softly.

"I always am," I tell him with a smile.

He gives me a small smile back, but it doesn't seem genuine. I think there is a story behind why he is doing it, something else I can't ask him about. I don't mention anything else about it.

When it's time to cross, he ushers me across the road rather quickly. Maybe he got knocked down or something before so he is overly cautious. I can feel he is tense, but when we get to the sidewalk again, I feel him relax, and he removes his hand from me.

Luca and I arrive at our destination and go inside. We look around for a seat, luckily finding one. The place is busy, so there's only a couple of tables free.

"Do you know what you want?" he asks.

"Yes, pancakes with fresh fruit and syrup, oh, also a latte," I say with a grin. "You?"

"Pancakes with bacon and maple syrup and a black coffee," he says with a chuckle.

The waitress comes over to take our orders and checks out Luca in the process. He must get attention everywhere he goes. I am sure he is used to it, and also loves it.

"Well, you piqued her interest that's for sure."

"I did notice, but all of my attention is on one woman today—you." I bet he doesn't say that often. I'm positive he is only saying it to be nice.

"Yeah, sure, we will see about that by the end of the day," I can't help but tease him.

"I appreciate your faith in me, angel," he says with a pout.

I reach over and prod his nose. His pout quickly turns into a smile. I have to admit I have developed a soft spot for him, even with our ups and downs the last couple of weeks. When he isn't being an ass, you can't help but laugh and smile around him.

"You are welcome, man hoe," I laugh.

"A proud one at that," he replies slyly.

I shouldn't be surprised he is proud of it. At first, I give him a disapproving look, but it only makes him laugh, and then I end up laughing along with him.

The waitress comes back with our drinks, and told us our food won't be too long, then gives Luca a flirty look before eventually she walks off.

"Have you seen much of New York?"

"No. I have only lived here for half of my life, but I haven't had much time to see things or have someone to go see them with me," he states.

"Well, you have me now! I can be your tour guide."

"Sure thing," he tells me with an easy smile.

I don't know what will happen with us in time, but for now I am sure we can be friends. He may push me away again in future. He isn't an easy man to open up which has become clear in the short time I have known him.

"When are you back at work?" he asks.

"Tomorrow. I've been rostered on for five nights."

"Oh, the joys."

"Yes, but I am ready to go back to work."

"Lucky you. I could do with a couple of weeks off to get away from the city."

"Then why don't you do that? It is your business. I am sure you can get people to look after things."

"Maybe," he says with a shrug. "It will be no fun to go alone. I have a couple of close friends, but they can't get up and leave like me. One has a wife and a young baby."

"I'm sure if you go to the right place, you will find people to keep you company," I suggest with a smile.

"I will think about it," he says with a shrug.

"Don't you have any family you could go with?" He hasn't mentioned family, so I don't know if he has any.

"No, I don't have any family."

There is a blank expression on his face, and no emotion in his tone when he speaks. I want to say something, but the waitress comes over with our food.

"Thanks, gorgeous," Luca said.

He winks at her. I know he is deferring from the topic of conversation. Family seems to be a sensitive, so I will add it to my list of what not to talk about.

Yes, I'd like to know him better, but it isn't going to happen any time soon, so I will take what I can get.

Chapter Twelve

LUCA

"Should I just go and leave you two alone? Maybe you can take her back to yours," Kayla says, sounding annoyed.

I may have been flirting with the waitress a little too much. I didn't mean to. It wasn't my plan, but when she asked about my family, my guard went up, and I used the waitress as a distraction in case Kayla asked me any more questions. I don't want her or anyone to know anything about my family because they are horrid people, and to me they don't exist and haven't done since I left home at fifteen.

"Don't be like that, angel. I am only having a little fun," I say with a pout.

"Whatever," she responds and pops a bit more food into her mouth.

I know I told her all of my attention would be on her today, but I didn't expect her to get pissed off at me for a little flirting. Maybe she is jealous.

"If I didn't know any better, I would say you are jealous."

"I'm not jealous!" she replies firmly.

"I don't believe you," I say with a smirk.

"Luca, shut the hell up and eat your breakfast, okay?"

"Yes, ma'am."

She glares at me when I call her that. I hold my hands up and laugh. I do what she tells me and turn my attention to my food, Kayla does the same and gives me the silent treatment.

The waitress comes back over to the table, and I see Kayla roll her eyes.

"Do you need anything else, handsome?" She purrs.

"No, I'm alright, sweetness. Thank you," I reply with a smile.

"If you change your mind, give me a shout, or even better, leave your number before you leave." The girl is adamant, that was for sure.

"Oh God, do you ever give up?" Kayla suddenly snarls. The waitress and I are taken aback by the unexpected outburst.

"Excuse me?" the waitress asks.

"You look desperate, go get some respect for yourself. What if I was his girlfriend? You have no clue why we are together, yet you continue to come over here and hit on him."

Christ! Where was this side of Kayla coming from?

"I don't need this drama at my work," the waitress hisses and storms off.

I look at Kayla with a raised brow.

"I have changed my mind. Maybe we should cancel today," she shrugs as she responds to my unspoken question.

She takes money from her purse, tosses it on the table before she walks out. I didn't think she was the dramatic type. I add my bills on the table and rush out after her.

"Kayla, wait," I yell out. She stops, and slowly turns to face me while I run over to her.

"What was that?" I can't help but question her.

"Sorry, I shouldn't have acted that way. It isn't me." She seems embarrassed about the entire thing.

"Then why did you act that way?"

"It gets under my skin when people act the way she did. No, there isn't anything going on between us, but she doesn't know it. It was disrespectful."

I think it stems from her past, when she was with her ex. It is understandable after what happened.

"It is how the world works, Kayla. But unfortunately, not everyone has a heart like yours," I reply.

It is true, Kayla is unique in many ways.

"I know," she says and lets out a sigh.

I open my arms to her, and she steps into them, I wrap them around her tight, and she snuggles into my chest. I hug her tightly to me and kiss the top of her head.

"Is that the only reason?" I whisper.

Kayla lifts her head to look at me, her eyes studying me closely.

"Maybe there is another reason." She pulls her lower lip between her teeth, not breaking eye contact with me.

"Which is?" She went to speak, but then changed her mind.

"It doesn't matter," she says with a smile and pulls away.

I have a feeling about what she was going to say, but I don't want to push her on it. What I want to do is bring her back to me and kiss her.

"Let's go get your car and head to Prospect Park," she says.

I nod, and we head back to the apartment to get my car. I rest my hand on the small of her back. Kayla is silent on the journey. I left her to it because she seems to be lost in her thoughts.

"Should we take something for lunch or get something there?" she asks.

"We can get something there."

We arrive at my car, and I open the passenger door for her. She thanks me and climbs in. I run around to get in the other side. It would be nice to see somewhere different. I haven't seen much of New York even though I have stayed here for years.

It's only a twenty-minute drive, which isn't too bad.

Kayla and I have been walking around for over an hour now. We've seen a lot of Long Meadow. It's beautiful. I have taken a few photos for memories because it will probably be the first and last time I see the place. It's peaceful too, which I like. Kayla seems to be in her element. She got so excited at every little thing; her eyes just lit up at the simple things. I wish I could see everything like she does.

"We should sit and enjoy the sun for a little while," she suggests.

"Good idea."

She seems relaxed now, unlike earlier. Neither of us mentioned what happened this morning and preferred it that way. We look around to find a spot which is easy enough because there seems to be plenty. We find one in the open so we can take advantage of the sun.

Kayla sits first, and I join her only seconds later. There are families, couples, groups of friends, and people by themselves surrounding us. Everyone seems content with where they are. I smile to myself while I glance around. It's nice to see there is such a thing as happy families.

I turn my attention back to Kayla to find her lying down on the grass. "What are you doing?" I ask with a chuckle.

"Laying down and looking at the sky," she says with a carefree giggle. "Lay down with me."

I hesitate for a moment, but in the end I join her. She tilts her head to look at me and smiles. I couldn't resist smiling back.

"It is beautiful here, isn't it?"

"Yes, it is."

Kayla is looking at the sky when she says it. I was admiring her when I agree. I swear, sometimes when I look at her, she takes my breath away, just another thing to add to my list of things that scare me when I'm around her. I quickly pull away before she catches me staring. I close my eyes and enjoy the sounds of nature filling my ears. My body is relaxed.

Suddenly, I feel Kayla's fingers brush against my hand. I don't react because I assume it's a mistake. My assumption is wrong because the next thing I know she puts her hand over mine and links our fingers. I open my eyes to look over at her, she is already looking at me.

"Why are you looking at me like that?" I ask.

"Why don't you smile often? You have a beautiful smile."

"Because I don't have much to smile about," I reply honestly.

"There's plenty to smile about, Luca, you just need to look closer."

I wish it's that easy. "Angel, when you have been through what I have, see the things I have, trying to find the good isn't that simple."

"Has your life really been that hard?"

There is a softness to her tone. I don't want to go into detail, but I will answer her question.

"Yes," I say. "And no. I don't want to talk about it."

"Okay, we don't need to talk about it. But keeping everything to yourself must be lonely."

"I manage," I say with a shrug. I'm used to being this way, it's normal for me.

Kayla rolls onto her side, and I do too. I bring my hand over and stroke her face. Her eyes close, and she smiles. I remove my hand, but we stay in the same position. Kayla reaches over, and runs her fingers through my hair and then down my cheek. My eyes fall shut as I move into her touch. She has such a gentle touch, and there is something so soothing about her fingers on my skin.

Her next move takes me by surprise. Her warm lips cover mine in a gentle kiss. I groan at the contact. It takes a second for me to kiss her back. I cup her face in my hand. Kayla scoots closer to me. She rests one hand on my chest. The kiss stays soft, but it is enough to drive me crazy. I grip her hip and hold her against me—the feel of her soft lips on mine is causing my heartbeat to speed up. I feel like I can't get any air into my lungs. It's making me breathless.

Kayla pulls away first, and I huff in protest. I wasn't ready for it to end, but I think we need a moment to breathe.

"Why did you do that?" I whisper.

"Because I wanted to. Shouldn't I have kissed you?"

"I just wasn't expecting it, that's all," I say, as I smile and stroke her hair away from her face.

"You and I both," she says with a carefree giggle.

I guess she hadn't planned to do it. We must have been caught up in the moment. She smiles at me and rolls onto her back again. She doesn't say a word after it. I lie there, trying to work out what just happened. Does she like me? It's evident there's something between us; our first kiss told us both that, but I don't know what it is. My original plan after I met her was to bed her, but now, I am confused. I have never had to think or work this hard when it comes to women. I usually get what I want in no time. I have not had a woman do this to me since Leah. God, she made me work for her, and I happily did because she was worth it.

Leah and Kayla were similar; by that, I mean they have the same heart, and Leah, like Kayla, always saw the good in the world. I close my eyes again and take a few deep breaths before I get emotional. I can't think about Leah, not right now.

"How about we start walking again? We have a lot to see," I announce. It'd be a good distraction because my thoughts will run away with me if I continue to lie here.

"Sure," she agrees with a grin.

I get to my feet first. I offer her my hand, which she takes, and I help her to her feet. I guide her into me and kiss her. She whimpers into my lips. It lasts only a few seconds before we part.

"Let's go," I suggest.

Kayla nods, and I rest my hand on the small of her back as we get back to our walk. Maybe as the day goes on I will work out what those kisses mean. Until that happens I will not overthink this and enjoy my day with Kayla.

Chapter Thirteen

Kayla

Luca and I are currently standing outside of my apartment door. We have just arrived back after a good day and night together. We stayed at Prospect Park until five o'clock, then went out for tea. After that, we drove back, and finished our night off with a couple of drinks. It's now after midnight, and Luca has work in the morning.

"Thank you for today, sweetness. I had fun," he says with a smile.

"Me too!"

I enjoyed my day with him. And the kiss we shared at the park, neither of us had brought it up, though I've been thinking about it all day.

"I should go." He lets out a sigh.

"Yes, you have work in the morning."

I don't want him to go. I want to invite him in, but I know it isn't the best idea. Luca steps in closer to me, wedging my body between him and the front door. He rests one hand on my cheek, and I believe he is going to kiss me. He seems to be inching closer, but he skips my lips and ends up kissing my cheek.

"Goodnight, angel," he says before taking a step away.

I stand there confused. What just happened? I was convinced he would kiss me, on the lips, not my damn cheek. Maybe he doesn't want me the way I thought. That could have just been something he said at the time. Then why does he act like he wants me? Ahh, I don't know anymore. Maybe I am being dramatic—I am not a dramatic person, or so I thought until my outburst at the waitress. I was jealous, but I didn't want to tell Luca that.

Luca gives me one last smile before he turns away and walks over to his place. He unlocks the door, and opens it to step inside. Before he closes it, he looks over at me.

"Sweet dreams, gorgeous," he said with a wink then closes the door.

I groan in frustration before turning to head into my place. I go inside, kick my shoes off, hang my coat, and get changed into my pjs, which consists of shorts and a tee.

As I stand in front of the mirror to take my make-up off, I notice how flushed my cheeks are. The cause of it, I'm sure, is Luca being so close as he was to me. I splash cold water on my face and was about to climb into bed, but something snaps in me.

No, I am not going to bed! Instead, I am going to do something, which isn't usually me. I am going after what I want for a change, and Luca is what I want in this instant. I walk quickly back through my apartment and make sure I have my house keys. I stroll across the landing and knock loudly on Luca's door. I don't care right now that I'm in my pjs and make-up free, he has seen me in a worse state when I was not well.

I impatiently wait for him to answer. I know he wouldn't be sleeping. I hear him unlock the door, and when it opens, he is standing there in only his boxers with a confused look on his face.

"Is something wrong?" he asks.

I don't answer him with words, instead I push him back into his apartment, kick the door shut behind me, and attach my lips to his before he even has a chance to speak. He growls into my mouth, grips my hips hard, and kisses me back.

He backs away after a minute, he's breathless, and looks at me with a confused look asking what is going on.

"Kayla, what are you doing?" he breaths out.

"I am done talking and acting like this isn't what we both want."

"Are—" he begins before I cut him off.

"Luca, just shut the fuck up and kiss me before I change my mind. Unless you don't want this? Then I will leave."

I act like I am going to turn and walk away. I don't get far before he pulls me to him and our lips meet again. I moan and move my body closer to press into his. He flips us around, my back firmly against the wall. He grabs my hands, pinning them to the wall above my head. He shifts his lips from mine onto my neck. His lips map the skin, and then his teeth graze it. I gasp and tilt my head to give him better access.

Luca moves his lips to my ear, the feel of his warm breath against my skin is enough to make me shudder.

"I have never wanted something as badly in my entire life, Kayla."

All I can do is whimper and nod in response.

"This needs to come off," he breathes out as he impatiently tugs at my tee.

I let him remove it. He pulls it over my head and tosses it aside. He steps back for a moment, his eyes admiring the new territory he hasn't yet seen. I have no bra on, so my top half is completely bare.

"Fuck, angel, you are damn sexy," he grunts out.

He comes at me again, his lips on mine and his hands go straight for my breasts. He grabs them, circling his thumbs on my nipples. I cry out and tug at his hair. Luca's fingers run down my ribs and over my stomach. It's a simple touch, one I have craved for weeks now, and it's enough to send pleasure straight down between my thighs—his hand stills at the waistband of my shorts.

He looks me straight in the eye and asks me, "Do you have anything underneath your shorts?" he pants.

I shake my head and roll my hips. I hope it will give him a hint of what I need. He smirks and puts his hand into my shorts. The second his fingers encounter my womanly folds, I moan profoundly, and my hips jerk. I am so wet for him—no—more like soaking.

"Mmm, is this for me, baby girl?"

His voice is low and seductive as his fingers tickle and tease my clit.

"Y... yes," I stammer out.

He separates my legs with his knees, and his fingers tease my entrance.

"Luca, please," I beg.

He slips one finger inside of me, then a second. I grip his arms, and he begins moving his fingers inside of me. Oh fuck, it feels good. I close my eyes, my head dips back, and small pants come from my mouth. His large fingers reach all the right places.

"Oh, God," I squeal.

I can feel my climax building up already. No man has ever gotten me off this quickly with his fingers; the only thing that usually works like this are toys.

"Does this feel good, angel?"

"Yes, so good."

His fingers begin moving faster, while his lips work my breasts, alternating between sucking and biting my sensitive nipples. My walls start to clench around him.

"Cum for me, gorgeous," he commands.

And right on cue, I do! I call out, my legs shake, and I erupt over his fingers, my legs nearly buckling from under me. He guides me through my high. I reach the end of my climax and rested back against the wall. My breathing is heavy.

"Fuck, I needed that."

I open my eyes to look at him. The second I do, he has this smirk, then he slips his fingers into his mouth and sucks them one by one.

"Mmm, you taste good," he grunts, and licks his lips.

I moan as I watch him do it. He steps back into me and rests his hand beside my head.

"Now, I need you to go to my bedroom and let me fuck you."

His voice is firm, it's a demand not a question. I nod, and he moves out of the way to let me go past.

"I want you to get naked and lay on the bed for me," he says. "I will be through in a second."

He swats my ass as I walk away from him. I go to his bedroom on wobbly legs, they're still weak from the pleasure he gave me. I want him so badly. I'm a little nervous because I will be completely exposed to him in a minute. I stand awkwardly in the middle of the room.

"Relax, beautiful."

Luca's voice comes from behind me, his warm lips kiss my shoulder. I moan as I nod. I take a deep breath and take my shorts off. I brush my ass against his length when I come back up. I hear him curse.

"Go lie down," he whispers in my ear.

I do as he asks, and go over to his bed and lie down. I rest up on my elbows to watch him. He stands at the bottom of the bed and drinks in every inch of my body. The way he is looking at me is intense. His eyes are full with lust and desire. I don't think any man has ever looked at me the way he is right now. It makes me feel good to be wanted so badly by someone.

I take him in also. He is so damn sexy! I want to put my hands and lips all over him. He grabs his boxers, and in a swift move he rids himself of them. I watch his every move, and the second his fully erect length comes into view, I feel excitement stir through me again. Fuck!

"Mmm, nice."

The words slip out of my mouth without warning, he is impressively sized in length and girth. My tongue darts out of my mouth as I admire him. Luca stands there confidently and lets me enjoy the view.

I lift my head to look at his face finally.

"Do you like the look of it, sweetness?" he asks me as he gently strokes himself.

"Yes. Get over here and fuck me with it."

"I plan on it for the next couple of hours."

"Don't make promises unless you can keep them," I can't help but bait him and let out a giggle.

"Oh, trust me, sweetness, I will be keeping my promise."

He crawls up the bed and towers over me.

"I am going to fuck you in a way no other man ever has. Your screams will fill my bedroom, and your body is going to crave me over and over again," he adds confidently.

My breathing becomes unsteady. My heart pounds in my chest, and in between my legs are throbbing.

"P… prove it," I stutter out.

Chapter Fourteen

LUCA

Prove it!

The second those words fall from her lips, something unleashes inside of me. Any control I have left disappears. I have wanted her for weeks, and now I'm finally getting what I want. Maybe if we have sex, it will get her out of my system.

I reach into the drawer at the side of the bed to get a condom. I tear it open and slip it on. I lean over her, our lips meeting in a heated kiss. I tease her with my cock, rubbing it up and down her folds.

"Luca, I swear—"

She starts, but I don't give her a chance to finish. I push my hips forward and thrust into her roughly—the sound of her squeal echoes through my room. Fuck! She is so tight and feels incredible around me. Kayla grips my arms. I begin moving into her, each time going deeper. I don't tend to fuck in this position often, but it feels too good to stop and change it up. It is too personal for me.

"Oh God, so good." She cries out, her entire body arching up from the bed, and her head falls back.

"Mmm, kitten, your pussy around me feels incredible." I pant out, slapping her thigh.

Kayla moans in response, scraping her nails down my back. I hiss, loving the feeling of the pain of it. I slip my arms underneath her, rest back on my knees and bring her with me, so Kayla is in my lap. Her arms go around my neck, her knees straddle me, and I hold her hips, guiding her back down on my length until I complete sink into her again. I grunt loudly as her walls clench around my throbbing cock. She begins moving against me.

"Fuck, Luca, you fill me up so good." She gasps. I capture her lips roughly with mine and spank her ass, making her moan into the kiss.

I wrap my fingers in her hair, tugging it hard and push up into her. She cries out in pleasure. Mmm, she liked that; I will have to remember that. I dip my head down, attaching my lips to her neck, kissing and nibbling on the skin until I hit a sweet spot and her entire body shivers. I suck on the skin, and her fingers fall into my hair, yanking it. Kayla isn't the only one who likes that.

I let go of her hair, running my fingers down her back, her body heating under my touch. Kayla uses her hold on my hair to bring my face closer to hers, letting our lips meet again. She picks up her speed, circling her hips. Fuck! That feels good.

"Easy, angel." I pant out. She keeps going like this I will be coming sooner than I would like.

I toss her onto her back again, needing to take back control. I bring her legs over my shoulders, kneeling between them and dig my fingers into her thighs. I run the tip of my cock over her folds and continue to do so until she begs me to get back inside of her. I smirk and do as she asks, entering her sharply, and she screams as we reconnect. She fists the sheets below her and closes her eyes, her breathing loud and heavy.

"Yes! Luca! Fuck!"

Damn, I am enjoying the sound of my name coming from her lips. Every stroke brings her closer to the edge. I go deep and quick. I keep my eyes open to watch her. There is nothing sexier than watching a woman climax and knowing you are the one responsible for it. Her head is tilted back; her eyes are closed; her lips are parted. I could feel her walls becoming tighter around me, her breathing was becoming unsteady. She is trying to fight it.

I stop, removing myself from inside her, but it will only be for a second. I let her relax her legs against the bed and then use my knee to push them apart, taking my place back between them, leaning over her, and she is quick to snake them around me again, grinding upwards, her pussy brushing against me. I re-enter eagerly, kissing her passionately and aim to finish her off.

"I know you are ready to cum for me, angel, don't try to fight the impossible. I am going to make you cum so fucking hard, again." I growl out confidently, getting into the perfect rhythm.

I sneak my hand between us, playing with her clit and let my lips wander any part of her body that I can reach, pounding into her. It doesn't take long before she starts to shake, and her eyes roll back. My name comes from her lips in a loud, strained squeal, and her climax hits, dominating every inch of her body. She squirms below me, her nails clawing at my back again. She is sure going to leave her mark on me. Watching her, feeling her is enough to end me, and I follow in a matter of seconds, exploding into the condom, Kayla's name escaping my lips between pants. Christ, I haven't come this much in a long time. We ride through our highs, Kayla stilling below me, her body limp, and I collapse on top of her.

"That was fucking incredible." She breaths out, caressing my back.

"Hmm, yes, it was..." I agree. It was more than incredible; it was mind blowing. I haven't connected sexually with a woman like that in some time.

I peck her lips and lay down next to her, disposing of the condom in the trash. Silence comes between us, both too breathless to talk. My plan to fuck her once and hopefully get her out of my system isn't going to work. You don't let pussy that good go too soon. I am not done with her for tonight, either.

"I told myself I wouldn't go here." She laughs, "You have trouble written all over you, Mr. and have done from day one." She adds, turning her head to look at me, a sexy little smile painted on her lips.

"I am irresistible. What can I say? And a little trouble never killed anyone, sweetness." I reply, "I would ask if you regret your decision of jumping into bed with me, but by the way you screamed my name, and how your body reacted to me answers the question." I add smugly.

With a snicker she says cheekily, "I could have been faking."

"No, you weren't faking. There was nothing fake about that." I wink. I know my work is always well done in the bedroom.

Kayla rolls her eyes at me and slaps my arm playfully.

"Could you be any more arrogant?" she questions, shaking her head.

"It isn't arrogance if it is the truth, angel." I answer, leaning in to kiss her, "You loved every single second of it." I mumble against her lips.

Kayla places one hand on my face and the other on my chest. She lets her lips move over mine, and using her strength turns me over, putting my back on the mattress and climbs on top of me.

"If I am going to make a mistake, I may as well make it worth it. Now, tell me, Mr. big shot, do you have another round in you, or are you a once a night type of guy, because if you are, this isn't going to work." She teases, a cheeky look on her face.

"No, I don't do once a night. I have more stamina than that." I reply, spanking her ass firmly, ensuring it will leave a mark.

"I think you are nothing but talk." She says, trying to be serious, but her words don't match the look on her face. There is nothing serious about it.

I am sure she is trying to get under my skin on purpose, and I am OK with that. I will prove to her I am not one of those lame-assed men who go once a night and last two minutes.

"Oh, Kayla, you are in for it now, angel. I swear by the time I am done with you—you are going to ache in places you didn't know possible. Anytime you fuck another man, you will find yourself comparing them to me because they won't be able to pleasure you in the way I do." I groan out, my cock beginning to harden again.

"Is that a threat or a promise?" she purrs, rubbing herself against me.

"It is a promise," I respond sternly. "Get me a condom, and I will show you," I demanded.

I have plans for us for the next few hours at least. Kayla reaches into my drawer, takes one out and opens it, putting it on. She lifts her hips, rests her hand on my chest.

"It is time to keep your word, Luca," she says, sinking down on my cock, her head falling back, closing her eyes the second she does, "your cock is so damn huge." She adds, pausing to adjusting to it again.

I will keep my word, and by the end of tonight, she will be coming back for more, and I will happily oblige to her.

"Now do your thing, gorgeous." I breathe out, grasping her hips.

We have a fun night ahead of us, and I am excited for every single second of it!

Chapter Fifteen

I wake to the sound of Luca moving around his bedroom.
"What time is it?" I ask tiredly.
"It is only six o'clock, go back to sleep, angel."
I'm exhausted after my night with Luca. I didn't think it was possible to have so many orgasms in one session. It was incredible! My body has never felt pleasure like that before. Luca sure knows what he's doing.
I slowly sit up and bring the covers up to my chin because I'm still naked. Luca stands in front of the mirror doing his tie. I watch him closely. He looks so different in his suit, with his hair all perfectly slicked back. He's very handsome.
"I will get up and go to my place to sleep," I say.
"Nonsense, just stay put."
"I honestly don't mind," I smile.
"Stay. You can leave when you are ready. All you have to do is make sure the door is locked on your way out."
I could argue with him on this, but I'm too tired. I nod and run my fingers through my tousled hair. Luca seems to be having an issue with his tie and is getting frustrated with it.
"Do you want me to help with that?"
"If you don't mind. I usually wear clip-on ties. It makes life so much easier," he laughs.
I wrap the sheet around my naked body, climb out of bed and go to him. He turns around and smiles at me. I hook his belt in my fingers to bring him closer to me.
"Easy, gorgeous," he says with a cheeky smirk.
I playfully roll my eyes at him as I giggle. I do his tie for him, then pat his chest. I'm about to go back to bed, but Luca has other ideas. He pulls me into his arms and plants his lips on mine. I moan instantly.
"You need to get to work," I mumble.
"I have time."
He swiftly removes the sheet from around my body, tossing it on the floor. He walks me backwards and pushes me onto the bed. My back hits the mattress while my legs dangle off the bed.

"Sorry, sweetness, I need to undo your hard work."

He loosens his tie and removes it. He also got rid of his suit jacket and shirt.

"You are going to be late."

"I am the boss. I am allowed to be late."

Suddenly, he drops to his knees in front of the bed. What is he doing? His warm lips brush against my leg, and he begins to kiss his way up.

"Luca, what are you doing?" I breathe out.

I watch him with curiosity. He hooks his hands under my legs and brings them over his shoulders. He glances up at me, smirks, licks his lips, and then his head disappears between my thighs. Oh, now I know what he is doing.

I soon feel his warm breath fan my skin of folds. I gasp, and my back arches up from the bed. His tongue flicks over my clit, one, two, three times until he finally gently tugs it.

"Oh fuck," I pant.

He runs his tongue down my folds and grasps my legs in his hands. I am sure I will probably have his fingerprints on me after this. He dips his tongue inside me and works it quickly.

I fist the bedding underneath me as I squirm. Luca's tongue is magic. I have only ever had a man go down on me once in my entire life, and it never felt anywhere near as good as this. Now I realize my ex had no clue what he was doing, no wonder why I didn't like it. But right now, in this moment, I love the pleasure Luca is giving me. He starts massaging my thighs, the speed of his tongue picking up.

"Yes," I cry out.

I curl my fingers in his hair and push my hips up from the bed. My climax is approaching quickly. Luca moans against me, the vibrations dancing over my folds.

"Luca, I am so close. Fuck, your tongue is exceptional."

He stops and pulls back. I glare down at him.

"I need to get my cock inside of you, angel, before I get over-excited and make a mess."

His lips gleam with my juices. He slowly moves his tongue around his lips and groans loudly. He stands, reaches over to the drawer to get protection before he comes back to stand at the bottom of the bed.

"Get on all fours for me."

He has the same authority to his tone as last night when he told me what to do. I like it, it turns me on. I get onto all fours. I hear him behind me, undoing his trousers, and the rustling of the foil condom packet. Moments later, I feel the bed behind me dip down.

"Mmm, I like this view."

He slaps my ass hard, and I yelp. I push back against him because I need him to finish me off. He holds onto my hips, stroking my folds with his length before he enters me quickly. Luca lets out a deep, throaty groan and starts to move into me.

He thrusts into me with ease since I'm already dripping wet. He goes in quick, hard, and deep. His fingers wrap in my hair, and he yanks my head back. In response I squeal in excitement.

"Fuck, your pussy wrapped around my cock is like heaven, angel."

He spanks my ass again, harder this time. I was ready to explode around him. It only took another couple of minutes before the sound of his name falling from my lips rang through the bedroom. My entire body shakes as my orgasm dominates my body.

"Do you like me fucking you like this, Kayla?"

"Yes, so good," I reply with a strained voice.

"Good," he grunts as he thrusts into me over and over again. Luca manages only another minute before he cries out, and his climax hits. I collapse down on the bed, Luca's body falling on top of mine. Both of us are breathing heavily.

"The best way to start my day," he says then kisses my shoulder.

We take a moment to get ourselves together, then he removes himself from inside of me and gets to his feet. I roll onto my back, my body too weak to move any more than that.

"I am going to clean up, and then I need to go."

I nod and hurry back up to the top of the bed. Luca comes through from the bathroom a few minutes later and re-dresses himself. He reaches down and pecks my lips.

"See you later?" he questions.

"Depends on when you get home. I am working tonight."

"That's right. Well, if I don't see you tonight, I will see you tomorrow, okay?"

"Yes," I smile.

"I will text you. Now, go back to sleep."

"Yes, boss man," I cheekily say with a giggle.

He says one last goodbye before he rushes out. I hope he won't be too late. I lie still on the bed, trying to get my energy back. The man is like a pro when it comes to pleasuring a woman. Though I worry now he may become my new addiction because I have had a taste of what he can do. I am still unsure about it because he could change at any time. I still sense he is trouble, but now I have gotten involved with him, there is a good chance there is no going back.

Once I have caught my breath, I stroll through to his bathroom to get myself cleaned up. I do what I need to before I go back to bed. I need to get some more sleep. I curl up, and it doesn't take long until I drift off. Every part of me is exhausted.

I have found ways to keep myself busy for most of the day. I came back to my place from Luca's around eleven o'clock. Now I'm going to see Elaine and have a coffee with her at her office. She is too busy today for us to go out for one.

I stop by the coffee shop to get us both a coffee and while there I grab some sandwiches too since Elaine probably hasn't eaten at all today. She is terrible at looking after herself and forgets to eat if she is too busy. I say hello to the receptionist as I made my way up to her office.

I peer into the room from the doorway to make sure Elaine isn't with a client or on the phone. She isn't, but she seems to be working on her computer. I knock lightly, and she looks up. She smiles and motions for me to come in.

"I come with coffee and food," I say grinning.

I hand over hers before I take a seat. She looks at me with a raised brow.

"What?" I ask with a laugh.

"You totally got laid last night. You have that sex glow around you, and you can't stop smiling," she smirks. "Spill, who was it?"

I feel the heat rise in my cheeks. The girl knows me too well. "Luca," I whisper.

"What? You fucked Luca?" she asks, totally shocked.

"Yes, many times last night," I can't resist buffing my nails in glee against my shirt with a cheesy grin on my face, "and once this morning."

"How did that happen? I want details."

I start from the beginning and tell her the entire story. I share with her how amazing the sex was. She seems intrigued by it all.

"You made the first move? That isn't like you!"

"I know. I don't know what took over, but damn, it was worth it."

"So, the rumors are true. He is an animal in bed," she says with a laugh.

"Yes. And should you really be discussing the details of a client's sex life?" I snicker.

"No, probably not. I won't tell, if you don't."

"My lips are sealed," I say, smiling so much it hurt my face.

We change the topic of conversation while we have lunch. I stay for only half an hour because Elaine needs to get back to work, but we have arranged plans for later in the week.

As I exit the building, my phone beeps in my bag. I reach for it and see a text from Luca on my screen.

Hey, angel. What are you doing? Did you get back to sleep? X

Hey, handsome. I've just left Elaine's office. How is work? And yes, I got back to sleep for a few hours X

Come and see me since you are already out X

Okay, send me your work address, and I will stop by. Do you want anything? X

A decent coffee. I need to get a better machine for this place. I will see you soon X

Luca texts me his work address. It isn't too far away from where I am, so it works out perfectly. I stop at Starbucks to get Luca a coffee, and I get myself a cup of tea. I don't need another coffee so soon.

I'm surprised he wanted me to come to his office. I thought he would prefer to keep his personal and business life separate. I wasn't expecting to see him again today. My body is still aching from last night—in the best way possible—of course.

I slowly stroll my way to his office. I might have gotten a little lost on the way, but I eventually found it. The building is massive. It's modern looking, expensive too. The scent in the air was a mixture of coffee and cleaning products.

"Hello, how can I help you today?" The pretty receptionist says with a smile.

"Good afternoon. I am here to see Luca; he's expecting me."

When I tell her why I'm here, she looks me up and down, mutters under her breath before rudely giving me directions. What is her problem? I wouldn't be surprised if he slept with her. I find his office easily enough; his door is already open.

"Hey," I greet.

"Hey, gorgeous, come in."

I smile and enter. He took his coffee from me and then told me to sit.

"Glad you came." He winks at me.

To anyone else, it probably sounds innocent, but to me, I know it isn't innocent at all. I hope that isn't why he invited me here, for sex, because it isn't happening, not in his office where everyone can see us.

Maybe I have the wrong end of the stick, but I will soon find out, won't I?

Chapter Sixteen

LUCA

I rest back in my office chair and put my feet up on my desk.

"You seem nervous, angel."

It is true, Kayla does seem nervous. It made me wonder if it was because of what happened last night and this morning. And what a fun night and morning it had been. I loved her screaming my name and hearing her beg for more. It was worth the wait, that was for sure. I hope it happens again.

"No. I am fine. I'm just surprised you invited me here, that's all," she said, then shrugs.

I'm surprised too, because I usually keep my personal life away from work. I have never invited anyone to my office. Even when I had sex with a couple of the women who work here, it didn't happen in my work space. People are only allowed in here when it has something to do with business.

"Why?" I want to know why she was surprised by it.

"Because something tells me you don't mix your work and personal life."

"No. I don't. I never invite anyone here."

"Then why did you invite me?" she asks.

"Because I wanted to." It's a straightforward answer. I can't give her any more than that. I don't even know why I invited her over here.

"So about last night and this morning," I said.

"What about it?"

"We should do it again." I thought I might as well put it out there, so I know where we both stand.

"And what makes you think I want to do it again?" she asks with a smirk.

I take my feet off the table, stand, then go around to where she's sitting. I lean against my desk.

"By the way you kept screaming my name and begging for more."

"I could've been faking."

Yes, I know she wasn't. The only time someone has faked it with me was the first time I had sex when I was sixteen because I was terrible. It was my first time, after all. I was quick to learn after that, and I haven't had an issue since.

I reach down, rest my hands on each side of the chair. My face is only inches from hers.

"You were not faking, sweetness. You enjoyed every single second of it," I say confidently. "And I know you want me again."

"Cocky much?"

"No, it's the truth. If I kissed you right now, you would let me."

"Are you sure about that?"

I have a feeling she is baiting me. I nod, closing the space between us I kiss her. She moans and kisses me back. She fists my suit jacket. I knew she wouldn't pull away when I kissed her.

I bring Kayla to her feet and hold her close to me. She slips her arms around my neck and presses her body to mine. I run my hands down her back then grab her ass. She groans, enjoying our kiss.

We are getting right into it, until someone knocks on my office door. What the fuck? This time it is me who groans, only it's in annoyance, and I reluctantly separate from Kayla.

"What?" I snarl.

I look over Kayla's shoulder to see the receptionist. She doesn't look happy.

"You have a call, sir. I tried to put them through, but it didn't work."

I had put all my calls on hold, so I didn't need to deal with anyone while Kayla is here.

"Okay," I say, annoyance lacing my voice.

She mutters before leaving.

"I should go, let you get back to work."

"You don't need to. I won't be long," I reply.

I don't want her to leave, not right now anyway. Kayla kisses my cheek, and tells me she will see me later or tomorrow then leaves. I'm pissed off. Millie knows if she can't put any of my calls through it's because I chose it. I will have a word with her later. I have a feeling she did it since she knew Kayla was here.

I readjust myself since I was a little excited. I brush my fingers through my hair before I take a seat back at my desk to take the call. It's one of my investors. I wasn't expecting their call until tomorrow.

I was on the phone for half an hour. Once I end the call, I decide it's time to leave for the day. I can't be assed staying here all day. Everything necessary has been dealt with, anything else I can do at home. I have people here to keep an eye on things when I'm not around. I gather my stuff and head out.

I stop by Millie's desk.

"You know not to interrupt me, Millie, when I put all my calls on hold. Don't do it again."

"Who is she?" she asks.

I had hooked up with Millie a few times. I know it wasn't my best idea, but she is gorgeous, and I couldn't help myself.

"None of your business," I reply. "I am leaving for the day. Take messages; any important calls forward to my cell."

I don't give her a chance to respond and walk out. My plan? I will stop by Kayla's and see if she wants to continue from where we left off in my office.

Though if we continue to have sex, she needs to know it's only that and nothing more. I don't want to complicate things. I can cope with friends with benefits arrangements, but nothing more than that. I don't know if she would be up for it, but I will work it out.

Kayla and I are naked in her bed. Kayla cuddles into me with her head on my chest. We have been in her bed for the last few hours. We take a break in between to get some tea, other than that we haven't moved. There is a silence between us, a comfortable one. Kayla is tracing her fingers over my stomach where my scars are. I hope she won't ask what happened to me because I will lie to her if she does.

"What happened?" The words I don't want to hear come from her lips.

"It was a childhood accident."

It can't be further from the truth; there was nothing accidental about my scars. She lifts her head to look up at me. She studies me closely, and I'm not sure if she believes what I tell her. I watch her mouth open to speak, but I'm not going to give her a chance since I know she will probably ask about the "accident," and I don't know what to tell her.

"I should probably go and let you get some sleep before work." I swiftly move away from her and pull my clothes on.

"You don't need to go. I am not tired, Luca."

"You need to try and get some sleep," I reply firmly.

I peck her lips and rush out before she can stop me. I get into my apartment, close the door and rest against it. I close my eyes and take a few deep breaths. Kayla is probably still lying in her bed thinking what the fuck just happened. I didn't plan on leaving as abruptly as I did, but I had to get out of there before she started asking unwanted questions.

I stop myself leaning on the door and go to the kitchen. I pour myself a double scotch and down it in one go, pour another and do the same again. I need to find a distraction before I ended up drinking the entire bottle.

I'm distracted from my thoughts when my phone vibrates in my pocket. I have a feeling who it is without even looking at it. I sigh and take it from my pocket—Kayla's name is on the screen. I hesitate for a second before opening it.

What the heck was that all about? Why did you rush off? And don't say because I need to sleep cause that's bullshit, and we both know it.

I don't know why I thought that excuse would work. I have to tread carefully with the way I reply. I don't want to upset her. Maybe I should be honest with her, well, sort of anyway.

I am sorry I ran off again. I don't like talking about my scars or how I got them. I knew you were going to start asking questions, ones I am not ready to answer X

Then you could have just told me that, Luca. I wouldn't have asked anything more, but whatever. I will see you around.

Damn it! She is mad at me. What does she expect from me? I would understand it if we were together, it would give her the right to get pissed at me, but we aren't, so I don't see the issue. Now I'm annoyed.

I lift the bottle of scotch along with my glass, put some music on at high volume and toss myself on the sofa. I fill my glass to the brim. I rest my head back on the couch, and turn the music off because it isn't doing me any good. I sit in silence, sipping on my drink.

Drink by drink, the time passes until the bottle is empty. I have lost track of how long I have just sat here. The light is now fading, the darkness closes in. All of a sudden I hear a loud knock on my door. I don't shift until there's another knock, but it's harder this time.

I groan in frustration, and stand, when I do, I stumble slightly. The drink has affected me more than I realize. I stagger my way to the door and open it. Kayla stands on the other side with a concerned look on her face.

"So, you are okay then?" She asked then lets out a sigh.

"Why wouldn't I be?" I stupidly ask. Why does she seem so concerned?

"Because when I tried to call, you didn't answer. I knocked earlier, you didn't respond. I have been here hitting the door for the last ten minutes."

"What time is it?"

"Half past seven," she replies.

The last time I checked, it was four o'clock. I must have blacked out. I do that sometimes. I can have a blackout for hours without realizing it.

"Sorry, I must have fallen asleep."

I'm not going to tell her I suffer from blackouts. I would rather keep all my fucked-up traits to myself.

"Okay. I should go to work," she says.

"Why were you trying to reach me?"

"Honestly, I don't know. Something in me told me to come to make sure you were alright. How much have you had to drink, Luca?"

How did she know I have been drinking?

"I only had a couple," I shrug. Another lie to add to the list of things I tell her.

"Just be careful what you drink, please? And call me if you need to talk."

Kayla kisses my cheek before she strolls off. I stay where I am, trying to get my head around what had just happened. How did she know something wasn't right? I find it strange that her instincts are drawn to me. I give myself a shake and go back into my apartment.

I know the best thing for me to do right now is to go lie down, maybe sleep for an hour. If I stay up right now, I will drink more, which would be the worst idea. I drag my ass to bed, strip down, and climb straight in. I will get a shower later once I wake up because I can't be assed right now. I pulled the covers right over my head, and get lost in my mind.

I pray for sleep to take over, but as usual, it doesn't work when I want it the most. I take some deep breaths in hope it will relax my body and mind. Eventually, after a bit of time, my eyes become heavy.

Chapter Seventeen

Kayla

I'm finally getting the first break on my shift. It's four in the morning. Tonight, work has been horrible. There was a horrific crash, and sadly we lost one of the drivers. It doesn't matter how long you have worked in this line of work, losing a patient doesn't get any easier.

I go to the staff room, get myself a coffee and grab my yoghurt from the fridge. I collapse down on the sofa and sigh. I check my phone and see I have a missed call from Luca a couple of hours ago, and a text he sent only ten minutes ago. I open the text.

Hey, angel, how is work? X

Hey, you, what are you doing awake now? Work is terrible tonight. We lost a patient, and another two are critical X

I set my phone aside and take a sip of my coffee, I need this. A few seconds after I put my phone down it starts to ring. I glance over at the screen and see Luca is calling. I pick it up and answer.

"Hi. What are you doing awake at this time?"

"I have been awake for hours. How are you doing after such a bad night?"

"I'm okay. Sadly it comes with the job, and it doesn't get any easier."

"I am sorry, Kayla. I can't even begin to imagine what it is like seeing the things you do."

"It's nights like this that are the worst."

Luca talks to me on the phone for a few minutes but then decides he wants to video chat instead. I still have twenty minutes left on my break, well, if no one needs me before then. Luca's face is soon flashing up on my screen. I hit the answer button and lay down on the sofa. He looks exhausted, and his eyes are bloodshot due to the drink.

"Hey, beautiful," he says with a tired smile.

"Have you slept at all, Luca?"

"I slept for a couple of hours earlier," he shrugs. I think he should see a doctor about his sleep patterns because they are terrible. Your body needs sleep. It is important. Luca swiftly changes the subject away from him, like always.

"Can I do anything to make you feel better?" he asks.

"Thank you, but no, I will be okay. I only have a few hours left until my shift ends."

Luca moves with the phone in his hand to lay down on what I assume is his bed. I try not to get too distracted by his naked upper half since he is shirtless. He smirks, which tells me I got busted looking at him.

"I know you want me, gorgeous, but I don't think you are in the appropriate place to be thinking about it."

I let out a small chuckle, shaking my head. He grins at me when I do. I think he is happy that he got me to laugh. He has made me feel slightly better than I was before I spoke with him.

"So, you aren't mad at me anymore?" he asks softly.

"I wasn't mad at you, Luca. I was confused, and then worried."

It was strange earlier when I was still at home. My gut instinct told me to check on Luca. I'm glad he was okay, well, he appeared to be, but he has obviously had a lot to drink. I sensed there was something wrong with him when he finally answered his door to me. I wish he would stop being so closed off. It's evident he is keeping a lot locked inside of him, and it isn't healthy. Unfortunately, I can't make him open up to me.

"I am sorry that I worried you." He let out a sigh.

"It is okay. The main thing is there didn't seem to be anything seriously wrong with you."

"I am fine. I will always be fine."

He smiles when he says it, but I can see through it. He is far from okay; he has too many demons in his head. No, I don't know what he has been through, but I can guess it hasn't been good.

"Do you have work tomorrow?" I ask.

"If I can be bothered going into the office," he says with a laugh before continuing, "or I may work from home. I will see how I feel."

It must be great being able to choose when you do and don't go into work. I laugh and shake my head at him. Luca shrugs, not seeming too bothered about it all. Luca stays on the phone with me until I have to get back to work. We have arranged to see each other tomorrow if we have the time. We say our good nights He is going to try to get some more sleep, I don't know if he will manage, but at least he is going to try.

I finish my coffee, dump the paper cup in the trash, and give my hands a good scrub before going back out to the Emergency Department. It's calmer now. I do a brief check-in with the patients. Most of them are sleeping. They will buzz if they need anything. Many of them will be going home in the morning, or if they are in for longer they will get moved into one of the stations. My main base is here, but I do help in other hospital stations if I am needed. We are short-staffed at the moment, so we all help out when and where we can.

I take a seat at the nurse's station to get some of my paperwork done while it was quiet. It will help pass the time.

My shift finally came to an end, and I can't get out of the hospital soon enough. Unfortunately, another person involved in the car accident passed away only a couple of hours ago. I was feeling extremely sad. The doctors did everything they could, but she didn't make it.

I put my earphones in to listen to my music as I walk home. It always helps me cope when I do. I swear by music being one of the best therapies there is. I get lost in the music until I arrive at my apartment.

I have a quick chat with my doorman before I go up to my place. Just as I'm coming down the hall, Luca is coming toward me, probably going to work. He is in his suit, so it's the only place he could be going.

"Good morning," he beams.

"Morning," I reply tiredly.

"Are you okay?"

"No, not really. We lost another person from the crash last night."

A wave of utter sadness takes over me again, and I feel the tears in my eyes. I know because I'm exhausted, my emotions are all over the place. If someone tells you who works as a nurse or doctor that losing a patient doesn't affect them, they are lying or are in the wrong line of work.

Luca's next move surprises me. He wraps his arms around me and hugs me tightly.

"I am sorry to hear that," he whispers as he strokes my hair.

I bury my face into his chest and hug him back. It feels nice to be held while I'm upset. I miss it. Luca pulls away first, and I look up at him. He reaches his hand up and wipes the tears from my face.

"Come on, angel, let's get you inside."

"You have work, don't you?"

"It can wait a couple of hours."

I nod, giving him a grateful smile as we head to my front door. I let us in.

"Go take a shower, get into something comfortable, and I will make us breakfast and coffee."

I go to protest, but he gives me a stern look. What he is suggesting sounds like a good idea. I kiss his cheek before going to my bedroom. I get what I need and go have a shower. I step in, my back against the wall and sigh as the warm water falls over my body, it feels good. I need it.

I stay there for a good twenty minutes before exiting, getting dried off, and pulling my sweats on. By the time I go to the kitchen, Luca is setting breakfast out on the table. He has made eggs, bacon, toast, and coffee. It looks and smells delicious.

"Nice timing."

"Thank you for making breakfast," I say with a grateful smile.

"It was no bother, now sit down and eat."

I take a seat, and he sits across from me. We make small talk while we eat. It's good having some company. I go to gather the dishes after we finish eating, but Luca reaches over the table, putting his hand on mine and tells me to stop.

"I will get them. You go to bed. I will be through soon."

Is he coming to bed with me? He better not think we are going to have sex, because we aren't. I am tired and not in the mood.

"You will be through?" I ask.

"Yes. I don't mean for sex, Kayla," he tells me with a chuckle. "Just a cuddle because I believe you need one right now."

He is right, I do. I just don't expect him to be the one to give them to me. I give him a gracious smile and stroll through to my bedroom. I quickly jump into bed and get comfortable.

Luca comes in fifteen minutes later.

"Everything is tidied up. I am all yours until noon, then I need to go into the office," he informs me with a smile.

"Thank you."

Luca strips down to his boxers. He hangs his suit and tie carefully over the chair. He slips in beside me. "Come here, angel."

He extends his arms out to me. I scoot over the bed and happily let him embrace me. I nuzzle my face into his chest, and he brings the covers over us. His fingers slip under the back of my tee, and he begins to caress my back gently.

"Rest, sweetness," he whispers.

I kiss his chest, causing him to groan. I giggle and apologize. I close my eyes, then Luca starts singing softly to me. His voice is beautiful and soothing. I had no clue he could sing.

"You can sing?" I ask him.

"Sometimes, though I haven't sung to someone in years."

"You have a beautiful voice, Luca."

He mutters out a thank you, and kisses the top of my head. I don't speak another word after it, instead, I get lost in his voice. I relax instantly and my eyes become heavy.

"Sweet dreams, angel."

Those are the last words I hear as I drift off. I'm happy to have him here. I wonder if he will still be next to me when I wake up. It will depend on the time that I wake up I suppose.

Chapter Eighteen

Kayla

I shoot awake, sweating and panting. I just had the steamiest, erotic dream I have ever experienced. It would make some of the pornos out there look innocent. The person in it? None other than Luca himself. I can feel heat throughout my body, and my legs are throbbing.

I try to steady my breathing as I run my fingers through my messy hair. I glance next to me to check if Luca is still here because I don't know what time it is. He is still here sound asleep. I pick up my phone to check the time, I see it's only half past ten in the morning. I thought I had slept for longer than that.

I need to sort my horniness out. I could wake Luca, he would have no problem fixing it for me, but I don't want to disturb him, he needs sleep. I won't get back to sleep, until I fix my issue. I do have another option. I quietly sit up in the bed, and go into my drawer, it has a couple of sex toys. I don't use them often, or not at all really, unless I am in serious need of release, like right now.

I chose the bullet, it always works well and quickly. I creep toward the bathroom.

"Where are you going?"

The sound of Luca's voice makes me jump. I didn't even know he was awake. The toy falls out of my hand, and rolls across the floor. It stops rolling on his side of the bed, right in front of him.

Oh God, this can't be happening! I feel my entire face heat. He looks down at the floor, then up at me, a smirk resting on his lips.

"And what were you going to do with this?"

He picks it up from the floor and waits for me to answer.

"Um, throw it out." Throw it out? What kind of lame-ass excuse was that? Unquestionably, I could have come up with something better, or told him the truth. It's evident he didn't believe me going by the raised eyebrow. I can understand why.

Luca gets up, the bullet still in his hand and makes his way over to me. He steps into me. I try to move backwards, but my back hit the wall.

"What has gotten you all fired up, angel? And why didn't you wake me up?"

"I... I... I may have had a dream," I breathe out.

Luca presses his body to mine and rests his hands on the wall on each side of my head.

"I assume it was a dirty one?" he asks, and I nod. "About?"

"You," I blurt out.

"Did you enjoy it?"

"Yes." I can't turn around and tell him no. He would know I'm lying.

"Did it make you wet?"

I nod in response. He leans in, putting his lips on my neck. I moan, and I bring my hands up and tangle my fingers into his hair.

"Again, why didn't you wake me up?" His voice is low and husky.

"Because you need to sleep."

"And? You have needs, clearly."

He grazes his teeth along the skin of my neck and swats my thigh with his hand. I whimper because my body is already sensitive, and he is not helping matters. Luca brings one hand down my body and into my joggers. He brushes his finger over my folds.

"Damn, sweetness, you are soaking," he groans "Do you want me to sort that for you?"

"Yes. Please," I beg.

Luca separates my legs apart further, dipping his hand down, and I feel him slip one finger inside of me, followed by a second. He begins working them quickly. I cry out, moving my hips in sync with his fingers. Luca pushes my joggers down, and they puddle around my ankles.

"Do you use this often?"

I know he's referring to the toy. I shake my hand to answer. He switches it on to the highest function. Is he going to use it on me? I don't wonder for long when he moves it over my folds, then holds it—straight on my clit.

"Oh, God," I gasp.

This is another first for me. No man has ever used sex toys on me. It feels so good, it's such a turn on. Between his fingers and the bullet, my climax is rapidly building.

"Come for me, angel. I know you are ready to."

Luca captures my lips in his, kissing me roughly and picking up speed. It's enough to end me! I squeal as my legs begin to tremble, and I erupt around his fingers. He doesn't remove his lips from mine until I finish my pleasurable high.

I nearly lose control of my legs due to them being weak. Luca holds me, anchoring me in place to stop it from happening. He gives me a sly look, confident because he knows what he does to me.

"As much fun as it was using this little thing on you, and I would love to do again, sometime, right now, I would love to fuck you with my cock, right against this wall." The tone of his voice is low and seductive. It causes a shiver to go right through my entire body and straight to my core.

"Then fuck me, Luca."

I rid him of his boxers, and he steps out of them. His full, hard length comes into full view. I moan at the sight because I know what he can do with it. I stroke his member. He growls loudly as he tilts his head back.

I kiss him, and the second I do, he comes at me. He pins my hips to the wall with his while he removes my cotton tee, tossing it aside.

"Condom." I breathe out.

I don't want us to get carried away and forget one. I'm on birth control, but I would like to make sure we are doubly safe. He nods and pulls away from me. He sets the bullet down and goes into the drawer to get a condom. It reminds me I need to get more, especially with him around. I take the time to catch my breath for a second.

I look over at him, he is putting it on before he comes back to me. He hooks his hands under my thighs, lifting me up off the floor, and my back's tight against the wall again. I wrap my legs around him and grab onto his shoulders to keep myself upright.

Our lips meet in a heated kiss, and he thrusts his tongue into me vigorously. My squeals echoed through the apartment as he filled me up completely. Luca starts drilling into me.

"Yes! Like that, fuck. Just like that," I shriek.

He is being rough, but it's what I need. I believe he does too. I roll my hips with him so we are moving simultaneously. Luca lets out a loud, throaty groan. My walls are already tightening around him. I'm close again. With his strokes deep and fast, he's brushing against all the right spots.

Luca's name escapes from my lips in a scream. He holds onto me firmly and brings us off the wall. He crashes his lips to mine and carries me toward the bed. He pushes up into me as he does. It feels incredible, and my grip on him strengthens. He sits on the bed, with me still wrapped around him so I was now straddling him.

"I need you to ride my cock, baby girl," he pants out.

I use his shoulders at leverage and start to rock my hips against him. My head falls back as the pleasure soars through me. I went from back and forth to circling my hips.

"Fuck, baby, that feels good," he grunts.

His hand comes down against my ass. I cry out and pick up my speed. I start bouncing up and down on his length. Our bodies move so well together. We're in perfect sync and climax together.

Luca falls back against the bed and takes me with him. He holds me against his chest as we catch our breath. He caresses the small of my back with his rough fingertips.

"I swear, angel, your pussy is addictive and one of my favorites."

"I am sure you say that to all the girls," I can't help but giggle.

"Don't be a smartass."

He laughs and swats the back of my thigh. I am positive I am not the only woman he has said that to. I go to move off him, but he is having none of it.

Instead, his arms come strongly around my body.

"Stay put, please."

The words came out in a whisper. It seems to me they weren't easy for him to say.

"Okay," I happily reply.

I keep my place on top of him. I bury my face into his neck. Luca lets out a sigh while he continues to stroke my back. I close my eyes, letting myself enjoy the feeling. Next thing, I feel him kiss the top of my head, which takes me by surprise. Neither of us speak for a little while.

"We should get cleaned up, beautiful. I will need to head to the office soon."

I can hear the disappointment in his voice when he said it. I don't think he is ready to move, but he has to. I nod and hesitantly climb off him. He doesn't shift though.

"Are you coming?" I ask him with a laugh.

"I just did, not too long ago… too hard."

"That is not what I meant," I say, continuing to laugh.

"I will move in a second. I am admiring the view for right now."

I rest my hands on my hips and cock my brow at him. He smirks while his eyes map my body. Once he is happy with his "admiring," he finally gets to his feet. He steals a kiss, linking our fingers, and leads us to my bathroom. He turns the shower on and lets me step in first, then he follows.

We start to shower, both of us not wanting to stay in it too long. I don't want to distract him and be the reason why he ends up not going to the office. We get out, wrapping towels around ourselves, and stroll back to my bedroom.

I sit on the side of the bed to dry off, Luca just stands in the middle of my bedroom, totally stark naked, and dries himself off without a care in the world. I enjoy a perv for a moment before I go back to what I'm supposed to be doing.

"What are your plans for the rest of the day?" he asks.

"To get some more sleep, then nothing much."

He opens his mouth to speak but then changes his mind. I can see he's trying to work it out in his head if he should say what he was going to.

"Do you want to go out for tea, around six o'clock before you need to go to work?" he asks nervously.

"Yes, that would be nice," I tell him, unable to stop my smile.

I wonder to myself if it's only tea or a date. I won't ask him, just in case it makes him change his mind.

"Do you like Greek food?"

"I do, yes," I reply.

"Then I know the perfect place we can go to," he grins.

Luca finishes off getting dressed. I put some clean pjs on since there is no point getting dressed when I'm going back to bed.

"Right, I need to go. I will see you later." He comes over to me and kisses me softly.

"See you later," I smile.

"Goodbye, beautiful."

With that, he disappears out of my bedroom and then out of my apartment. I sigh and rub my face with my hands. I have no clue what is going on between Luca and I.

I clean up our mess and climb back into bed. I'm shattered. I set my alarm for three o'clock and get myself comfortable. I may sleep until then, or I will wake before. But three is a good time for me to get up. It will give me a chance to catch up on a bit of housework and washing before I get ready for "tea" with Luca tonight.

Chapter Nineteen

LUCA

I'm in my apartment getting ready for tea with Kayla. I may be regretting my suggestion for us to go out together. I got caught up in the moment at the time. I should never have asked her. I don't want her to get the wrong impression of what is going on between us. I can't cancel now, not only is it too late, but also, if I do, I think she would be done with me—entirely. Maybe I should make it clear to her what is going on between us.

I finish off getting ready and gather my things. I take a deep breath as I walk across to her place. I don't know why I am so nervous about this. We have shared tea before, a few times. I'm probably overthinking, as always. I finally knock on her door.

It only takes her a moment until she comes to the door and opens it. The second she comes into view, I forget how to breathe. My heart is beating at an impressive speed. A pink dress covers her beautiful body. It is nothing too fancy or out there, but it suits her and clings to her perfectly. She has the barest touch of make-up, and her hair is pulled back in a high ponytail.

"Hey, handsome," she says with a grin as she checks me out.

"Um, hello." I finally breathe out. Kayla looks at me strangely, probably wondering why I'm acting like an idiot!

"Are you ready to go?" I want to distract her before she asks me for a reason about my ridiculous behavior.

"I just need to grab my coat and bag."

Kayla would need to go straight to work from tea, and that's why she needs to bring her bag with her. She gives me a soft smile before going to grab her things. As she does, I take the time to get myself together. By the time she comes back, I'm back to my usual self. Her coat's on and buttoned up, which makes it easier for me not to get distracted by her in the dress.

I place my hand on the small of her back as we head out of the building.

"I have booked a table, so we shouldn't need to hang around," I say.

"Good idea since we don't have long before I have to go to work."

I guided us to my car. I'm only taking it because it will save us time, unlike walking. I open the front passenger door to let her climb in first.

"Belt up, sweetness."

I close the door and rush around to the other side to get in. It will only take us ten minutes to get there in the car. I decide to use the time to talk with her and hope she doesn't change her mind about going to tea after I do.

"Kayla, I need to make something clear."

"Luca, I know. But, don't worry, I don't think we are dating or anything just because we are going out for tea." She says with a laugh.

"You don't?" I ask her. I am surprised because many women, not all of them, would assume this is a date. I like how she doesn't.

"Luca, I know better than that," she replies with a shrug.

The tone in her voice is strained a little. I don't know what to think of it. Yes, she said she knows we aren't dating, but does she want to? Is that why her voice sounds like that?

"Okay." I keep my answer short because I don't want the conversation to continue. Something about the way she said it got to me, it made me feel like an asshole. I shouldn't feel this way though. I have been honest about not wanting more than sex from the get-go, I'm not the dating kind.

Kayla sighs, turning away from me and stares out the window. We don't speak another word for the rest of the drive. I find a parking spot easily for us. I get out first, I'm about to go around to open the door for her, but she is already getting out of the car. I wait for her to join me.

I reach for her hand, linking our fingers I lead her inside. I feel her looking at me, probably wondering why I'm holding her hand, especially after what was said in the car. I refuse to meet her gaze.

The front of house staff greets us with a smile.

"I have booked a table for two; it should be under Maddox."

"Yes, follow me," she replies with a smile.

She leads us through the restaurant to a table at the back, which is what I requested. I prefer to be far from everyone else, less noisy this way, and no one is close enough to listen to our conversation.

"Someone will be by in a moment with the menu." She smiles and leaves us to it.

I drop Kayla's hand and bring the chair out for her to sit on. She thanks me, and sits down, and I sit across from her. She slips her coat off, and my response is the same as when I picked her up.

"Why are we so far away from everyone? Are you ashamed to be seen with me?" she questions me.

I couldn't tell by her face if she was joking or being severe. "What? No, of course not. Why would I be ashamed?"

"Because you can't be seen having tea with a woman, it may give people the wrong idea," she states.

I go to defend myself, but before I can, she lets out a laugh.

"You are messing with me!" I say with a laugh.

She smiles widely at me. I shake my head and stick my tongue out at her. A waiter comes over with our menus.

"Can I get you both a drink?" he asks, his attention is mainly on Kayla.

"Can I just have water, please?" she asks with a smile.

"Sure," he responds. He doesn't take his eyes straight off her, only when I clear my throat does he look my way.

"I will have diet coke."

My reply came out as more of a snarl than my normal voice. I'm glad when he left. I turn my attention back to Kayla to find her staring at me with a raised brow.

"What?"

"There was no need to be rude to him," she said with a sigh.

"I wasn't rude!" I protest. I know I was. I didn't like the way he looked at her. Now I understand how Kayla felt when we went out for breakfast.

"You were," she argues.

"I don't know what you mean," I say with a shrug. I pick up the menu to take a look, and she does the same.

"Any idea what you want?" I ask.

"I am thinking of a pasta salad."

"Shouldn't you eat something more substantial, especially with such a long night ahead of you?" I suggest.

"That is substantial, and it will leave room for dessert too. If I eat a larger meal, then I won't manage dessert," she says with a laugh.

"That is true, and you got to have dessert, right?"

She makes a valid point, so I will let her get away with it. The waiter comes back with our drinks and takes our orders. Kayla places hers. I decided on the keftedes with basmati rice and feta salad. I rest back on my chair and stare at her for a moment.

"Is there a reason you are staring at me, Luca?"

"Yes. You look beautiful in that dress."

I watch as her cheeks turn a delicious crimson, and she stammers out a thank you. I try not to smirk because I am making her blush. She rolls her eyes at me and takes a sip of her water.

Maybe going out for tea with Kayla isn't going to be so bad, I thought. So far, so good.

We arrived at the hospital. Tea was delicious, and the conversation seemed to flow easily, which is always nice.

"Do you want me to walk you in?" I asked.

"No. I will be okay. Thank you for tea."

"You are welcome, angel. Thank you for your company," I tell her.

"See you, at, um, some point?" she asks.

"I will see you tomorrow, maybe."

"Okay. Enjoy the rest of your night, Luca."

She says goodbye and moves to get out of the car. I reach for her, grab her arm, not too rough, and she turns to me. The second she does, I press my lips to hers. Kayla moans in response, her fingers going directly into my hair as she kisses me back. I groan and put more pressure onto her lips. Her lips always feel incredible against mine.

Kayla abruptly pulls away from me, both of us breathing heavily.

"I should go inside."

"I hope your night is better than last night," I say hopefully.

"Me too. Goodnight, Luca."

She got out of the car and I don't stop her this time. I wait until she has gone inside before I drive off. I don't want to stay anywhere near the hospital for longer than I need to. I hate the place, and there is nothing but bad memories associated with it. I can deal with being there for a small amount of time, but that's it.

I wasn't ready to go home because if I do, I will be alone, which is never a good idea. I find somewhere to park and get my phone out. I scroll through my contacts and find who I'm looking for. My buddy, Spencer. I hit the call button, and he answers in a few seconds.

"Hey, what's happening?" he says.

"Alright, pal. Are you busy?" I ask.

"Nah, just chilling. Holly and Aiden are away at her mums for the night."

Holly is his wife, and Aiden is their son, he's nearly two.

"Do you want to grab a beer or something?" I suggest.

"Sure, meet you at Flannigan's Irish Bar in about half an hour?"

"Yes, see you then."

We hang up, and I start the car to go home. I will just park it and then walk to the bar, it's not far from my apartment. It will be good to see him. I haven't seen him in weeks, which is understandable since he has a family. I have known Spencer for about eight years now. He was there the best he could be during one of the most challenging times of my life, but he still didn't know much about my life before we met.

No, I am not going down that road. I give myself a shake. I was going to forget everything tonight and just have a nice time catching up with Spencer. I will only have a couple of beers. I don't want to drink too much, because if I start, I won't stop.

Chapter Twenty

I arrive at the bar and look around for Spencer. I hear him calling out my name and follow the sound of his voice. He's at one of the tables with two beers. I smile and make my way over to him, taking a seat across from him. He slides one of the bottles over to me. I raise my bottle and thank him before I take a sip.

"How are things?" he asks.

"Yeah, I'm doing okay. You? How are Holly and Aiden?"

"We are all good," he tells me smiling. "So, do you want to tell me how you really are?"

I sigh, run my fingers through my hair. I could lie to him, but there's no point.

"I have my good and bad days," I reply hesitantly. More bad than good, but he doesn't need to know that.

"Did you go talk to someone like I suggested?"

"What's the point? It isn't going to bring Leah back." I reply, my voice shaky.

"No, but do you think this is how she would want you to be living your life?" he asks softly.

No, if she knew how I was living my life, she would be so disappointed in me. Leah was unique, that was for sure. She had a way of lighting up an entire room. She would smile at strangers in case they were having a bad day. Leah always lived to the fullest and treated everyone the same. She had a heart of gold. And she loved in a way I didn't know existed until I met her. Leah loved me completely; my past didn't matter to her. She knew the right things to do and say if I was having a bad day.

"Spencer, I stopped living life the night I lost her. Now, I just get through each day."

"Luca, it has nearly been three years. I know you can't get over something like that overnight, but you need to get yourself out of the darkness. You can't keep shutting yourself out from the world."

His voice is calm and sympathetic. I know he is trying to help, but he can't understand what I am feeling. I lost the love of my life because some fucking idiot ran a red light. She got taken away from me without any warning. The bastard behind the wheel destroyed multiple lives, including mine.

"I will do what I need to, Spencer." I try not to show the annoyance in my voice.

"Sorry, but she would want you to be happy, and you know that."

"I know she would," I reply. "Can we please change the subject?"

I don't want to talk about this anymore. I didn't come here to talk about what happened. I tried to escape from it.

"Yes. Of course," he said, backing off and smiling at me. "But you know where I am if you need me."

"I know. Thank you."

I change the subject. I get him to fill me in about work and his family. He happily tells me everything. Spencer is a good man. He's a great husband and father too.

"Holly and I are going to start trying for a second baby." He beams. His entire face and eyes light up as he tells me.

"That's great news. I hope you both get what you want soon." I smile.

"Thank you," he said.

I'm happy for him. I really was. Though, at the same time, it made me feel sad because I know I will never have any of that. I was supposed to have all of it with Leah. I was going to ask her to marry me the day after she got killed. I still have the ring, and I think I will always hold onto it. I drift off thinking about it.

"Luca, what is going on in that head of yours?"

The sound of Spencer's voice brings me back.

"Nothing, sorry. Do you want another drink?" I ask.

He nods, and I head to the bar to get us both a scotch. I look around as I wait to get served, seeing if anyone grabbed my attention. I spot a couple of women, but then I realize something, I don't want to go home with anyone, not tonight. So instead, I get our drinks and join Spencer back at the table.

"So, what is new with you? How is the new place?" he asks.

"It is good. I like the building. It is quiet." I smile as the thought of Kayla comes to mind, the way she squirms below me and cries out my name.

"Good to hear."

"I have a little thing going on with my neighbor who lives across from me."

"Do tell? And what do you mean by a little thing?" he asks with a raised brow.

"We are having sex and hanging out. We went out for tea tonight, but it wasn't a date."

I make sure I emphasize the not a date part. I start telling him the entire story of how we met, and how our first meeting didn't go well. I fill him in on us hanging out and what she does for a job. I find myself rambling about her.

"She is beautiful, sweet, and makes me laugh."

The words didn't come out normally, not the way I usually talk. I am gushing about her, over her. I think it is my cue to stop. By the time I'm done, Spencer is leaning back against his chair, his arms folded across his chest, and a smug look on his face.

"What?" I ask, confused.

"You like her," he states with a smirk.

"I do not! It is purely sexual," I protest.

"Bullshit! If it were only sexual, then you wouldn't be spending as much time with her. You wouldn't be taking her out for tea." He responds confidently.

"You are delusional," I chuckle. Crazy man thinking I like Kayla. It isn't like that.

He says drily, "And you are in denial."

"Shut up and drink your drink," I say with a laugh.

He holds his hands up, but I can tell he didn't believe a word I said to him. He can think what he wants, but I know the truth.

Spencer and I have just left the bar, both of us heading home.

"If you want to admit you like Kayla finally, you should bring her to Aiden's birthday party next weekend," he says. "You are still coming, right?"

"Yes, I will be there… alone," I reply sternly.

"If you insist," he says with a shrug.

He hugs me goodbye and reminds me to call if I need him. He goes one way, and I go the other. I am not asking Kayla to go to a kids' birthday party with me. Plus, she'd probably be working. I slowly make my way home, I'm in no rush to get there. I enjoy the night air while walking. I arrive at my apartment building and hesitantly enter, then go up to my place.

I slide off my jacket, kick my shoes off, and toss myself onto the sofa. I take my phone out of my pocket to check it since I haven't looked at it since I met up with Spencer a few hours ago. I keep my phone out of the way when I am in company.

I see a text from Kayla on my screen, and it makes me smile.

Hey, how is your night going? Thankfully my night is calmer X

Hey, angel. I met a buddy of mine for a couple of drinks. That's good then X

She sent me the text about an hour ago, so I don't know if she will reply soon. It depends on how busy she is, I guess. She texts back only moments later.

Did you have fun? And did either of you get lucky, ha-ha X

Yeah, it was good to see him. And no, we didn't. He is married with a kid. I wasn't in the mood X

Oh… then it is good he didn't get lucky, lol. You weren't in the mood? Are you feeling okay? X

I'm fine. I don't need sex every night, you know ha-ha X

It is true what they say then, uh? Every day is a school day. And today, my lesson is you aren't a sex addict after all lol X

Not quite there yet, angel. Though, I could have it every night if that is something you are up for ;) X

Yeah, like you could stick to fucking one woman, no offence ha-ha, X

None taken, and you are probably correct X

Kayla and I text back and forth for at least half an hour before she's got to go see to a patient. I toss my phone on the sofa next to me, close my eyes, and just lay there. A part of me wishes if I lay here long enough sleep would take over me. It doesn't work, which becomes apparent when over an hour has gone by.

My phone starts ringing. Who is calling me at this time? I glance over and see it's a video call from Kayla. I grab it and answer. Her beautiful face soon appears on my screen.

"Hey, sweetness," I grin.

"Hey, baby boy," she greets me.

Baby boy? That was a first, her calling me that. I know she is joking. I just don't know what to think of it.

"Baby boy?" I question with a raised brow.

"Yes. You call me things like angel, baby girl, sweetness, and whatnot all the time. It's only fair I get to call you something else from time to time," she declares with a grin.

"That's fair, I guess," I say, laughing.

"Are you going to try to get some sleep?"

I can hear the concern in her voice when she asks the question.

"I will try, but it probably won't work."

"If you want, you can come to mine tomorrow morning. You seem to sleep better when you aren't alone," she suggests, her voice soft, yet nervous.

She has a point, that's true, though it isn't the fact I have someone next to me. I have spent many nights with women and didn't sleep. Kayla is what makes the difference, but I will keep that information to myself.

"I don't want to be a bother to you."

"You won't be, Luca. I wouldn't mind," she reassured me, smiling.

Maybe I will take her up on her offer. It just means not going into the office until sometime in the afternoon.

"I will think about it," I responded.

Kayla nods and smiles at me. She stays on the video call until her break is over.

"I've got to go. Maybe see you in the morning?" she asks. She sounds hopeful when she does.

"See you in the morning. Goodnight, gorgeous."

"Goodnight, handsome."

She blows me a kiss before she ends the call. I sigh loudly to myself and decide to go to bed. I have at least seven hours to go until Kayla will be home. I don't like this feeling of needing her. It isn't right.

Chapter Twenty-One

I hadn't seen Luca for a few days, I've spoken to him however. He's been busy with work, and I have been too. Thankfully my days rostered on have come to an end, and I have a couple off now. I'm ready for them. I'm going out for tea tonight with Elaine and Dane. I don't like being the third wheel, but I enjoy spending time with them both, so I pushed the thought of that to the back of my mind. After a couple of glasses of wine, I am sure I won't be caring. We're having tea at mine and Elaine's favorite Italian restaurant.

I'm in the middle of getting ready when I hear a knock on my front door. I pick up my dressing gown and wrap it around myself since I only have underwear on. I wasn't expecting anyone. I peer through the peep hole and see Luca standing on the other side. I didn't know he would be stopping by tonight, he didn't mention it when we spoke earlier. I open the door to him, and he flashes that stunning smile at me.

"Hey, you, this is a nice surprise," I say with a massive grin.

"Sorry, if I have disturbed you. You are going out, I assume, with your hair and make-up done."

"Yes, I am going out, but I'm still getting ready. Come in," I say.

He nods and steps into my apartment. I motion for him to follow me to my bedroom. He takes a seat on my bed and I sit back on the floor to finish my make-up.

"Do you have a date?" he asks through gritted teeth.

Hmm, I don't think he likes the idea of me going on a date with another man. "No. I am meeting Elaine and her boyfriend for tea."

"And you aren't going with someone?" he questions.

"No, I will be the third wheel for the night," I tell him with a laugh. I see a look of relief take over his face when I confirm I will be going alone. I can tell he is trying to fight to keep the smirk off his face. We fall silent, but he watches me as I get ready in the mirror.

"Do you want some company?" he blurts out.

I turn around to face him. "For what?" I ask, confused.

"For tea, so, you don't need to be the third wheel. If you don't want me to come, that's fine," he says with a shrug.

I like the idea, at least with him there with me I won't be alone. I know Elaine won't mind if I bring someone with me. Though, I am sure she will be surprised when I walk in with Luca.

"Yes, that would be nice," I finally responded.

"Cool," he says casually. "I will go get changed, and then come meet you back here."

Luca leaves to go to his place. I send Elaine a quick text to let her know I am bringing someone, I don't mention who. I take the chance to get my dress on before he comes back. I've chosen a simple red mid-length dress with thin straps, my gold heels, and bag to match. I straighten my hair and pin my bangs back away from my face. I give myself a once over in the mirror and go to the living room to wait for Luca to return.

He arrives back not even ten minutes later and walks in.

"I am ready to go if—oh fuck."

I don't think that was the way he was supposed to end his sentence. He was looking at me with wide eyes. The same look covered his face the night we went out for tea when he first saw me in a dress. His eyes are staring at me like I was some piece of art.

"Are you okay?" I ask.

I'm trying to keep a straight face when I ask, my voice is innocent, but I want to smirk so badly. I can only imagine the thoughts running through his head.

"Mmm." Is the only response I get from him. His eyes finally meet mine, and they seem darker.

"Shall we go?" I question, tilting my head to the side, tugging my lower lip between my teeth.

"Yes, we should go right now, or we will be late."

His voice is low and ragged. I giggle and nod. I walk out of my apartment, quickly closing and locking the door before he changes his mind and drags me to the bedroom.

"Where are we eating?" he asks. I assume he's trying to find a way to distract himself from his previous train of thought.

"Enzo's Italian Restaurant," I say excitedly. Yes, I know, I am weird getting excited over a restaurant, but the food is delicious.

"You're cute when you get excited, sweetness. Your entire face glows."

I didn't know he paid such close attention to me unless I am naked.

"It does not," I say with a laugh, blushing.

Luca lets out a loud laugh, wraps his arm around my shoulder and kisses the top of my head. I look up at him to find him looking down at me, the most beautiful smile painted on his lips. This smile seems to reach his eyes, something I haven't seen before. I give him a dorky grin, and he covers my lips with a soft kiss. It didn't feel like the usual kisses we shared. Instead, there is something warm and gentle about it.

Even when our lip's part, he keeps his arm around me, holding me close to him. I don't mind. We make our way out of the building and toward the restaurant.

There's no point in taking a cab to get there, the walk wasn't far from here.

"Did you inform Elaine that you are bringing me?"

"No. I told her I was bringing someone, not who, though."

"Oh. I am sure she will be surprised when I walk in with you. Possibly not a good surprise for her," he says laughing. "Should I be worried about her boyfriend?"

"Why, because you've hit on her more than once, you mean?" I ask, wriggling my brows at him.

"Um, yes, that." He suddenly seems nervous, and this was shown by the way he rubs the back of his neck.

"You will be fine. Yes, she probably told him, they don't have secrets. He won't worry, though, the relationship they have is solid," I responded honestly. It's the truth, neither of them see anyone else as a threat because they know what they have. I watch as he relaxes.

"Thank God." He laughs, with his hand on his chest.

I roll my eyes at him and shake my head.

"Don't roll your eyes at me, angel," he replied sternly, then swats my ass.

I jump and yelp, not expecting it. I fling my head around to glare at him but end up laughing as he is pulling a funny face at me.

"God, you are annoying." I huff, then playfully slap his arm.

"Don't lie. You love it. Your life would be boring without me in it." He stands tall, and his voice drips with confidence.

"Whatever makes you feel better, buddy."

I laugh and pat his head. He raises his brow at me. I shrug, stick my tongue out at him and turn away. We soon arrive at the Italian place and make our way inside.

I look around and see Elaine and Dane at a table, stealing kisses. I smile as I watch them. I want what they have. Luca removes his arm from around me, instead, he rests his hand on the small of my back as we join them at the table.

"Hey," I say, greeting them. They pull apart and look up. I see a look of shock appears on Elaine's face.

"Luca? You were the last person I expected it to be," she says with a laugh.

"Hello, Elaine. I hope you don't mind that Kayla brought me along," he says rather sweetly.

"No, not at all. Luca, this is my boyfriend, Dane. Dane, Luca, he's Kayla's—um —fuck buddy."

She is unsure how to introduce him, but I am sure she could have said, my friend. Luca let me slide into the booth first, and he came in next to me. This may be a little awkward to start with, but all will be well after a couple of drinks.

"Just as well I changed my mind about trying to set you up on a blind date tonight, or things could have gotten awkward."

A smirk twitches onto her lips, and her eyes fall on Luca. What is she up to? Is she trying to see how Luca will react? I can see him out of the corner of my eye, his jaw is clenched, and his hands seem to be holding onto the table tight.

"You were? Why? I made it clear that I don't want you to set me up," I groan and screw up my face.

"I know, I know. That's why I didn't do it," she tells me with a laugh. "Luca, are you okay?" she adds slyly. She is baiting Luca on purpose! I will have a word with her later.

"I am fine. Why wouldn't I be?" he asks, confused.

"No reason."

The waiter came over to take our drink order, so the conversation came to a stop. Thank God! I didn't want it to continue. We place our drinks order, and the second the waiter walks away, I change the subject.

***

The night has been going well so far. Everyone is relaxed and getting along. The food was delicious, as always.

Elaine and I are going to the lady's room.

"What the hell was that all about earlier with Luca?"

"I wanted to prove a point," she states nonchalantly.

Prove a point? What is she talking about? I think she has had one too many glasses of wine.

"Prove what point?" I ask, looking at her baffled.

"That he likes you. That it's more than sex between you two." She sounds so confident with her words.

"I don't think so. He only wants sex, he doesn't want anything more."

"You sound disappointed with that, Kayla. Do you like him? I mean, really like him?" she asks softly.

"I don't know if I am being truthful. I am still working things out." I sigh and rub my temples.

It wouldn't matter anyway because he isn't willing to try more than what we have going on. And how can you be with someone who refuses to tell you anything about themselves and keep secrets? It would never work.

"Maybe you should work it out soon, Kayla, before you get in too deep and get hurt," she says gently, I can hear the concern in her voice.

"I know. I will be fine," I say with a smile, hoping it will be the truth.

She nods, but it's evident she isn't sure and was worried about me.

"I think there is a new bromance brewing with Dane and Luca," Elaine announces. She's picked up on how I don't want to talk about Luca and I anymore.

"Yes, they seem to be hitting it off great," I agree. They are getting on amazingly. Though Dane did tease him at first about hitting on Elaine, the four of us ended up laughing about it.

"We should go for a couple of drinks after this."

Elaine and I finish up in the bathroom and make our way back to the table. Dane pecks Elaine's lips, and she cuddles into him as we wait for our last course. Luca rests his hand on my knee under the table, a simple touch, but it's enough to make me shiver.

"Do you guys want to go for a few drinks after we finish here?" Elaine looks between the guys when she asks. Dane nods and smiles in reply. "Luca?" she questions.

"Yeah, sure. I don't have any plans for tonight, anyway."

It would seem we had the rest of our night planned out.

Chapter Twenty-Two

LUCA

The four of us are still at the bar having a good time. I had stopped drinking about an hour ago. I didn't want to get drunk or have Dane and Elaine to see me like that. The others have slowed their drinking down since we are all busy chatting and laughing.

"How long have you two been together?" I ask.

I couldn't remember if Kayla or Elaine mentioned it to me before. If they had, I have forgotten. I know one thing, Dane and Elaine are madly in love. You can see it in the way they look at each other, touch each other, and steal kisses. It's beautiful to watch. I remember those feelings; they can make you feel like you are in an entirely different world.

"We have not long celebrated our first anniversary."

Dane has a massive smile on his face and pride in his voice when he answers me. He wraps his arm around Elaine, brings her in close and kisses the top of her head. She glances up at him, with pure love. It's strange for me to see Elaine this way, all sweet, and loved up. I'm used to seeing her as a hard ass that you don't mess with, who doesn't back down, and says what she thinks. I know she needs to be that way when it comes to her work.

I am a great believer that when it comes to our partners in life, there are sides that come out only for them, or when we are around them.

"I am waiting for them to hurry up and get married," Kayla pipes in from next to me, pointing between them both.

"You and me both, girl," Elaine smirks.

She turns to Dane, with a cheeky smile on her lips.

"See what you have done, now, dude," Dane chuckles.

"Sorry, you are in for it now, though," I tell him. I can't help the laugh because both girls are now looking at Dane.

"I will do it when I am ready. When it is least expected," he responded and prods Elaine's nose.

She rolls her eyes and pouts at him. He reaches over to kiss her, and her pout quickly turns into a smile. When they part, Dane looks at me while the girls are distracted and winks at me. Hmm, I think he will be proposing sooner than Elaine knows. I smile and give him a nod.

"How about we go get the drinks, sweetheart?" Dane suggests.

He and Elaine head to the bar to get the next round, but I make sure they know I only want water. I turn to face Kayla, who seems to be in a little world of her own. I rest my hand on her knee, squeezing. She jumps a little and looks at me.

"Are you okay, angel?" I ask her. I don't know what she is thinking about, but to me there seems to be a sadness to her.

"Yeah, I'm fine. Thinking is all," she says, shrugging it off. There's more to the story than that. I lean in, stroking her face.

"What is on your mind, sweetness?"

"I want what those two have, but I don't think I will ever have it," she replies, sounding disappointed.

"I am sure you will have all of that, Kayla," I tell her with a smile and squeeze her knee again.

"Maybe…" she trails off and turns away from me.

I don't see why she wouldn't have all of that. Why wouldn't she get to be a wife and a mother? She's incredible, and the right guy is out there somewhere. And if he's an asshole, he will have me to deal with, if I am still around. Yes, something is going on with Kayla and I, but I would step back if the right man came along for her. I wouldn't like it, but I would stop seeing her because it's what she deserves, and I can't give her that. It would be selfish of me to get in the way of her happiness.

I drift off in my own thoughts.

"What's wrong with you two?"

I snap out of my headspace when I hear Elaine ask, so does Kayla.

"Hmm, nothing. Sorry, I was thinking," Kayla says with a soft smile.

Kayla has gone back to smiling. I rest back on the chair and slip my arm around Kayla's shoulders. She gives me a side glance, but I can see there is a grin on her lips. Then, I feel a pair of eyes on me that weren't Kayla's. When I check to see who it was, I notice Elaine's watching us.

She has a strange look on her face while she does. The best way I can explain it is she knows something I don't, or something I don't want to share. It didn't take long for me to work out what it is. She's addressing the Kayla and I situation. I shake my head, I have a chuckle, and then break eye contact with her.

Whatever Elaine is thinking, she should stop. I divert the attention away from me, and start talking about random topics. The bar closes in an hour, so I just need to get through it without anyone saying anything else.

We exit the bar, all of us ready to head home. I step outside and groan. It's pouring rain! I hate the rain!

"Yay! Rain!"

Is Kayla seriously excited about the rain? Who likes the rain? I glance over at her, her entire face gleams with excitement. She steps out into it, staring up at the sky, her hands are held out like she's trying to catch the raindrops. I watch her, trying to work out what she is doing.

"From the look on your face you don't know about Kayla's love of the rain?" Elaine chuckles.

I don't know much about Kayla, to be honest, only the basics. I shake my head in response.

"Kayla has always loved the rain. I don't know why; she has never given an exact reason, but she did mention how it makes her feel free," Elaine replies as she watches her best friend, smiling.

I study Kayla while she is fascinated with the rain. It didn't seem to bother her that she was getting drenched by it. My lips twitch into a smile. She looks happy and not at all phased strangers are looking at her like she is weird.

"I hope you don't mind getting wet, Luca, because she will make you walk home. You will not be getting a cab unless you want her to walk home by herself, which wouldn't be very gentleman-like of you," Dane tells me with a chuckle.

"You're joking, right?" Surely Kayla doesn't want to walk home in this?

"No. You can try to convince her otherwise, but you will be wasting your time," Elaine answers.

It looks like I am walking home then. I will not allow her to walk home alone. The three of us left Kayla to it for a few minutes. We only interrupt her because Dane and Elaine want to get a cab home. Kayla and I say our goodbyes to them. I stay in place by the doorway of the bar.

"Are you staying here all night, Luca?"

"Can we please get a cab home, baby girl?" I say with a pout.

I'm hoping she will look at my pouty face and agree. Kayla saunters over to me, steps in close, I thought she was going to kiss me, but she has other ideas. She fists my tee and drags me out into the rain.

"No, we are walking," she tells me firmly.

I go to protest, but before I can, she presses her lips to mine. I lose my train of thought the second her mouth connects to mine. Everything around me seems to disappear as she kisses me softly. I moan, wrapping my arms around her and keeping her close. Abruptly she separates from me.

"Let's get going, baby boy." She beams. She offers her hand to me. I hesitate for a second before I take it and let our fingers link. We get on our way back to our apartments, a comfortable silence falls between us. The rain didn't seem to be bothering me anymore.

"Why do you like the rain as much?" I ask curiously.

She drops my hand, turns around, naming all of the reasons why she loves the rain as she walks backwards. It's everything from the smell of it, to how it feels on her skin, to how it makes everything look pretty. The list continues. Who knew there are so many reasons why someone could love the rain? I listen as she rambles on.

Then out of nowhere she loses her footing. I dive at her to stop her from falling, but I am too late; she hits the ground, landing on her ass. I rush over to her and kneel in front of her.

"Are you okay, angel?" I ask in a panic.

I hate seeing people hurt themselves in any way. She doesn't answer my question due to her laughing.

"Kayla, it isn't funny. You could have hurt yourself!" I sigh and shake my head.

"Luca, relax, babe. I am fine."

She boops my nose as she talks, and I find myself laughing along with her. I peck her lips and jump to my feet.

"Get off the ground, silly girl," I tell her with a laugh.

She really is the sweetest. Kayla eventually stops laughing and lets me help her up.

"Now, do you think you can make it home without falling again, or do I need to carry you?"

I playfully prod her side when I ask.

"I will manage."

I wrap my arm around her shoulder and bring her close to me, just to be on the safe side. I don't want her falling over a second time. I don't even know how it happened the first time.

"At least this way you won't do it again," I say with a chuckle.

"Hey! I am offended," she huffs.

I kiss her, and the huffing stops. Kayla halts us in our tracks, swings her body around and slips her arms around my neck to kiss me back. I tangle my fingers into her now dripping wet hair, and put more pressure onto her lips. Kayla runs her hands over my shoulders, down my chest, and grips my tee in her hands. I am drenched, my tee clings to my body. She presses her body tight to mine. Things are going toward heated until she moves back.

My breathing is heavy. So is hers.

"I love kissing in the rain!" Her voice is a little higher pitched than usual because she is excited.

"Another thing to add to the list, huh?" I smile.

"Yip!" She pecks my lips and reconnects our hands. She lay her head on my shoulder as we continue our journey back.

"Do you want to stay at my place tonight?" she whispers nervously.

"If you want me to?"

"I do," she answers as she looks up at me.

"Okay, then," I say with a nod.

I could have said no, maybe I should have, but the truth is I didn't want to say no. I want to spend the night with her. And it scares me.

The rain seems to be getting heavier, and I hope it will make Kayla speed up, but nope, she keeps the same pace. I can't wait to get these wet clothes off, they are sticking to me, and it's horrible. I won't be surprised if we end up with a cold after this.

"How does a warm shower, a sandwich, and hot chocolate sound?" Kayla asks, breaking the silence.

"Damn good, because I am freezing."

"Don't be a pussy," she teases.

I glare at her, trying to seem mad, but it doesn't work because I end up chuckling.

"Don't worry, baby boy. I will heat you up." Her tone is seductive, and a sexy smile plays on her lips.

"Mmm, I look forward to it." I am anxious to get her alone again.

Chapter Twenty-Three

Kayla

Luca and I rush into my place, we're laughing, and desperate for some warmth, trailing water behind us as the rain drips off our clothes. I put the heater on because I know it will warm us up quickly.

"I am locking the front door and hiding the key in case you decide to go back out into the rain dragging me with you," Luca says with a chuckle.

"Don't pretend you didn't enjoy it," I tell him with a smirk.

The grin hasn't left his lips since we left the bar, well, except for when I fell, but other than that he has been happily enjoying the rain with me even if he denies it.

"No one likes the rain, sweet cheeks. Only weirdos like you," he teases.

I flip him off while giggling, and he locks the door like he said, and takes the key out. He makes me turn around and hides the key. I'm officially locked inside my apartment. I guess there could be worse people to be locked in with.

"We should get out of these wet clothes," I suggest.

Yes, I love the rain, but it's getting uncomfortable with my cold, wet, dress sticking to me because of it. Luca nods, reaching for the bottom of his tee and tries to take it off. Unfortunately, he isn't doing a good job of it. I stand and laugh at him. He stops what he is doing and glares at me.

"Help me, please?"

He pouts and gives me his sweetest expression. I snicker and go to him. He looks good with the tee clinging to him, showing off his muscles. I can't help myself and perve, then lick my lips. He looks damn hot, and wet. I help him remove the tee and toss it away.

I trail my fingers down his bare chest. The second my fingers touch his skin, he closes his eyes and groans. I step into him, pressing my body to his and kiss him. I knead my fingers in his hair as we kiss, and Luca slips his arms tightly around me. The feel of his lips always gets me excited so quickly. We part a moment later, but neither of us speak. We just stare at each other, our eyes connected, and our breathing uneven. Luca reaches in, swiping the hair away from my face.

"What are you doing to me, Kayla?" His voice is strained when he speaks and a scared look pools in his eyes.

"What do you mean?" I quiz, tilting my head to the side.

"Nothing, it doesn't matter, angel," he smiles.

I go to speak, but he silences me with his lips before I can. The second his lips touch mine, I become weak, and the words he said disappear from my head. We begin fighting with each other's clothing, item by item getting dropped on the floor until we are only left in our underwear.

Luca's lips fall on my neck, kissing it softly. I moan, and my head tilts back.

"You make me weak, Kayla, and I don't know how to deal with it," he mumbles against my neck.

I don't even know what to make of that. His teeth sink into the skin of my neck, making me cry out. I grab his hair roughly and bring his lips back to mine. I need a distraction, or I will start overthinking the words he said to me.

Luca moves his hands down my body, goosebumps appearing anywhere he touches. He hooks his hands under my thighs and lifts me off the ground. I wrap my legs and arms around him, steadying myself.

"Hold on tight, sweetness," he says with a laugh at my reaction.

Luca turns us around and carries me to my bedroom. He lays me down on the bed, towering over me. His fingertips trace my thighs, over my stomach, and the valley between my breasts. My entire body reacts to him. I whimper and arch into his touch.

"God, you are so damn beautiful," he breathes out.

I look up at him, his eyes burning into mine. I motion for him to come closer to me. He does as I ask, and I capture his lips with mine. He kisses back, but there is something different in the way he kisses me. He is being relatively gentle, something I don't get much from him.

I rest my hand on his chest, pushing up on it, and flip us over, so he is below me. I sit on his stomach, feeling his excitement dig into me. I reach behind me, unclip my bra, and slowly remove it. Luca is watching my every move closely. I drop it on the floor, and his hands go straight to my now naked breasts. He sits up, with me still on his stomach and massages them in his hands. I cry out as my head dips back and involuntarily roll my hips against him at the same time.

Luca's hand slips down my body, his hand on my panties, but I swat his hand away.

"Kayla, I want to touch," he whines.

"Not right now. I am in control tonight, baby boy," I purr confidently.

"Mmm. Well, get to it, angel," he smirks and slaps my ass.

I lean forward, making my way down his chest, over his stomach. Luca shudders below me. I reach where his scars are, paying particular attention to them. I kiss every single one, and then caress them with my fingertips. I wish I knew what happened to him, but he won't tell me, and to me it seems the story behind them isn't a nice one.

I look up at him to find him staring at me with an intensity that makes me pause.

"Please. Don't do that," he whispers. I sense it's upsetting him, so I stop. I move away from the scars, kissing over the rest of his stomach instead. I curl my fingers in his boxers, and he lifts his hips to let me remove them. I take them off, leaving him naked below me.

I flicked my tongue over the tip of his length. He groans, and his hips jerk. I inch him into my mouth, slowly.

"Fuck!" He pants.

I work my lips along his length, and Luca's fingers fall into my hair as I do. I use my hands since they are free, touching him anywhere I can reach.

"You are so good at that, Kayla," he says between heavy breaths.

I moan against him in reply and pick up the speed of my lips. He fists the bedding below him, loud growls coming from his lips. I remove him from my mouth, only long enough to run my tongue along the base, and then take him back in.

"Fuck! I'm close, baby," he gasps out, and his cock twitches in my mouth, his pre-cum, it tastes amazing.

I continue what I'm doing, and it doesn't take long until he cries out and releases into my mouth. I drink him up, riding him through his high, and only stop when he stills.

I kiss my way back up his body, taking my place on his stomach again. I watch his chest rise up and down, his body gleaming with sweat droplets. He opens his eyes to look at me. I lick my lips, moaning.

"Mmm, dirty girl," he says with a smirk.

"I'm only warming up," I respond seductively.

Luca pulls me down against him and kisses me roughly. He pushes my panties down, and I kick them off. I rub myself against him, letting him feel my wetness. He grabs my ass, holding me tightly to him. We get into a heated make-out session, and I feel him harden against me. He's ready to play again.

I sit up, taking a condom from my drawer. I tear it open then roll it onto his length. I place my hands on his chest and lift my hips. He grasps them, and guides me down on top of him until he has entirely filled me. I cry out, and my back arches. I take a moment to adjust, my body still not quite used to his size yet.

Once I relax around his cock, I start to rock my hips. He fills me up so damn good. Luca sits up, my legs on each side of his body. I cling onto his shoulders and continue to move. He puts my hands on the back of my neck, holding me in place to make sure I am looking at him. I close my eyes, moaning in pleasure with how good it all feels.

"Kayla, look at me," he demands.

I do as he asks and open my eyes, letting mine meet his. The look filling his eyes is enough to send a shiver down my spine, a look of sheer want, lust, and pleasure. He uses his free hand to touch the rest of my body, his touch feather-light, but it still feels incredible.

I flick my hips quicker, until suddenly, he takes them in his hands and slows my movements down. Luca lays me on my back, bringing one of my legs around him. I'm expecting him to pick up the speed, or thrust into me rougher, the way he tends to usually, but he doesn't. His strokes are deep yet slow and tender, something I haven't experienced with him.

"Luca, that feels good, baby," I whimper out. It's doing things to my body, things I can't explain in words, that I haven't felt before. Luca buries his face in my neck, massaging my thighs as he gets into a perfect rhythm. I move my hips in sync with him, something that makes us both cry out because it feels so good.

I cling to him as our bodies move perfectly. Everything about what is happening right now feels different! Even the way our bodies are responding to each other. The passion surging between us is on an entirely different level. I slip my other leg around him, my hold on him tightens.

"Kayla, I need you to come for me, baby. I can't hold back much longer."

His voice is strained, his breathing deep. He lifts his head and rests his forehead on mine. He guides his hand between our bodies, going to my clit. He rubs it and kisses me. My walls clench around him, and my legs quiver. He pushes into me harder, more rapidly.

"YES! Uh! Luca!"

My screams echo in the room as my orgasm dominates my entire body. I feel the pleasure in every single nerve. I erupt around him, my nails digging into his back. Luca calls out my name, and his climax takes control of him. Grunts, groans, and curse words escape from his lips as he releases.

"Fucking hell" He pants out and collapses next to me on the bed.

We lay there, neither of us say a word, the only sounds to be heard is our breathing. I don't know how to explain what we just shared, but one thing I do know, out of all the times we've had sex, that was the best, which is saying something since the sex between us is consistently mind-blowing.

"I will be back in a minute," Luca exclaims, before he abruptly gets up from the bed and rushes to my bathroom. Something tells me I wasn't the only one feeling the difference in what we just shared, and he did too. I guess now he's freaking out.

I sigh and run my fingers through my damp hair. I wish he would explain to me what has happened in his life to make him so afraid of letting anyone close. I'm half expecting him to come through, say goodbye, and walk straight out the door. I hope I am wrong.

I crawl to the top of the bed to lie down while waiting for him. He comes back only moments later, and I prepare myself for what is to come. I get proven wrong because he smiles and climbs onto the bed, lying down next to me.

"Come here, angel," he grins and pats his chest.

He isn't leaving! I scoot over and put my head on his chest. He cuddles me closer to him.

"You aren't leaving?" I ask cautiously.

"Not tonight, beautiful," he replies, and kisses the top of my head.

I smile to myself and snuggle in tight. I'm glad he decided to stay.

Chapter Twenty-Four

LUCA

Kayla is in the kitchen making us hot chocolate and a snack. I offered to help, but she told me no. I didn't want to argue with her, so I stayed put in her bed. It gives me time to process what happened between us tonight. I planned on fucking her the way I usually do, but something changed in me the second she kissed me, touched me. I didn't want to be that guy, the asshole who uses women for pleasure, not tonight.

I feel things with Kayla, things I refused to let myself feel for nearly three years. Yes, the thought of letting my guard down, even a little, still scares me, but I won't worry about that now it's an issue for tomorrow.

"Did you find something to watch?" The sound of Kayla's sweet voice snaps me out of my thoughts and makes me look up.

"Yes, a documentary on tigers," I tell her with a chuckle. "It's the only decent thing on at this time."

"That's fine. I love tigers." She beams, smiling from ear to ear.

She joins me back in bed and hands me a mug of hot chocolate; she has added cream and marshmallows to it, yummy! She set a plate between us with cheese, crackers, and fruit. It probably isn't the best idea to eat cheese at three o'clock in the morning, but we are hungry, and neither of us seem tired. I thank her with a peck on the lips.

I hit play on the controller to start the program. Kayla rests her head on my shoulder, and I put my arm around her. We turn our attention to the TV, and a comfortable silence comes between us. It doesn't take long for her to get lost in the show. I am trying to watch it, but I get distracted by her. I'm admiring her without her knowing it. She is breathtakingly beautiful!

I then get an idea in my head. I wasn't sure if it's a good one, but I will go for it. "Do you have any plans for next Saturday? Are you working?" The words slip out quickly, and shakily. I am nervous asking her!

Kayla looks at me, with curiosity in her eyes.

"I have no plans, or work on Saturday. I'm working Friday night, so I will need to sleep for a few hours on Saturday morning, but other than that I'm free."

I take a deep breath and decide to go for it. What is the worst that can happen? She could say no. "I have a kids party to go to on Saturday. My friends Spencer and Holly, their son, Aiden, turns two. It will be a party for the children during the day, but at night it will be for the adults, we can have a few drinks, and things like that," I say. "And I am wondering if… um… you'd like to come with me?"

I hope she will say yes, but if not, I would understand. The thought is probably daunting since she won't know anyone there.

"Yeah, sure, that would be nice, and something different for my Saturday." She answers without hesitation.

"Okay, good. Thank you." I grin, kissing her softly.

Spencer is going to be surprised and happy when I tell him I'm bringing Kayla along. Holly is going to have a mini freak-out when I show up with someone. She asked if she could set me up on dates with her friends for the last year, but my answer has always the same—No! I wasn't ready. I hope they don't get the wrong idea though. I still don't know what is happening between us, and I don't want anyone else having an opinion on it until I know. I wonder if Kayla thinks of it as a date. Possibly she does. I won't correct her either way.

We finish our hot chocolate, and snacks, then lay down on the bed. Kayla curls into my side, and I bring the covers over us. She slips her hand under the covers, directly down to my scars. She caresses them with her fingertips. I close my eyes, a loud breath falling from my lips. Most women who see me naked either don't notice them, or comment on them just to be nosy. I appreciate her for not bringing it up.

"I got them when I was a kid. It was my so-called father's way of making sure I remember what happens if I step out of line."

I speak calmly, but I have anger inside of me when I think of him. I hate the bastard!

"Your own father did that to you?" she asked sadly.

"Yes, with boiling water. I was around eight or nine at the time. He convinced the hospital I had an accident, so nothing was done about it," I whisper.

A horrible shudder goes through me. Talking to Kayla about this made me anxious. Leah was the only person I ever talked to about my childhood. She never judged me. My first ever girlfriend when I was a teenager broke up with me when she first saw them. It knocked the hell out of my confidence.

"Luca, I am sorry you had to go through that. No one deserves that," she whimpers, looking at me with sad eyes.

"It was a long time ago. It was a recurring thing in my house. I became numb to the pain and learned not to cry. I ran away when I was fifteen."

I can hear my voice breaking as I share my secrets. I need to stop talking about this, it's too much. Kayla rolls onto her stomach, resting her head on my tummy and reaches up, softly stroking my cheek.

"How did you survive alone at that age?" she asks, concerned.

"That, angel, is a story for another day," I respond sternly.

I'm not ready to share my life story with her. I don't want to depress her, or scare her off.

"Okay. If you ever want to talk, Luca, you know where I am." She says and kisses me softly.

"I know, sweetness," I responded gratefully.

Kayla rolls off me, taking her spot next to me again. I am glad she didn't push me to continue talking. I look down at her to see her starting to drift off.

"We should go to sleep, angel. You can barely keep your eyes open."

I stroke her hair, and she looks up at me.

"I'm tired now." she says with a soft giggle and rubs her eyes.

I switch the TV off, letting her get comfortable before doing the same with the light.

"Promise you won't sneak away when I'm asleep, Luca."

"I promise. I will be right here when you wake up," I reply.

She presses a soft kiss to my lips before she turns her back to me. I shift over to lay behind her. I snake my arm around her and bring her back against me. She seems to fit perfectly with my body in every way. I rest my hand on hers and link our fingers.

"Goodnight, angel, sweet dreams," I say, kissing one of her shoulders.

"Goodnight, baby boy."

I like it when she calls me that. In a matter of minutes, I hear her breathing even out, and she falls asleep. I close my eyes and wait for the same to happen to me.

I wake, reaching for Kayla, but she isn't next to me. The spot is empty. Where did she go? And what time is it? I reach for my phone, and the screen reads eleven o'clock in the morning. No, that can't be the time. I have to look again to make sure. It was right enough. I feel good after a solid seven-plus hours of sleep.

I sit up, stretch, and climb out of bed. I glance around for my boxers and finally find them, putting them on, and go in search of Kayla. The moment I step out of her bedroom, I smell food cooking. My stomach growls at the possibility of something to eat.

When I arrive in the kitchen, Kayla is standing at the cooker. She is singing away to herself.

"Morning, beautiful. Why didn't you wake me?" I ask as I make my way over to her.

"Good morning, handsome. You looked so peaceful and comfortable. I didn't want to disturb you," she replies, smiling over her shoulder at me.

I slip my arms around her from behind, kissing her shoulders. She lets out a soft moan and leans against me.

"What are you cooking? And can I help?"

"Cheese and red pepper omelet, do you like it? And no, I got it. It's nearly ready. You can make fresh coffee if you like."

"Yes, I like it," I say, kissing her neck. "I will get the coffee brewing."

I kiss her cheek and head off to start. I'm proud of myself for not leaving during the night, even if deep down I wanted to. It seems to be a step in the right direction for me. I just don't know if it will last.

I start the coffee, while Kayla finishes plating breakfast up for us, as she sets the plates down on the table, I pour us both a cup and join her.

"This looks delicious, angel," I tell her with a grin, digging straight in.

Kayla lets out a soft giggle and does the same. It's good to have breakfast with someone again.

"Do you have plans for the rest of today?" she asks in between forkfuls.

"Nope! I am hoping I can spend the day with you. Unless you have plans?"

"No, I don't have plans. So, I am all yours for the day. What would you like to do?" she asks with a smile.

"Hmm, I don't know, maybe go shopping, have lunch, and go to Central Park?" I suggest.

"Yeah, that sounds nice." She replies, her entire face lighting up.

I nod and get back to my food. I want to try and be a decent guy for Kayla. No, I am not ready for anything serious, not yet. I don't want to purposely hurt her, she doesn't deserve that. I've let my guard down around her a little, which is something I haven't done in a long time. She's an incredible human being with a huge heart, and she will be good for me. I will be good for her—to her, if only I could stop the demons from my past taking control. My heart is nowhere close to healing, and until it does, I can't give another person my full attention, or my heart, because it would be unfair to them.

Maybe we can take it slow and try dating. I'm not sure, but I can think about it, and then perhaps talk to her. I think the first thing I should try to do is stop screwing around, it would be best not only for me, but for Kayla too. She doesn't want to be with a man who fucks around, and I don't blame her. If I want more with her, then I need to stop that.

I have a lot to think about.

Chapter Twenty-Five

KAYLA

"Everything is ready, right?" Luca asks nervously.

"Yes. Will you relax?" I ask with a laugh.

Why is he so nervous? Because his friends Spencer and Holly are coming for tea tonight, and to meet me. Luca insisted I meet them before the party because at least I'd know them rather than being at a party with a bunch of strangers. He's more nervous than me for some reason. I don't understand why he's freaking out so badly, they're his friends. Maybe it's because he's introducing them to me, and he doesn't want them getting the wrong idea regarding us.

We've been spending a lot of time together the last few days. The nights I wasn't working, he stayed with me. The nights I was working, he would be waiting for me to come home to have breakfast together before going to work. I've no idea what is between us, and I refuse to question it in case he freaks out and runs off again. Whatever it is, it's working for us, though.

"Sorry. I will stop acting like a crazy person," he says with a laugh, flashing his best smile at me. "Do you want a drink? Maybe scotch?" he adds, with a smirk.

"No. I do not want a scotch," I laugh, shaking my head at him, "but, I will have a glass of wine, please."

"Aw, you suck!" he huffs.

I smirk back at him saying, "Yes, and very well."

"Mmm, yes you do, naughty girl..." He trails off.

I stand, watching him as his mind goes to a dirty place. I laugh and throw a cushion at him.

"Hey, you were the one that turned it dirty, not me," Luca says, laughing.

I flip him off and playfully roll my eyes at him. I follow him to the kitchen to get our drinks because he will put too much in my glass if I leave it to him. I reach up to take a glass from the cabinet, and when I come back down Luca is right behind me. I brush my ass against him as I do, causing him to groan.

"Can I help you?" I question him innocently as I turn to face him.

"I wanted to make sure you didn't fall is all..."

That is a lie! I know this by the sly look on his face.

"Bullshit!" I'm calling him on this.

Luca steps in, closing the small gap between us, trapping me between him and the counter.

"Why else would I be behind you, angel?" he asks, wriggling his brows at me.

"Because you are a perv who seems to be obsessed with my ass," I answer. It's true, he has taken a liking to my ass recently.

"Mmm, it is a nice ass, sweetness. I can't help myself, especially with the angles I have seen it from," he replies, sneaking his hand around to grab it.

I slap his chest and shake my head. He gives a dorky smile, and then presses his lips to mine. I moan, slipping my arms around his neck and kissing him back. He grabs my ass, bringing me flush against his body. He is getting me revved up, and we don't have time because his friends will be here soon.

"Luca, we should stop," I mumble into the kiss. "Your friends will be here soon."

He groans in annoyance but eventually parts from me, and steps back.

"Now look at what you have done," he exclaims, pointing to his evident excitement.

"You started it!" I protest.

"And I will finish it—later," he says with a wink.

He excuses himself to readjust his issue. I take a second to get myself together and make our drinks up. I take a seat on the sofa, Luca coming back through only a few minutes later.

"Better?" I laugh.

"I guess, but I'd rather have sorted it in a different way. I can always tell them to come a little later than planned?" he asks me hopefully.

"No, they are probably on their way here. Stop thinking with your dick," I tell him snickering.

He mutters under his breath and screws his face up, then comes to sit by me.

"We can play later, baby boy," I purr.

"I guess I can wait until then," he says with a pout.

I peck his lips, then hand him his drink. He takes a long swig of it while I sip on mine. I don't want to get drunk and make an ass of myself in front of his friends. I chat randomly to distract his dirty mind, thankfully it works.

"Can you come shopping with me tomorrow to get a birthday present for Aiden?" he asks.

"Yeah, sure," I say with a smile. I'm sure between the two of us we can find something for the little one. He thanks me with a kiss. The second we part there's a knock at the door. Luca downs the last of his drink, stands, takes a deep breath, and answers the door.

I'm suddenly nervous. I gulp down the rest of the wine. I get to my feet, fixing my clothes and hair. Luca soon appears with his two friends.

"Holly, Spencer, this is Kayla. Kayla, my two closest friends, Holly and Spencer," he says, smiling warmly at me.

"Hey, it is nice to meet you both." I smile back, trying not to show my nerves.

"You too!" Holly gushes, before she rushes over to hug me.

I hug her back and feel myself relax. Spencer says hello with a handshake. Once introductions are done, Luca gets them both a drink.

"We can have the first course after our drinks," he says, passing them a drink.

"That's fine. It gives me a chance to get to know your date," Holly says with a smirk.

I wait for Luca to correct her, to my surprise, he doesn't. He just smiles and nods. Holly sits beside me, and the guys take up the sofa.

"So, how did you two meet? Was it in this building?" she asks.

"No, we first met at my friend's law firm. Luca was a jackass," I say with a laugh.

"What did you do?" she asks, glaring at him.

"Nothing! I hit on her." Luca shrugs before adding, "You know my weakness for beautiful women."

Holly and I look at each other, shake our heads, and laugh. I think she knows there's more to it than that. She knows him better.

"How long have you been married?" I ask curiously.

"We've been together for six years, married for three," Holly gushes. "Have you ever been married?"

"No. I was engaged once, but he turned out to be a liar and a cheater."

"I'm sorry, Kayla. Some men are assholes! I was lucky to meet Spencer. He is a good man." She looks over at her husband when she speaks, with the biggest smile on her lips. He smiles back.

"Nah, I am the lucky one, sweetheart," Spencer replies, winking at her.

I can tell they are madly in love, even after only knowing them for such a short time.

"Has what happened put you off getting married one day?" she quizzes.

"No, I still want that one day. A husband, kids, and a house."

"I hope you find what you are looking for," she replies confidently.

"She will," Luca pipes in. I turn to look at him, giving him a grateful smile.

"Everyone deserves happiness like that, no matter what we have been through. No matter what we have done." Holly looks straight at Luca when she says it.

"Not everyone." Luca replies. "I will get the starters plated up," he adds and walks away into the kitchen.

Holly sighs and watches after him sadly. I'm positive there is way more to the story than I know, something Luca doesn't want to share with me.

"I will go help him," I whisper. I excuse myself from them and go to stand next to Luca.

"I got it, Kayla. You don't need to help."

"I want to." I smile at him before asking, "are you okay?"

"Fine," he responds.

I choose not to say anything else about it, not wanting to upset him. So, we are silent as we plate up the salads. I hope it isn't going to be like this for the rest of the night.

Thankfully the mood picks back up after our first course. Whatever was bothering Luca doesn't seem to be doing so now. He appears to be in his element with his friends around; it's lovely to watch. I really like them both. Holly is a sweetheart, and Spencer is hilarious.

"You guys ready to get your asses kicked?" Holly snickers.

"No, because we will win," Luca replies.

The four of us are kneeling on the floor at the coffee table—the girls at one side, the guys at the other. We are having a drinking competition. We have three shots of tequila each.

"After three…" Holly says.

We all nod, and she counts to three, then says, "Go!" Everyone starts making their way through the shots. Holly and I slam the last glass down on the table before the guys have a chance.

"Ha! We win!" I exclaim.

"Not fair! You cheated!" Luca complains.

"How did we cheat? You are just terrible losers," I tease.

The guys cross their arms over their chests and huff at us.

"Oh, get over it already," Holly laughs, rolling her eyes at them.

We offer another try, but they refuse, scared they will lose again. Spencer came to our side to offer his wife a hand up. She kisses him over and over until his pouty face turns into a smile. He wraps his arm around her, leading her to the sofa, sits down, and brings her onto his lap. They are such a sweet couple.

Luca goes into the kitchen to get everyone another drink. I suddenly feel his eyes on me, and when I look up, he beckons me to him. He probably wants a hand to bring the glasses through. I happily go because Spencer and Holly are getting carried away kissing.

"Yes?" I question him.

Luca reaches for me, places his hands on my hips, and roughly pulls me into him. His lips cover mine without warning. I whimper, kissing him back. It's a heated kiss, the type to cause a shiver to run through my body.

"I think tonight is going great," he says, removing his lips from mine.

"Me too! They're good, fun people," I tell him with a smile.

"We should rejoin them. If they are left alone too long, I don't even want to imagine what they are doing on my sofa."

Spencer and Holly are behaving when we arrive back.

"I thought I would need to get the cold water out," Luca says with an evil laugh.

"No, not yet, but there is a good chance we will be leaving soon. We don't get many nights alone," Spencer responds.

"You do what you need to," Luca agrees nodding.

Luca takes a seat on the chair, and to my surprise, he takes me with him so I'm on his lap. I squeal, not expecting it, and make the other's laugh.

"We should put some music on. I want to dance!" Holly announces.

We have got some music on, but it's on a low volume, and not the kind to dance to.

"I second that!" I grin, liking her suggestion. I'm a little drunk, which means I will happily get up and dance.

"For my two favorite girls..." he says trailing off looking between the two of us before continuing, "of course." Luca chuckles looking pleased with himself he played us like that.

He changes the music using his phone to something a little more upbeat. I think the night is just going to become more fun.

Chapter Twenty-Six

LUCA

Kayla and Holly are happily dancing around the living room. I love how great they were getting along. I feel no matter what happens between Kayla and I the girls will continue to be friends. Spencer and I are on the sofa drinking and enjoying the show.

"I like her, she is sweet, and you seem happier when you are around her," Spencer says, looking at me.

"Yeah, she is incredible. I like having her around, but I can't be what she needs, not completely," I responded sadly.

"Yes, you could be, Luca, if you allow yourself to. You need to give her a chance, buddy." He replies with an encouraging smile and pats my shoulder.

"Maybe…" I know he is right, I should give us a chance, but it isn't that simple. I can't help but smile as I watch Kayla from afar. God, she is beautiful, perfect even. I would dance with her if we were alone, but I will not do it with my friends here. She must have felt me looking because she turns toward me, grinning from ear to ear, and I return it.

"She really likes you, you know that, right?" Spencer whispers.

"You think?" I questioned him.

"No, I know. And you like her too, a lot. Don't even try to deny it," he tells me chuckling.

"I don't know what you mean," I shrug, but a smile came over my lips.

Spencer shakes his head at me before slapping me on the back of my head. I glare at him, and he looks at me slyly. I flip him off and go to get some more drinks. On my way back, Holly tries to grab me and make me dance with them, luckily, I get away unscathed.

"God, you guys are boring!" Holly huffs at us.

"I was thinking the same thing." Of course, Kayla agrees.

"I am enjoying the show, angel," I reply, and wink at her.

Kayla sticks her tongue out at me, then lets out a loud laugh, and goes back to dancing. It feels good the four of us hanging out. I used to spend a lot of time with Spencer and Holly but pulled away from them after what happened, and only saw them occasionally. Once they had Aiden, it became less, which is understandable, they have a baby to care for. Plus, I didn't want my sadness around the little one. I love Aiden; he is my little buddy; he calls me Uncle Luca. Unfortunately, I probably don't see him as much as I should. I feel like it's my fault.

The girls stop dancing, probably needing a breather since they have been doing it non-stop for the last half an hour or so. Kayla comes over to me, steals the glass straight from my hand and drinks it.

"Hey, that was my drink!" I protest.

"Not anymore," she says sassily, then giggles.

I reach for her, pulling her onto my lap.

"Smartass…" I chuckle, swatting her ass.

Kayla prods my nose and then kisses me softly. I soon forgive her for stealing my drink. I slip my arms tight around her body and kiss her back. She moans and then pulls back.

"Shall we leave?" Spencer asks.

"No, sorry, we will behave," Kayla says, blushing.

She goes to remove herself from my lap, but I refuse to let her. I give her my best puppy dog eyes, and it works. She stays on my lap but moves position so she is no longer straddling me.

"Aiden is going to be excited to see you, Luca," Holly tells me with a smile.

"I can't wait to see him." I can't help but smile. "I haven't seen him in a while," I added, sadly. The latter part was for Kayla to know. I spoke without thinking it through again.

"I know, but sometimes these things can't be helped," Holly replies softly.

She is only saying it so I won't feel guilty, but I do. I don't want to ruin the atmosphere, though, so instead I nod and smile.

"What is Aiden into at the moment? Just so we know what to look for, for his birthday present?" Kayla questions.

"Paw Patrol and Dinosaurs are his favorite things at the moment," Spencer answered. At least we have an idea of what we are looking for now. I don't have a clue.

"I love my boy, I do, but I don't want to spend the night talking about him because once I start, I won't stop. So, change the subject, more adult talk," Holly suggests.

We change the subject to a different topic, which consisted about life, work, and sex. Kayla is surprised and slightly embarrassed when we begin talking about sex openly, but she soon relaxes.

To an outsider, it would seem like Kayla has been friends with Holly and Spencer as long as I have. Holly and Spencer are two of my most favorite people in the entire world, and seeing them get on with Kayla makes me happy. It's a good thing, especially if something does happen between us.

"I am curious, are you two dating other people? I know you aren't "official"."

The truth is I haven't been with anyone else since Kayla and I started sleeping together. I don't think she has been with anyone else either, not to my knowledge.

"I'm not dating, or sleeping with anyone else, that isn't my style," Kayla answers first.

All eyes soon turn to me. Holly raises her brow at me. I think if I told her I was still screwing other people, she would slap me.

"No, I am not either. Um, I haven't been with anyone since things started up with Kayla." I watch as shock takes over everyone's faces. "I don't know if I should be offended with the lack of faith you all have in me." I laugh.

"Sorry, buddy, but we all know what you are like," Spencer says with a chuckle.

I want to argue with them, but there is no point because they are right.

"Someone will make an honest man of you yet." Holly grins at me.

I laugh and shake my head. I think it's time we change the subject again. I'm used to it from Holly. She wants what is best for me. If Holly gets me alone, even for a second, she will be quick to lecture me, to tell me to get my ass into gear and make things more official with Kayla. I need to avoid being alone with her.

It is one o'clock in the morning and we are walking Holly and Spencer to the door. They're ready to go home for some alone time.

"See you both Saturday at the party," Holly grins.

"Yes. I look forward to it," Kayla replies.

We hug them both goodbye. Tonight has gone better than I ever could have imagined. Kayla goes to the kitchen and starts to clear up. There's a lot to do. I come up behind her, slipping my arms around her waist, and kissing her cheek from over her shoulder.

"We can tidy up in the morning, angel."

"Or we can do it now, so we don't need to do them in the morning," she laughs, looking over her shoulder at me.

I turn her around to face me, and she slips her arms around my neck.

"I can't be bothered," I whine.

"If we do it tonight, we will have nothing to do in the morning except get naked and have hot, morning sex," she purrs, "but, if you would rather do it tomorrow…." she trailed off.

Is she really bargaining with me using sex right now? Damn! The woman knows me too well.

"Fine! We can do it now."

"That is what I thought," she replies, smiling widely.

"Shocking! Using sex like that." I chuckle because of how playful she is.

"You love it, don't pretend like you don't, baby boy."

Kayla pecks my lips, and then pushes me away from her, insisting we get to work. She's so bossy at times. I like it, though. At least working together, it won't take long. Kayla starts on the dishes, while I take care of the trash, then go to help dry the dishes.

"Thank you for doing this tonight with me, Kayla."

"I had a lot of fun. I know it wasn't easy for you to do what you did," she replies and kisses my cheek.

"I had fun too." I smile, rubbing her back.

I lean in, kiss her softly, and then we get back to what we were doing. Once we are done, I switch all of the lights off, wrap my arm around Kayla's waist and lead her to my bedroom. I strip down and climb into bed, waiting for Kayla to join me, but she doesn't.

"What's wrong? Don't you want to stay?" I ask, disappointed.

"I do want to stay. I will be back soon. I have something for you," she answers, a sexy smile playing on her lips.

I watch after her curiously. She smirks at me and disappears into the bathroom. I sit up, resting my head on the wall and wait for her to come through, anxious to know what she has for me.

I hear her move around my bathroom. What is she doing? Finally, after about five minutes, I hear her footsteps approach the bedroom. The second she arrives in front of me, I groan loudly. A silk dressing gown covers her perfect body.

"Mmm, do you have anything on underneath?" I breathe out my question, licking my lips.

Kayla doesn't answer me, instead, she unties it, letting it fall open.

"Oh fuck," I moan, gripping onto the sheets as I see the sexy little black baby doll she has on. It's lace and see-through. It doesn't leave much to the imagination, and she looks so good in it. I feel my excitement rise at the sight.

"Mmm, what do you think?" she asks seductively, biting her lip.

"You look hot in it, and my cock agrees…" I moan.

She slowly removes the dressing gown from her body, letting it fall to the floor.

"I need you to come here, right now, angel," I demand.

Kayla nods, sauntering over to me with her hips swaying sexily. She stops at the bottom of the bed for a moment. I take in the sight of her. She's so beautiful. Eventually, she crawls up the bed, kneeling between my legs.

"I don't think you realize all the dirty things I want to do to you…"

The words cause a shiver to run through my entire body. The confidence showing, the lust pooling in her eyes were turning me on, big time. With how sexy she looks right now, she can do anything she pleases to me, and I will let her.

Chapter Twenty-Seven

Kayla

I move from between Luca's legs to sitting on his stomach. I roll myself against him, feeling his growing excitement prodding me. He groans loudly and grabs my thighs, hard. I am sure they will bruise, but I don't mind. I like it.

"Do you like it, baby boy?" I purr, "I bought it for you." Circling my hips on him while I talk feels so good.

"Yes," he breathes out. "Just for me, uh?"

His rough fingertips run up the back of my thighs, slipping them under the baby doll, brushing them over my ass.

"Mmm, yes," I respond, leaning down to attach my lips to his neck.

I graze my teeth along the skin. Luca wraps his fingers in my hair, tugging on it to lower my head down and bring my lips to his. He kisses me roughly, holding me tightly to him. I slide my hand between our bodies, into his boxers, and stroke him. He moans deeply, as his hard cock twitches in my hand.

"I love how quickly I can get you hard." I can't help my smirk, while I continue to stroke him.

I watch him as I do; his eyes are closed, and his breathing becomes heavy.

"That is because you turn me on more than anyone else ever has" he answers honestly.

"And you turn me on in a way I didn't know was possible."

I take one of his hands in mine, open my legs, and run his hand between my thighs, showing how wet I am for him.

"Fuck, you are drenched, angel," he stammers out. "I desperately need your tight, wet pussy wrapped around me."

His dirty mouth arouses me. I am not used to men talking to me like that.

"Then I will happily give you want you want."

I remove myself from on top of him, only long enough to rid him of his boxers. Luca pushes the baby doll up around my hips. I reach over to the drawer, taking a condom out. I quickly rip it open and put it on him.

I capture his lips with mine, grinding against him. I move the right way, and he glides into me with complete ease, the both of us crying out as we connect once again. I sit up, resting my hands on his chest, and begin to work my hips.

"Fuck, yes, that's what I need. I have been craving you wrapped around me all day," he grunts.

I moan in response. He slaps my ass, making me cry out. He holds onto me as he sits up. I hold onto his shoulders as I swirl my hips. He reaches in, capturing my left nipple in his mouth, sucking and nibbling on the tiny bud. I fist my fingers in his hair, my head dipping back, and a deep groan from my lips circulates the room. He switches to my right nipple and does the same.

"Ahh, yes, fuck, Luca…" I breathe out, picking up the pace of my movements.

"I love my name coming from your lips, angel." He pants, his lips going to my neck, biting down on it hard.

I squeal, my hold on his hair rougher. I pull at it, hard to tilt his head back, and crash my lips to his in a heated kiss. Luca runs his hands all over my body, adding to pleasure while I ride him. He parts his lips from mine, looking me straight in the eye.

"No one has ever ridden my cock quite like you."

The look in his eyes tells me everything I need to know. I have never had a man look at me the way he does with such desire. It's the sexiest thing I have ever seen. Luca grasps my hips, thrusting his upwards, getting deeper inside of me, hitting the right spot. I grip the head board for leverage to hold myself in place, moving my hips in rhythm with his.

"Oh, God! Yes! Right there. Luca! Don't stop," I beg.

In one swift movement, he has my back against the mattress, and stops. What the hell? I thought I made it clear he wasn't allowed to stop. He removes his length from inside of me. I go to protest, but before I have a chance, he slips a finger into me, followed by a second, curling them inside, soon finding one of those special spots again. He works his magic fingers on me.

I cry out, arching up from the bed, and move my hips in sync with his fingers. I feel my walls tighten around them, my climax starting to build. Then, again, like only a moment ago, he stops.

"What the fuck, Luca?" I complain. He smirks and swats my thigh.

"Get on your stomach…" He demands with a low growly voice. I nod, curious about his next move. I do what he asks. He came up behind me.

"That's a girl," he pants, spanking my ass.

He brings my ass up, then thrusts roughly back inside me. I gasp, clenching my fists onto the bottom of the bed. He pushes deeper into me, slowing his strokes, teasing me.

"Luca, I need you to fuck me harder! Please, baby, I need to come," I beg.

He tangles his fingers in my hair, tugging it as he thrusts harder as I ask.

"Just like this, baby?" he asks in between his heavy breaths.

All I can do is nod and groan in response. My entire body shakes, pleasure dominating every inch of me. I scream out his name, tightening around him, and releasing. My toes curl, my body becomes weak, and my head spins.

"Luca, I need you to cum. I can take much more," I gasp out in between pants.

And right on cue, he grunts out my name as his climax takes over. I hear his heavy breathing behind me, mixed with cursing and groans as he comes to an end, collapsing down on my back. I can't move, I don't have the energy.

Luca kisses my shoulder before pulling out, and rolling down onto the bed next to me.

"That, that was incredible," I say, managing to turn my head to look at him.

"Mmm, yes it was, sweetness," he smirks, kissing me softly.

"I can't move. I think if I try, I will fall," I say with a ragged giggle.

"That is what I like to hear," he responds, a sly look on his face. He is obviously proud of his work, and so he should be.

"Don't look as smug," I laugh, slapping his chest playfully.

"Take your time, angel, but I am not done with you. Not yet. Do you think you could handle me again?"

"Yes, but give me ten minutes," I reply with a raised brow.

"Okay, gorgeous," he chuckles and kisses me.

Luca climbs off the bed and goes to dispose of the condom. It gives me time to catch my breath. I close my eyes, trying to steady my breathing. I hear him wandering around.

"Can I get you anything?" I hear him ask.

I look up to see him standing over me, his length right in my eyes. I soon perk up. A burst of energy comes out of nowhere, and I get onto my knees. He looks at me with surprise.

"What? I got my energy back, unexpectedly." I say, licking my lips.

"The magic of a cock in your face?" he asks, laughing loudly.

I let out a laugh too at the choice of his words. I motion him to me and attach my lips to his cock, caressing his length with my mouth. I back away and climb up the bed. Luca is quick to join me and tower over me.

"I could fuck you all night…" He hisses, his body lying on mine.

I will go as many times as our bodies allow.

I cuddle into Luca after our two-hour sex fest. Every part of me is tired and aching but in a good way. He is drawing circles on my back with his fingers. I have my head on his chest and can hear his heart pound, mine is the same.

"Can I ask you something?" he questions.

"Yeah, sure," I reply, looking at him.

"You always seem surprised how good sex with me can make you feel. You have been with other men."

"I have, yes. I haven't been with many, but none of them ever made me feel the way you always do. Oral sex isn't something I have participated in often, but my ex went down on me once, and I hated it, but when you do it, I enjoy it. It makes me feel good." I answered.

"Shocking! I dislike men who don't take the time to please their partners. Yes, it takes a little more extra stimulation for women than for men, but it shouldn't matter. Sex is an act that is supposed to make everyone involved feel good, not just one person." He says, "it is nothing but selfishness. Stick with me, angel. I promise I will always make you feel good," he adds, winking at me.

"Not everyone thinks the same way you do," I respond, "and I know you will always make me feel good. Aren't you getting bored with me yet?"

I know him only having sex with me is not the norm for him. It's a change from what he is used to.

"Of course not, don't say shit like that, Kayla. I am nowhere near bored with you. I meant when I told you no one has ever turned me on the way you can. I didn't just say that in the moment, or to make you feel good. It is the truth," he replies honestly, and plants a peck on my lips.

I hope he means what he's saying.

"Okay." I grin and snuggle back into him.

I hear him sigh, and then his lips land on the top of my head. I smile at the gesture. I like it when a man does that, it is sweet. I don't say anything to him though. We stay put for another ten minutes before going to clean ourselves up.

"We should get some sleep, beautiful. We have a busy day shopping tomorrow." Luca suggests as we climb back into bed.

"Good idea." I agree because I am exhausted. I go to move onto my side, to turn my back to him, but he stops at me when I look at him to see what he is doing.

"Please, don't turn your back on me." He asks with pleading eyes.

"It's only to go to sleep, Luca," I reply, slightly confused.

"Can you not sleep in a different way?" he asks nervously.

"Luca, you need to tell me what you want, baby boy. I am not a mind reader."

He sighs, and by the look on his face, I can tell he is trying to work out what to say.

"Like the way we were before we moved to clean up," he blurts out.

It's evident the words coming from his lips aren't easy for him. I smile then nod my head as I roll into him. I curl into his side, my head retaking its place on his chest.

"Like this?" I quiz.

"Yes."

He switches the light off, wraps his arms protectively around me and brings the covers over us. He kisses me goodnight, and silence fills the room. I close my eyes, listening to the sound of his breathing, and it helps me start to drift off. In a matter of seconds, his breathing evens out, telling me he has already fallen asleep. He isn't usually that quick. He is probably exhausted.

"Goodnight, handsome, sweet dreams." I whisper, "I wish you would tell me what is going on in that head of yours."

I sigh and let sleep eventually take over me. I will sleep well tonight for two reasons. One, because he has tired me out, and two, because he is next to me. I tend to sleep better with him close. I know that went both ways because the only time he seems to get a decent sleep is if I am right there with him.

Chapter Twenty-Eight

LUCA

It's Saturday, meaning today is Aiden's party. I am looking forward to seeing him. Kayla is in my bed getting some rest after coming off her night shift. She was going to go home, but I convinced her to come to mine. I will need to wake her soon to get ready because we need to leave in an hour and a half. I have prepped lunch already, just a sandwich and a salad, something light since we will eat at the party. I have put them in the fridge until she got up.

I go through to my bedroom to check on her. She is still sound asleep. I rest against the door frame and sigh. She is so beautiful! I stand there, watching her. I'm catching feelings for her, ones that are more than sexual. I tried to stop that from happening, but I failed. You can't control your emotions. And right now isn't the best time for me to start feeling like this. The right thing for me to do is put distance between us, but I can't. I don't want to. I am confused about it all.

I quietly stroll over to the bed and sit on the edge. I stroke the hair away from her face, making sure not to wake her.

"I am sorry if I end up hurting you, angel. It won't be on purpose," I whisper, kissing her forehead.

She stirs but doesn't wake, thankfully. I pull away and leave the bedroom before she catches me. I close the bedroom door and go to my piano. I sit down and start playing. I make sure not to press the keys too hard, or play too loud. I close my eyes, letting my fingers dance along the keys. I get lost in the music, gently humming along.

"Wow! That is beautiful." I hear Kayla say from behind me.

I didn't even hear her come in. I jump, stop playing, and swing around to look at her. She is standing in the doorway in one of my tees, which she looks darn good in.

"Did I wake you?" I ask.

"No. I woke and then heard you play. That was incredible." She smiles, making her way over to me.

I go to shut the lid down, but Kayla stops me.

"Please don't stop because I am here," she says softly, looking at me with hopeful eyes.

I haven't played for someone in so long. I am hesitant. I couldn't say no to her, not with the way she is looking at me. I sigh, nod, and pat the spot next to me. Kayla smiles brightly as she sits beside me on the bench. I take a deep breath and start playing again. I can feel her watching me as I do. She rests her head on my shoulder, and I try not to lose my concentration.

Neither of us speak for the next few minutes.

"Where did you learn how to play?" she whispers, the feel of her warm breath brushing my skin, causing me to shiver.

"An old friend taught me," I responded.

"You are so talented, Luca." She beams, kissing my cheek.

"Thank you," I smile. "Give me your hand." I add.

She looks at me, slightly confused but gives it to me. I take her fingers in mine and dance them along the piano, making her play a tune. I watch her face light up, and her eyes go wide with excitement. I let go of her fingers, encouraging her to do it herself, which she does. She manages two notes, but after that she hits the wrong ones and is off key.

"I don't think I have magic fingers like you when it comes to the piano," she giggles.

"It takes time and effort, angel. I can try to teach you if you like." I suggest. I may be a terrible teacher, but I am willing to try if she is.

"Really? I would love that! It may not work, but it will be fun to have a shot," Kayla says, her eyes gleaming.

"Yes," I reply simply, and kiss her softly. Her lips turn up into a smile while we kiss. I trace her thigh with my finger, making her moan. I pull back before we get carried away. We didn't have time to do that. I brush the hair away from her face.

"You go get showered, sweetness, and then we can have lunch before we leave."

Kayla nods, pecking my lips, and goes to get shower. I stay at the piano for another ten minutes before closing it, and head to the kitchen. I take the plates from the fridge, and start the coffee. Kayla won't be long in the shower. After a short while she came back dressed in a pretty blue summer dress, with her hair in a side braid.

"Food! Yum! I am so hungry." She smiles.

"It is only a sandwich because there will be plenty of food when we get there. I am sure Spencer mentioned a BBQ."

I slide a plate across the breakfast bar to her as we sit down. She thanks me with a smile and digs straight in, I do the same.

"Are you excited to see Aiden?" she asks between bites.

"Yes. I miss the little dude!" I smile.

"He means a lot to you, huh?"

"He does, yes," I responded.

"I can't wait to meet him."

I have a feeling Aiden is going to love Kayla. He is a little charmer and will break a lot of hearts in the future, I believe. I wasn't looking forward to being surrounded by so many people, but at least I'm not going alone, and it gives me a chance to see Aiden.

We have just arrived at Spencer and Holly's house. There's already a lot of people here. Their house is beautiful. They work damn hard for it, too.

"Ready to head inside?" Kayla queries.

"I am, yes."

We climb out of the car, and I grab the presents from the back seat. I offer Kayla my free hand, which she takes happily, and I lead us inside. You can hear the kids running around, laughing. It's nice to hear. I just walk us in because they won't hear if we knock, or ring the bell.

"They will probably be out back," I voice my thoughts out loud.

I spot the table where the presents are, setting ours down with the others. Kayla's grip on my hand seems to tighten the closer we get to the back door. She is nervous.

"Relax, angel." I say, squeezing her hand.

I feel her relax, and we step out into the back yard. I glance around, and spot Spencer and Holly.

"Luca, Kayla." Holly says, standing up and coming over to greet us with a hug. "I am so glad you made it. Help yourself to a drink."

Once we say our hellos, I get us both a drink as Kayla goes to sit with Holly. I join them, just as I was about to sit when I hear Aiden call out excitedly, "Uncle Luca!"

He comes running over to me. I kneel, and scoop him up in my arms. He flings his arms around my neck, hugging me.

"Hey, my little buddy. Happy birthday. I missed you."

"I missed you too." He replied.

He hugs me for a good few minutes before he wants to get back down. I'm expecting him to go play with his friends, but he doesn't. Instead, he heads straight for Kayla. He looks at her curiously, wondering who she is.

"Hello, I am Kayla. You must be Aiden," she says with a smile.

"Yes. It's my birthday," he says with a toothy grin.

"Happy birthday, Aiden." Kayla says to him, her smile seems bigger.

"Will you come to play with me?" he asks sweetly.

Kayla nods, and Aiden takes her hand. He looks over at me.

"You come too."

I take his other hand when he offers it to me, and he tugs us towards the grass. He decides he wants to play football. I happily join in, along with Kayla. I am sure she is glad she wore her vans with her dress because I don't think it would be easy if she was in heels. One by one Aiden's friends join in, and it becomes the kids against us two adults. We give it our best shot, but our energy is nowhere as high as the kids.

I stop to take a breather, but Kayla seems to be in her element, running around, pretending to miss the ball. She is smiling and laughing. I get lost watching her.

"Haven't you asked her to be your girlfriend yet?" I hear from behind me.

Holly appears at my side, with a grin on her lips.

"My girlfriend? I haven't even asked her out on an official date," I bark out with a laugh, one step at a time, especially for me.

"But you want to." She smirks, her entire lighting up even at the possibility.

I shake my head and roll my eyes at her. She nudges me.

"Ask the girl out already!" Holly states firmly. Then she adds, while patting my back, "It's only a date."

"I will, eventually. Back off." I laugh. Does she think I don't know this? If it was this easy, I would have asked before now.

Kayla comes over, out of breath from all the running around.

"I need a break," Kayla giggles, holding onto her side, "I have a stitch."

Aiden didn't seem to mind we have stopped playing; he's content with his friends. I slip my arm around Kayla's waist, and we join the other adults, finally managing to get a drink. Spencer and Holly introduce us to some of their friends. I was polite, but didn't talk unless someone talked to me.

"I will go start on food," Spencer announces, excusing himself.

"Do you want a hand?" I ask, pleading with him using my eyes.

I need to get away from everyone, there are too many people to deal with at once. Luckily he can read me like a book, and thankfully he accepts my help. I kiss Kayla softly before jumping to my feet and strolling over to the BBQ.

"Thanks for rescuing me." I chuckle in relief.

"You are welcome! I always got your back, buddy," he says smiling.

We get to work on the food, knowing everyone will be getting hungry.

"I am happy you brought Kayla with you."

"Me too," I agree, grinning like an idiot without even meaning too.

It will make my day easier having her here with me. It has been a long time since I have socialized like this. I used to love it, but that all changed when Leah was killed. I know she will be smiling down on me right now. I am sure she would approve of Kayla.

Chapter Twenty-Nine

Kayla

It has been a fun day. Now all the kids have gone home, and Aiden is in bed. There is only a small group of us left now. We are all sitting out the back, enjoying some drinks, and having adult conversation. I enjoyed seeing Luca with Aiden, he was so great with him. Aiden seemed to bring his softer side out. Luca has barely left my side the entire time we have been here. I wasn't sure if that was for my benefit or his. I know when we first arrived he was anxious, but he relaxed after a couple of drinks, yet I can still see he isn't one hundred percent comfortable.

"How long have you two been together?" Holly's friend, Liv, asks.

"We aren't." Luca answers quickly.

Could he have corrected her any quicker? I shouldn't be surprised because it was the truth. We aren't together. We aren't even dating! I don't know what we are. It's more than sex now. And I know I am not the only one thinking about it because Luca is also. I know this by his change in behavior. When we started having sex, we spent more time doing that rather than anything else, but now it's different. Yes, we still have a lot of sex, but we also hang out a lot, and stay with each other the nights we don't work.

"Oh, sorry. I just assumed," Liv replied.

I don't say anything, I was worrying I would say the wrong thing.

"I am going to get a drink. Does anyone want anything?" I ask, jumping to my feet.

"I will give you a hand," Holly says to me with a smile.

"Okay. Thanks." I smile back at her; there were a few people who wanted a drink.

I can feel Luca watching me as I head for the kitchen with Holly behind me. I start on the drinks, and she appears at my side. I can sense she wants to ask me something. I have a feeling what it's regarding.

"Kayla, are you okay?" She finally asks, looking at me.

I sigh and turn to face her. She is looking at me with concern on her face. I could lie, but I hate doing that. I may as well tell her the truth.

"I guess how easily Luca answered the question got to me…" I trail off.

"He does care about you, Kayla. You just need to be patient with him. He has been through a lot and is scared to let anyone close. Luca is vulnerable and still healing from what happened," she replied softly.

I would probably understand him better if I knew why he is this way!

"I don't know what happened because he never told me. He doesn't tell me anything." I reply, trying not to sound too disappointed.

"He hasn't told you?" she questions me, and I shake my head. "He must not be ready, but he will, eventually."

"Maybe." I shrug.

If he doesn't want to tell me, it is his choice. He doesn't owe me anything. I turn away from her, finishing up the drinks. I didn't want to discuss it any longer. I believe Holly knows that. We gather the glasses, taking them out to everyone. I take my place next to Luca. He slips his arm around my shoulder. Usually I rest my head on his shoulder when he does it, but I didn't, not this time.

"Kayla, what is wrong?" he whispers, caressing my arm.

"Nothing." I replied, not looking at him.

I can feel his eyes burn into me. He's waiting for me to say something more, but he is wasting his breath because I don't plan on saying anything. I half expect him to pull away, but he doesn't. Instead, he kisses the top of my head, then brings his lips close to my ear.

"I am sorry, angel…" He says sadly.

I glance up at him to find him staring down at me with a sympathetic look.

"For what?" I'm curious about what he will say.

"You know what, Kayla. It is obvious to me I upset you, and for that, I truly am sorry," he says, stroking my cheek, his eyes searching mine for answers.

I close my eyes and move into his touch. He reaches in and kisses me softly. I whimper into his lips and rest my hand on his cheek. He parts from me first.

"It doesn't matter. You just told the truth." I shrug, trying to act like it wasn't getting to me.

"We can talk later, okay?" he suggests.

"Sure…" I smile and nod.

I don't know what we have to say. I will worry about it later, for now, I just want to enjoy my night. Luca puts his arm back around me, and I rest my head on his shoulder this time. Everyone is chatting amongst themselves except me. I was listening and drinking instead.

Luca and I have arrived back at our building. It's one o'clock in the morning, and I'm exhausted. All I want to do is sleep. I know Luca said we would talk, but we haven't yet, and I wasn't in the mood, not tonight.

"Are you staying with me?" he asks, the nervousness evident in his voice.

"I think I will stay at my place tonight. I'm tired." I reply, running my fingers through my hair. He looks disappointed at my answer.

"Oh—okay. Are you mad at me, Kayla?" he asks softly.

I wasn't mad at him. I was something, but I don't know what. Maybe it was getting to me more than it should, but I can't help it. I have been patient with him, and I will continue to do so, but he needs to give me something.

"No. Why would I be mad?" I question, giving him a soft smile.

"Then why don't you want to stay?"

"Because all I want to do is sleep," I shrug.

"And we can." He trails off.

I don't understand why he is so adamant about me staying with him.

"Okay, but you can come to mine. I want my bed tonight."

"Whatever you want, angel." He grins.

I giggle at the excitement on his face. He reaches forward, kissing me softly. Once we part, I let us into my apartment. I take two bottles of water from the fridge and go into my bedroom with Luca right behind me. I strip out of my clothes and cover myself with a nightie. I can feel him watching my every move.

"Yes, you aren't getting any tonight, so don't get your hopes up." I say laughingly while looking over my shoulder at him.

"I didn't say I wanted anything." He chuckles, shaking his head.

No, but I bet he was thinking about it. I shake my head and climb into bed. Luca strips down to his boxers and climbs in next to me. The second he is close to me, he pulls me to him and wraps me in his arms.

"Can I at least switch the light off?" I snicker.

He nods, letting go of me. I turn the light off and curl back into him. He caresses my lower back, and my entire body instantly relaxes. I hear him letting out a loud puff of breath. He has something on his mind. I nuzzle his neck with my face.

"What is on your mind, Luca?" I ask, looking up at him. I can barely see his face because it was dark, but I feel his eyes looking back at me.

His rough fingers fall on my cheek, stroking it gently. I rest my hand on his chest and feel it heave up and down. He is anxious. He places his hand over mine and links our fingers.

"I am wondering if—um—you would like to go on a date with me. An official one…" He stammers out.

I can't see his face, but I have a feeling an anxious look would be on his face. I know we have been out to tea a couple of times and shared time with friends and together, but nothing has been official.

"I would like that a lot," I answer and cover his lips with mine.

His fingers run into my hair, and our lips move perfectly together like they always do. It's a sensual kiss, gentle yet passionate.

"Me too!" he replies, pulling away from my lips, "Now, get some sleep, angel, because you only got a few minutes this morning after your work."

"Yes, boss." I giggle, pecking his lips.

I turn my back to him. I know he doesn't like it, but it is the way I am most comfortable. He rolls over, snaking his arm around me then links our hands. He buries his face in the nape of my neck.

"I am trying, Kayla, I promise. But please be patient and don't give up on me." His voice breaking when he spoke. I feel his pain in my heart with each word. I squeeze his hand and snuggle tighter into him.

"I promise, but, Luca, you need to stop keeping me at arm's length. I sense you have been through a lot. I know there are reasons why you are so closed off, but we can't move forward if you don't let me in," I whisper softly.

"I will, but not tonight. You need to sleep, sweetheart."

Sweetheart? I like that! It is the first time he has called me it. I smile to myself. He leans in and kisses my cheek from over my shoulder. I close my eyes, shuddering under his lips.

"Thank you," I replied.

"Sweet dreams, angel."

"Goodnight, baby boy."

He didn't want to discuss things further, and I don't want to push him, not tonight. I hope he sticks to his word and opens up to me. We don't have a chance in hell if there are too many secrets. This will never work. I'd like us to have a chance, which won't work if he doesn't let me in. I am not expecting him to tell me everything all at once, that is too much for anyone, but piece by piece I would like to get to know the real him, know the reasons for how he is the way he is. Yes, he told me briefly about his childhood, so I know he probably had a terrible one, but there is way more to his story.

I listen to Luca's breathing. It's starting to even out. He has fallen asleep already. I'm happy about it because since we started spending our nights together, his sleep routine has improved, which is good for him. I close my eyes and let sleep begin to take over me. I know I won't be far behind him.

I was back at work tonight, so I need a decent night's sleep.

Chapter Thirty

Luca

I've been awake since six, and it's now after nine o'clock. Kayla's still sound asleep. I have had a productive morning. I have been to my place, went for my morning run, showered, and I'm currently making breakfast. I am cooking scrambled eggs, bacon, and toast. There is fresh coffee brewing, also.

I know today I need to talk to Kayla, open up a little as I promised. I won't tell her everything. I wasn't ready for that. I do not plan on mentioning Leah because that is too much, too soon. I will eventually tell Kayla about her. I know if I don't let her in even a little, there is a chance I will lose her, which is something I am not allowing to happen. I'm not going to let her walk out of my life. I hope an official date is a step in the right direction for us.

I'm grateful Kayla has been so patient with me. There aren't many women out there who'd do the same. I don't even deserve the time she has given me. It's only fair I give something back to her seeing how she shares all of herself with me.

I plate up the food, setting them onto a tray along with coffee and orange juice. I hope she doesn't mind me waking her up at this time. She can go back to sleep after breakfast if she needs to. I carefully stroll to her bedroom, making sure not to drop anything. I don't have the steadiest hands. I arrive safely and sit the tray on the drawers next to the bed.

Kayla is still sound asleep, lying on her stomach. She's sprawled out, snoring a little. It is cute, and I chuckle quietly. The covers are off, and her nightie has crept up. I climb onto the bed, kneeling between her legs. I dip my head down, pushing her nightgown up further. I trail soft kisses down her back, running my hands over her thighs. Kayla let out a soft moan.

"Morning, beautiful," I whisper, continuing to kiss her back.

"Mmm, good morning, love," she breathes out.

Love? I don't even know if she realized she said it. I didn't comment on it.

"I have made breakfast."

I climb off her and take my place next to her. She looks at me, smiling then puckers her lips at me. I smile back, leaning in, I kiss her softly. Kayla takes her time to turn over onto her back and sits up. I give her a second to wake up properly before lifting the tray to settle it on the bed between us.

"Oh, this looks good. Thank you." She grins.

"You are welcome, angel."

Kayla takes a plate from the tray, and I do the same. Silence comes between us while we eat.

"How long have you been awake? Didn't you sleep well?" she asks, with a concerned look on her face.

"I woke up at six. I slept great, but I couldn't go back to sleep once I woke up."

Kayla studies me for a moment before finally nodding. I believe she's trying to work out if I'm telling her the truth. I was so glad she realized it. She puts her attention back on her food. I do the same. I'd like to spend the rest of the day with her before she goes to work, but if she wants to sleep for longer, I will understand.

"Are you doing anything today?" she asked between bites.

"Spending my day with you?" I responded, giving her my best puppy dog eyes.

Kayla giggles, shaking her head, but then nods. I will take that as a yes. We finish breakfast, and Kayla gathers everything, putting them on the tray, and setting it on the floor. I go to move, but she stops me.

"Lay with me for a bit?" she quizzes, batting her lashes at me.

"Of course." I grin. I will happily lay with her all day if she wants.

I remove my tee and joggers, slipping in beside her under the covers. Kayla scoots closer, cuddling into me, and rests her head on my chest. I feel my heartbeat quicken when she does. She slides her hand under the covers, caressing my scars. I close my eyes and take a deep breath. It gets to me every time she touches me there. There is something intimate surrounding it.

"You still haven't told me how you survived on your own when you ran away from home." She whispers cautiously, as if she isn't sure if I'm ready to discuss it yet.

Maybe right now is the right time. If I tell her this story, perhaps she won't ask too many questions regarding anything else, and I will be keeping my promise to her. It is a long story from then until now, but I will break it down and share the main points.

"I lived on the streets for two years, picked up the odd job here and there so I could eat…" I respond, trying to keep my voice steady. I try not to think about those days because they were some of the worst years of my life. I thought it couldn't get any worse, until what happened to Leah.

"You were homeless?" Kayla whimpers out, looking up at me, her eyes full of sadness.

"Yes, but when I was seventeen, I got a job working at a hotel, and it was there my life changed forever, all thanks to one man." I smile, but my heart hurts at the same time I think about Jasper, "I know I told you I got my start in real estate, but I wasn't ready to talk about Jasper or my past."

"No, that is okay, I get it, you didn't want to open up," she smiles. "Who was he?" she asks curiously.

"Jasper, he owned the hotel, one of many properties throughout the US. He apparently saw something in me. He took me in, treated me like his own because he didn't have any kids." I smile at the memory, "I worked my way up, and by the time I was nineteen, I was the hotels' assistant manager and then eventually the manager a year later."

"You were a manager by twenty?" she asks, surprised.

"Yes, he taught me everything I know. And he paid to put me through college," I replied. "I didn't have much of an education before he came along because I skipped school, and then was on the streets at fifteen, but he made sure I did all the work, and helped me with it when I needed it."

"Wow, he sounds incredible. He sounds like a good man." Kayla smiles.

"Jasper changed my entire life in more ways than one. He was a good man with a heart of gold. Sadly, I lost him when I was twenty-three. He had a heart attack, he was only in his fifties, and it killed me. He was the closest thing to a real father that I ever had." I sigh, trying to keep my emotions under control.

Kayla leans in and strokes my face, "I am sorry you lost him, Luca; it couldn't have been easy."

"It wasn't. It killed me and sent me down a destructive path. I drank myself stupid, and took drugs, only to name a few things. And six months later, Jasper changed my entire life again. He left me a lot of money in his will so I could buy a home for myself, or start my own business, along with some of his properties."

I got myself together when he did because I didn't want to let him down. I still struggled some days, but I focused on work, ensuring I didn't ruin everything he worked his entire life for. I built it up, which is why I am where I am now business wise.

"So, he's the reason why you are where you are today?"

"Yes, he changed my life in many ways. If it wasn't for him taking a chance on me, I dread to think where I'd be today. I don't even know if I would still be alive," I say honestly.

I have considered taking my life more than once over the years. And if I hadn't met Jasper, I don't think I would have made it past twenty-one. I just wished he was still around.

"Don't say things like that." Kayla whimpers out, tears welling in her eyes.

The last thing I want is to upset her, but I am being open with her. I wipe away the tears before they have a chance to fall.

"Sorry, but it's the truth, angel." I sigh, kissing her softly.

"I know, but even the mere thought of you not being around hurts." She winces, her voice breaking.

I wasn't expecting her to get so upset with me saying it. I feel terrible now. I pull her into my chest, wrap my arms around her and stroke her back. I didn't think I would be in a position again where someone would miss me if I weren't around.

"Sorry, sweetheart. I didn't mean to upset you." I say, kissing the top of her head, and she snuggles in tighter, holding onto me for dear life.

"Don't ever say anything like that again, okay?" She mumbles against my chest.

"Promise, beautiful," I answer, nuzzling her neck.

Kayla looks up at me and runs her fingers through my hair and over my face before finally resting it on my chest. She covers my lips with hers, planting a soft kiss on them. I smile into her lips, cupping her face in my hand. Our lips disconnect, but Kayla keeps her place close to me.

"Have you seen your parents since you left?" she asks softly.

"No. And I don't ever want to see them again. They didn't even look for me, but I am not surprised. They didn't care about me, either of them. My father was the worst, and my mother wasn't much better." I hiss out through gritted teeth. I hated them both!

"They never deserved you in the first place. I am sorry you have been through hell and back more than once, Luca. I am glad you are here with me now. I know you still have your struggles, but you should be proud of yourself for getting to where you are." She smiles, telling me, "I am proud of you."

"Thank you, angel. It has been a long time since anyone has ever said that to me." I grin and peck her lips.

"I appreciate you opening up to me. I have a feeling there is still a lot more to your story, but I will not push."

"Yes, there is. However, I... I am not ready to share it all just yet. Is that okay?" I stammer out, fearful of her reply.

"It is. I know it wasn't easy for you to tell me everything you just did. I'm sure you will share anything when you feel you are ready. I promise not to push." She smiles, and her eyes tell me she means every single word.

I give her a grateful smile in return. I think that is enough of my life story for this morning.

"How about we get showered and head out, find something to do?" I suggest wanting to get off the topic entirely.

"Okay, but not right now, soon."

"When you are ready." I smile, not wanting to rush her.

I soon realized why she didn't want to move; she wanted more cuddles. I have no issues with that.

"So, when are we going on our official first date?"

"Whenever you are free." I reply, looking down at her.

"It will need to be either Tuesday or Thursday because I work every other night." She pouts.

"That sucks!" I huff. "How about we do it Thursday?"

"Yes, that will be fine. I look forward to it." She beams and kisses my cheek.

I dislike the idea of needing to sleep alone most nights next week, but we can't do anything about it. I probably won't sleep much those nights.

"I look forward to it too," I reply brightly.

I need to plan it! It needs to be perfect! She deserves it after everything. I will work on it. I don't want to only take her out to tea. I will find something more exciting for us to do.

Chapter Thirty-One

KAYLA

I haven't seen Luca since Sunday because of our work schedules, but I am going to surprise him at his office today. Yes, it has only been a couple of days, but I have missed him. Facetime just isn't the same as being in the same room. I know he is at his office today, he told me last night. I didn't let on that I was going to stop by. I have lunch and coffee for us both.

I head inside, going up to his floor. I have to check in at reception.

"Good afternoon. I am here to see Luca," I say with a smile, and the receptionist looks up at me, her entire face changes. She didn't look thrilled to see me.

"No." She snarls, glaring at me.

What is her issue? I have done nothing wrong to her.

"Excuse me?" I reply, annoyed.

"I said no! He is busy!" She hisses, "Why are you even here? You do know he will be bored of you soon, right? He is still screwing around, so don't think you are special."

Now I know her issue! She is jealous because she wants him. I shouldn't be surprised. I am sure he has probably had sex with her and possibly every female that works here.

"What is going on between Luca and I is none of your damn business! I am going to go through to his office, and if you try to stop me, I will inform him of your little display of jealousy." I snapped, fed up with her attitude.

I wouldn't tell him, even if she did. I do not want to be responsible for her getting into trouble or losing her job. She mutters under her breath, rolls her eyes and tells me to go through.

"Thank you." I smile politely.

I am not going to continue to stoop down to her level. I didn't say another word; instead, I headed straight for Luca's office. I hope he isn't busy. I peer through the window, making sure he wasn't with someone, or on the phone; he isn't. He was doing something on his computer.

I knock on the door, and he looks irritated that he got disturbed. Maybe this wasn't a good idea. I should have called ahead. He looks up, and the second his eyes fall on me, his frown turns into a smile, reaching from ear to ear. He motions for me to come in. The second I step into his office, he gets up from his desk and rushes over me. He wraps his arms around me, pulls me in, and kisses me softly. I wasn't expecting him to be this happy to see me.

"Hello to you too, baby boy." I giggle.

"This is a nice surprise! I missed you..." he replies nervously.

"I missed you too. I wanted to see you." I responded, hugging him back the best I could since my hands are full.

He steps back, clearing his throat, and visibly pulls himself together. I think he was taken back with his own excitement.

"I bring burgers, fries, and coffee." I smile, holding them up.

"Thank God, the only thing I have had to eat or drink today is a smoothie."

He leads us to his desk, takes a seat in his chair, and I prop myself up on his desk. He took his food from the bag and passed me mine.

"I hope you don't mind me stopping by?"

"Of course not! Seeing you makes my day better," he says grinning as he squeezes my knee. "It has been a stressful couple of days." He sighs, running his fingers through his hair.

I can see he's stressed, and he looks tired too. I assume he hasn't been sleeping great. He has bags under his eyes. I set my food down, jump off the desk, and stand between his legs. He places his hands on my hips and glances up at me.

"You haven't been sleeping." I sigh, stroking his face, and he shakes his head.

I feel terrible because I haven't been there the last couple of nights even though it was no one's fault.

"I tried, I swear, but it didn't work." He said sadly, a look of disappointment covering his face.

I climb onto his lap, snaking my arms around his neck, and kiss him softly. Once we part, I rest my forehead against his. "You can come and stay with me tonight, or I can come to you. I have missed you next to me in bed."

"I'd like that. You come to mine. I will cook us tea, and we can make a night of it," he suggests with a smile.

"I have a better idea; how about I cook tea since I am off today, and you will probably be working until six o'clock or later?"

"You don't need to do that, angel, but yes, I am working until seven o'clock." He pouts.

"I want to," I exclaim.

Luca nods and places his finger on my chin, using it to tilt my head and take my lips with his. I moan, slipping my fingers into his hair, tugging it, and kissing him back. He groans, his hold on me tightens. Luca sleeping next to me isn't the only thing I have missed. I move my lips to his neck, trailing them upwards and sucking on the skin, leaving a small hickey.

"Mmm, angel, what are you doing? Marking what is yours." He breathes out, running his hand over my ass.

"I can't wait to get you alone later." I purr, rolling my hips onto him.

He growls, swatting my ass. I know I avoided it when he asked if I was marking what is mine because I didn't know if he was mine. I think we need to have our date first and then see how it goes. Yes, the things we have been doing, especially the last couple of weeks, it's like we are a couple, but I know we aren't. Luca clarified this on Saturday.

"Fuck, baby, I have missed you in that way too. I need my Kayla fix." He pants out, and I can feel his excitement stirring, "You have become my new drug of choice."

I whimper at his words and cover his lips roughly with mine. After a minute, I hesitantly pull away, only because our lunch will get cold. I will fuck him right here in his office one day. I understand when he says I am like a drug to him, because he is the same to me. I crave him in ways I have never had any other man.

"We should eat before it gets cold," I say between heavy breaths.

"I would rather be eating something else, but that can wait until later," he says with a smirk, licking his lips and wiggling his eyebrows at me.

I moan, squeezing my legs together because I know what he can do with that tongue. I give myself a shake and retake my seat on his desk. He rests back on his chair with a sly look on his face, knowing how turned on I am due to him.

"Don't look as smug." I say giggling, shaking my head.

He continues to look at me in the same way, taking a bite of his burger. I will get him back for this later.

I have left Luca's office to let him get back to work since he has a lot to do. I have plans of my own anyway. I need to get things to make dinner tonight, and something a little more fun and sexier to wear for afterwards. I enjoyed dressing up for him the last time, and it made me feel good and confident. It is a little something to make us both feel incredible. Luca gave me the key to his place to let myself in and cook dinner there for us. I could have done it at my place, but he insisted I do it at his.

I wasn't sure what to cook for us, but I will work it out when I get to the grocery store. I feel my phone vibrate in my pocket. I take it out, surprised when I see it's Luca texting. Maybe he forgot to tell me something. I open the text.

Why didn't you say anything when I asked are you marking what is yours? Are you seeing other people? You can tell me if you are, I would understand X

Hmm, he picked up on that. Why would he think I was seeing other people? I made it clear more than once it isn't my style.

Because I didn't want to scare you off, I have had no reason to believe you were mine after Saturday. Of course, I am not seeing anyone else. I am not like that, you should know that about me by now, baby boy X

I know I shouldn't have said what I did on Saturday. I am not ready for a real relationship, but I like to think I am yours, and you are mine. I should have known better than to ask if you are seeing anyone else. I am sorry, angel X

I feel a smile growing on my lips, and it soon covers my entire face. He sees me as his. I feel my stomach flip at the thought, my heart speeding up in my chest.

I like the thought of you being mine. I can appreciate what we have until we work out what this is X

I am happy you said that, beautiful. I still have some issues to sort through before giving you all of me. Is that alright? X

I will wait for as long as it takes, love X

Thank you! You are terrific, sweetness. I don't deserve you X

Yes, you do! We can work this out as we go X

Yes, we can! I've got to get back to work, angel. I will see you later X

See you later, baby boy X

I smile and put my phone away. I know all these changes can't be easy for him. I am not ready to give up on him. Going by what little he has said, I am guessing too many people in his life over the years have done that, so many people have left him, and I don't want to be added to the list because he deserves more. He needs someone to believe in him, show him he is worth it. It will take time, but eventually, those walls he has around him will come down.

We have a long, tough road ahead of us, but I am ready for it!

Chapter Thirty-Two

LUCA

I've arrived home after a long ass day! I'm anxious to see Kayla; she always makes my day better. I'm nervous, too, due to our text conversation after she left my office. I honestly missed her like crazy the last couple of days. Yes, I know things have been changing between us the last couple of weeks, but after being away from her for a couple of days, it made me realize even more how much I want and need her in my life. I am glad she seems to feel the same way and is willing to wait until I am ready.

I hear music coming from my apartment as I approach the door. I head inside, the scent of food catches my attention, and it smells incredible! My kitchen comes into view, and I see Kayla dancing around as she prepares dinner for us. She looks like she is having a ball. I love the way she can be so carefree. I smile as I stand watching her for a minute. God, she is so damn beautiful! I set my briefcase down and stroll towards the kitchen. Kayla hasn't yet noticed I'm home. I go up behind her, and slip my arms around her waist and kiss her neck.

"Hey, angel," I whisper in her ear, pressing myself against her.

"Mmm, hello," she moans and turns to face me. The second she does, I capture her lips with mine. Kayla embraces me, kissing me back.

By the time we part, we are both breathless. I smile, reach in and push her hair away from her face.

"What are you cooking? It smells great! And can I help?" I ask while I circle my fingers on her hips.

"Lasagna, and there is some fresh Italian bread to go with it." She grins, "and I made us a caramel cheesecake," she adds proudly.

"Oh, yum. What can I do?" I question her.

"Nothing. It is prepared, I just need to put it in to cook. So, you can go shower."

"Okay, if you're sure." I say, and she nods, "I won't be too long." I peck her lips and head into the bathroom. I won't have a long shower. All I want to do tonight is have dinner with Kayla, maybe a small glass of wine, and curl up on the sofa and watch a movie. I strip down and step into the shower. I close my eyes and enjoy the feeling of the warm water running down my body. I have been so stressed and tense the last couple of days, so this feels good. I am exhausted since I've only had about four hours of sleep since Sunday. At least I know I will get some sleep tonight because Kayla will be next to me.

I stay there for ten minutes, eventually I get out and wrap a towel around myself. I go to the bedroom, dry off and pull some joggers on. We aren't going anywhere, so there's no point dressing up.

When I arrive back in the kitchen, Kayla's sitting on the sofa, with two glasses of red wine on the coffee table. She looks over her shoulder, smiling, but then her eyes fall on my bare chest, and her lips turn up into a smirk.

"Enjoy your shower, baby boy?" she asks, finally looking up at my face.

"Yes, I needed it." I smile and take a seat next to her.

"Dinner will be about an hour."

Kayla lifts both glasses of wine and hands one to me. She turns around, places her legs over my lap and takes a sip from her glass. I take a sip too, and place my hand on her legs.

She grabs my hand, linking our fingers, "How was the rest of your day, love?"

"Stressful, but I feel better now," I responded, lifting her hand to my lips and kissing her knuckles. Her eyes close, and the smile grows on her lips.

I set our hands back down and lean in to kiss her lips. The kiss was soft and sweet, only lasting a moment.

"Thank you for making dinner, angel. Next time is my turn." I smile, caressing her face.

"No, bother. And I will hold you to that." She giggles, booping my nose.

"Hey!" I huff, prodding her side, causing her to squirm because she is ticklish. I could be mean and start tickling her, but I will play nice since she has made us dinner.

Kayla moves, curling into me, resting her head on my shoulder. I snake my arm around her and plant a kiss on the top of her head.

"Are we still on for our date?" she asks, kissing my neck.

"Yes! I have it all planned out," I answered confidently.

I have everything planned right down to the proverbial T. I want it to be perfect and unexpected, and that is precisely what it will be.

"And do you want to share those plans?" she asks with a smile.

I shake my head with a laugh and kiss her. I am not telling her anything. Kayla moves onto my lap, straddling me. Her lips come away from mine, and she kisses along my jawline and then my neck. I groan, holding her hips.

"You aren't even going to give me a hint?" she questions between kisses.

I should have known she would try to seduce the information out of me.

"Not going to work, angel," I breathe out my reply.

I feel her teeth sink into my skin. *Fuck!* I love it when she bites, and she knows it. I need to use my willpower, which is easier said than done when it comes to Kayla. She does it again, rolling her hips into me.

"Are you sure…" she purrs, trailing off.

I can feel myself begin to break but I can't. I need to take control back. I don't want to ruin the surprise.

"P... positive." I stammer out, trying to contain myself.

Kayla rolls her eyes at me and removes herself from my lap.

"You are no fun." She pouts, but I can tell she was trying to hold back a smile.

I chuckle, peck her lips and then pull away.

"It is a surprise," I spoke, trying not to look too sly.

She flips me off, lets out a loud laugh, and turns away from me. I feel this isn't the last I will hear of this tonight. She will try again!

****

Kayla and I are lying on the sofa, wrapped in a blanket and each other after sharing hot, passionate sex for the last hour. I haven't felt this type of belonging in a few years. I don't want to be anywhere else other than right here. The last few years have been like a blur, the same thing day in, day out, but not now. I'm enjoying all the changes, thrilled to have someone to share moments with.

"Tonight, has been perfect," I whisper, kissing along her bare shoulders.

"Yes, it has been," she agrees with a soft moan.

She rolls over to face me, smiling beautifully at me. She reaches in, stroking the damp hair away from my forehead. Neither of us speak a single word as we get lost in one another. I need to admit to myself I am crazy about this woman! All these feelings have hit me unexpectedly. I honestly believed I would never feel anything again.

I kiss her forehead, hoping it's enough to let her know how I feel without having to say anything else. Kayla closes her eyes, lets out a long breath, and shifts closer.

"Thank you for letting me in, Luca." She says softly, opening her eyes to look at me. She has the most beautiful eyes.

"I don't know why you have been so patient with me, especially since I acted like an ass more than once."

"What can I say? I'm a patient woman." She giggles, her entire face lighting up. She would need to be to deal with me.

I laugh and press my lips to hers. She slips her fingers into my hair, deepening the kiss between us. Kayla pulls back after a minute. "We should have a shower and then go to bed, love. You have a lot of sleep to catch up on." She suggests, caressing my face.

I nod, agreeing with her suggestion. It's only eleven o'clock, but I am exhausted. She pecks my lips, and then jumps to her feet, wrapping the blanket around her before offering her hand. I smile, taking it, and she helps me to my feet. I groan when I stand in front of her in all my naked glory. She keeps hold of my hand, leading us towards the bathroom for a shower. I know I had one earlier, but I am all hot and sweaty, and reek of sex, not that I mind but another one will do no harm.

"And we will only shower, just in case you have any other ideas, Mr.," she says with a giggle, looking over her shoulder at me.

"I didn't say a word otherwise." I will behave because, honestly, all I want is to cuddle up in bed with my girl. I can call her that now, which is good. I will eventually call her my girlfriend! Kayla didn't look like she believed a single word I said.

"I promise to behave," I reply, hand to my heart.

She eyes me for a second but then gives me a slight nod, her way of saying I believe you. Kayla switches the shower on, letting the blanket fall from her body as she steps into it. I take a deep breath, keeping my hormones under control, and finally join her.

We wash quickly and were climbing into my bed in no time. I'm eager for a decent night's sleep. Kayla stole one of my tees to sleep in; she usually does if she's here. She pretends that she forgot her pj's, but I know that is a lie; she just likes sleeping in my clothes. I don't mind.

"We are going straight to sleep," she says firmly.

"Yes, boss…" I laugh.

She switches the light off straight away and shifts to snuggle up. Kayla kisses me goodnight, "Goodnight, baby boy, sweet dreams."

"Goodnight, angel." I responded, wrapping her protectively in my arms.

I let my eyes close, hoping sleep will soon take over. I want to enjoy her here since she is back at work tomorrow. I wish she had two days off together for our date because it would make it even better, but I will take what I can get. I am confident what I have planned is something she hasn't experienced before.

Chapter Thirty-Three

I'm getting ready for my date with Luca! Who starts a date at eleven o'clock? I haven't got a clue where we are going, but Luca told me to pack an overnight bag, wear anything I like to start with, and to make sure I have a dress for going out to tea in my bag. I managed to get a couple of hours of sleep, so that will need to do for now. I am not tired, though. I'm excited about our date, so the buzz is putting a spring in my step. Luca has gone out to get us coffee while I get myself organized.

I have everything done, more or less. All I need to do is get dressed jeans and a hoodie will do for now because I think we will be travelling in the car, so I may as well be comfortable. I dress and make sure I have everything I need, before I head to the living room.

Great timing, I think as Luca calls out, "Did you miss me, angel?" He only left twenty minutes ago.

"Nah, I enjoyed the peace." I teased back, sticking my tongue out at him.

Luca pouts and gives me sad eyes. He is cute when he pouts. I have never seen a man pout so much like he does. I thought it was more of a girly thing. I laugh and go to him, kissing him softly. He soon stops pouting.

"So, where are we going?" I hope he will finally tell me.

"Nice try, sweetness." He laughs, booping my nose.

I groan and take my coffee from him. He found my annoyance rather amusing. He grabs my bag from the sofa.

"Come on, gorgeous. We should get going." He tells me with a panty melting smile, "And I promise to have you back in plenty of time tomorrow so you can get some sleep before work."

I nod, grab my coat, and we head out. We get to the car and he tosses our bags on the back seat before he opens the door for me. I climb in, Luca makes sure I get my seatbelt on before he starts the engine.

"The first stop is in about ten minutes," he says with a smile, keeping his eyes on the road.

The first stop? Are we going to more than one place? Now I am even more curious. I decide not to question him because he won't answer me, I just enjoy my coffee. I became confused when we pulled into what looked like a private airstrip.

"Um, Luca, where are we?" I ask, looking around.

He doesn't respond with words, only smiles as he parks the car. I glance around. I've never been here before. I didn't even know it existed.

"I will be back in a minute. You can stay in the car or wander around," he says before getting out.

I stay where I am until I know what's going on. I look over and see Luca talking with someone, after a few minutes, they shake hands and he rushes back to me.

"The jet is ready to go," he says.

"Wait, what? The jet? Are we going on a jet? That can't be right?" I'm shocked, and look at him wide-eyed.

"You heard me, angel. I borrowed it from a friend." He grins, "And it is ours until tomorrow."

"You're being serious. Oh my God, this is crazy! I can't believe this!" I'm sure I resemble a fish right now, "This is crazy. You know that, right?" I laugh in total disbelief, "Is this something you often do?"

"No, this will be a first," he positively beams, "I'm excited to share this with you. Now come on, sweetness, it's fueled, and the pilot is ready to go."

I finally get out of the car, Luca grabs our bags from the back, and he locks it up. He reaches for my hand with his free one, links our fingers, and guides us towards the jet. I am still in slight shock. The second we got onto the plane, my eyes grow wider, and I'm in complete awe. It is beautiful and looks way more expensive on the inside than what it does from the outside.

"This is incredible!" I gush, taking it all in.

There are ten white leather seats, they look welcoming, there's a trolley with food and drinks next to a kitchenette as you come in through the entry. Luca tells me to make myself comfortable, which I happily do. He makes us both a plate with fresh fruit and yoghurt.

"Enjoy, beautiful," he says with a smile, handing me a plate, and takes a seat next to me.

In no time we were taking off. This is surreal! I swear I'm half expecting to wake and for this all to be nothing but a dream.

"Now, can you please tell me where we are going?" I quiz, batting my lashes at him.

"Tybee Island. Have you ever been?" he asks, and I shake my head, "It's a small barrier island, close to Savannah. It is beautiful."

"No, I have never been. I've heard of it! I love the beach!" I say excitedly.

"You are going to love it. It will only take two hours or so for us to get there, so relax, angel." He says, kissing my cheek.

"Happily." I say with a grin.

I can't believe he has made all of this effort for our first date! I am utterly blown away by it. I smile, resting my head on his shoulder. I am utterly smitten with this man! No one has ever done anything like this for me before.

Luca and I have just arrived at our hotel room for our one right on the beach with a view of the ocean! It's beautiful, the walls are decorated with a beautiful blue and white wallpaper, there is a calming feeling that surrounds it. The bed Queen size and more that big enough for two with velvet and silk bedding and so many pillows they will probably end up on the floor. I could never afford a room like this, you can tell by just looking at it, it would be expensive.

"I can't believe you did all of this for me, Luca. It's too much."

"No, it isn't. I wanted it to be perfect. You deserve it after putting up with me." He pulls me in close, holding me to his chest and kisses me softly. I melt into the kiss, fisting his tee, and it seems to make him hold me tighter.

"We should stop, angel, and go explore, get some lunch, and start our date. But later, you're all mine." He pulls back, and we both catch our breath. His idea is for the best because we will lose track of time and miss most of the day if we start. We quickly put our things away, saving them from getting creased. I am eager to get to the beach.

Luca rests his hand on the small of my back, and we stroll out. It only takes a matter of minutes, and we are right at the beach. I like that it's practically empty of tourists, it's a weekday, after all, but it's like we have the place to ourselves.

"Shall we take our shoes off and enjoy the sand between our toes, my lady?"

"Hell yeah!" I say beaming, and clap my hands.

We slip our shoes off, sauntering down to the water. I am glad he seems to like the beach as much as I do. I didn't think he would be the type. We get to the water's edge and walk along it. I love the feel of the water running over my feet. Luca connects his hand with mine, our fingers entangling. It's tranquil listening to the waves crashing.

"We should go skinny dipping when it is dark." He smirks, nudging me and wiggling his eyebrows at me.

"Hmm, we will see," I giggle at his antics, rolling my eyes.

I should have seen that one coming! It would be another new experience for me, maybe I will think on it. I rest my head against him as we continue our walk. He kisses the top of my head the same way he always does.

"I have booked a table for dinner at six o'clock this evening."

"Hence the dress?" I ask, and he nods.

A comfortable silence falls between us; nothing needs to be said. It's a perfect moment. When Luca suggested we go on a date, I sure didn't expect this. I thought it'd be dinner and a movie, something I would have been happy with. But this is a whole other level.

"Are you hungry, sweetheart? Do you want to get some lunch?"

My heart flutters every time he calls me that.

"Lunch would be nice, but something simple like hot dogs or nachos and we can sit at the beach and eat! Why waste time in a restaurant when we can eat with such an incredible view. We will be in one later for tea, so lunch alfresco sounds like a good idea."

"I like the sound of that, angel! Give us a chance to enjoy the fresh air and sunshine."

Yay! I am thrilled he wants to do the same thing. Surely there are places close by to get the basic food we want.

"Shall we go on the hunt for food?" he questions, and I nod.

We have only been here, not even an hour, and it's already the best date I have ever had! My gut tells me it is only going to get better.

Chapter Thirty-Four

LUCA

"I can't believe we are doing this." Kayla giggles with joy as she strips down.

We are at the beach after a great night, and to end the evening we are going skinny dipping. It's late, and no one is around, so we may as well enjoy the chance. We stop by the hotel to change out of our formal clothes and into something more casual, and grab a blanket to take with us.

"I can't believe you've never skinny dipped." I chuckle, removing the last of my clothing.

I stand there, naked, and Kayla looks at me, cocking her brow. There's enough light from the moon for us to see each other, which helped.

"I am not getting completely naked! I will leave my underwear on!" she says, shaking her head.

"You are sort of missing the point, angel," I say laughing as I step into her space, "but, if you want to keep your underwear on, then that is your choice."

I am not going to pressure her to get naked. It would make me an asshole. Kayla will do whatever she feels more comfortable with. She glances around and turns back to me.

"If you ever speak of this to anyone, I will make you pay." She says firmly, with her hands on her hips. Her efforts undermined by the smile trying to break through.

"Speak of what, sweetness?" I respond innocently, finding her "attitude problem" highly amusing.

Kayla rolls her eyes at me then reaches behind her and unclips her bra, taking it off and setting it down with the rest of our clothing. I watch her closely, and she makes sure to lock her eyes with me as she hooks her panties in her fingers, before slowly sliding them down. Mmm, she is getting entirely naked with me. I like it!

Kayla runs straight into the water, letting out a squeal as she feels the waves, after a second, she dives under. I quickly follow her. It's a little chilly, but it didn't matter after a moment. When I come back up, I see her swimming toward me. She flings her arms around my neck and presses her lips roughly to mine, her nipples hard against my bare chest, driving me crazy. I hold her close to me, kissing her back, the taste of her lips a mixture of sweet and salty. Just when I am getting into it, she backs away.

"Kayla!" I whine, reaching for her.

"If you catch me, then we can have sex right here on the beach." She says seductively.

"Deal!" I groan, diving at her, but she's too quick. She laughs loudly as she starts to swim away.

I will catch up with her! I swim after her, and to start with she's too far ahead, but I'm about to change it. I duck under the water, which makes it easier to swim. I catch up with her, grabbing her from behind and bring her back against my front.

"That was too easy, angel." I chuckle, swatting her ass.

She gasps, flings herself around, and her lips soon reattach to mine. Hmm, I believe she let me catch her on purpose. Kayla rolls her hips into me, and I soon get the hint, so does my dick because he starts to rise to the occasion.

"Hold on tight, gorgeous." I pant between kisses.

Kayla clings to me, and I head out of the water, ensuring my hold on her is secure. I carry her over to the blanket we previously set out and I lay her down, coming to rest on top of her. I let her snake her legs around my waist, rubbing against her.

"Do you feel what you do to me constantly?" I breathe out, digging my fingers into her thighs; in response she gasps and rolls up against me.

"Yes, you do the same to me, Luca." She gasps, caressing her fingers up and down my back, "I need you to take me."

I am so ready for her. I capture her lips with mine, and then I realize something. I don't have condoms with me; they are back at the hotel. I groan in frustration.

"What's wrong?" Kayla asks, looking up at me confused.

"I don't have any condoms, baby girl. I left them in our room." I sigh and sit up.

"I am on birth control. Do you always wear condoms when you have had sex with other women?" she asks.

"Always!" I reply, it's the truth, I do. I never ride bareback.

Kayla tugs her lower lip between her teeth, a come hither look in her eyes, "Fuck me, Luca!" she demands.

I lay my body back down on top of hers, balancing myself with my hands as her legs go around me. Shifting so I am supported by one hand, I use my free hand to hold her thigh tightly, thrusting forward and enter her smoothly, gliding in due to her wetness. I love the way I make her soaked so easily. Kayla cries out, arching up from the blanket. Fuck! This feels incredible, her slick wet pussy wrapped around my cock without anything between us. Our lips meet in a heated kiss as I work in and out of her, my strokes seeming to move in rhythm with the crashing waves.

"Mmm, fuck, angel, this feels so good," I grunt out, picking up a little speed.

I am trying to contain myself because I lose all control with her.

"Yes, yes it does. So good, Luca, harder baby, I need you to go harder." She begs, her nails scraping down my back.

I don't hesitate to give her what she asks for. I thrust into her harder, every stroke much deeper than the previous one. I dip my head down, kissing and biting all over her neck, the sea water mixing with her skin is heady. She starts to roll her hips in sync with mine, driving me crazy.

"Fuck, I love your pussy." I pant out, slapping her thigh.

"Ahh, Luca, you fuck me so good. Oh God, I am close, make me cum," she squeals.

Letting go of her thigh I slip my hand between us, playing with her clit while I continue to fuck her. It doesn't take long for her walls to tighten around my shaft. Her legs shake, and my name falls from her lips, as her sweet juices cover my cock. I bury my face in her neck, and her lips fall at my ear, kissing it, her warm breath tickling the skin.

"Luca, cum for me, baby boy. I want to feel you release inside of me. Mmm, your cock fills me so good." She says between pants. I am not used to her using dirty words, but damn, it's turning me on.

Kayla continues to whisper dirty talk into my ear, and I feel my climax approaching. It takes only another minute before my length throbs, my balls drawing up tight, I call out her name loudly, as I release into her. I collapse against her, and we cling to each other as we catch our breath.

"You're amazing!" she says, playing with my hair.

I lift my head to look down at her and smile.

"No, you are amazing," I whisper, kissing her forehead. Kayla sighs and closes her eyes, "We are great together."

I peck her lips and lay down next to her. Kayla shifts closer and rests her head on my chest. I put my arm around her, and she curls into me. I caress the small of her back, feeling her shudder under my touch.

"I could lay here with you all night under the stars and listen to the sound of the waves," Kayla says.

"I could too, sweetheart, but sadly we can't," I huff. I don't want to go home tomorrow, another thing that can't happen. I feel safe here, like I have no worries.

"We should probably get back to the hotel, uh?" Kayla asks, sounding as disappointed as I feel.

"I guess." We hesitantly got to our feet, pulling our clothes back on and gather everything up. I take her hand in mine, and we silently stroll back to the hotel. It's only a five-minute walk.

"Are you tired?" I question her as we get in the elevator, she shakes her head, "Good because I am not ready to go to sleep and call it a night."

"Neither am I. What would you like to do, instead?" she asks.

"Find something to watch, order some snacks, talk, and have another round before we go to sleep," I suggest.

"Sounds perfect, love." She beams, kissing my cheek.

I could stay up all night with her, just talking. Today has been one of the best days I think I've ever had.

It's four o'clock in the morning, Kayla has just drifted off. We spent hours talking about nothing in particular. It was nice. I lay there, just watching her as she slept. She is perfection, so beautiful and pure—inside and out. I still believe she deserves someone better than me, but somehow, I am the one she wants. Next week will be a terrible week for me, but I hope I don't lash out and mess everything up with Kayla. That's the last thing I want, but it will be three years since Leah was killed, and every year I go off the rails for a week. I drink, take drugs, party, screw around, and push anyone away that is close to me.

The right thing to do is tell Kayla about Leah, but I can't! I'm still not ready; not only that, but I also don't want Kayla to feel like I am comparing them—that she needs to compete with Leah. Leah was the love of my life, but I know the time will come when I will need to let myself love someone, let someone else love me. I don't know if it is crazy, but I want Kayla to be that person, maybe, but I can't share that with her. It would be too much pressure on her.

I sigh, run my fingers through my hair and plant a feather-like kiss on Kayla's forehead.

"I do care for you, angel. You mean a lot to me, and I want to be with you." I whisper, hoping she won't hear me. I don't think I am in the right mind quite yet to share this information with her.

I pull her closer and shut my eyes. I am tired and ready to sleep. We need to check out by eleven o'clock, later today, and the jet will be prepared to fly back by midday, which means Kayla should get a few hours' sleep before her night shift. I wish she had more days off so we could have stayed here longer, but next time we can arrange it for us to get away for a few days rather than only one night. Hmm, I wonder where I can sweep her off to next? I can borrow the jet anytime I want for as long as I need. Maybe I can take her further afield, Europe somewhere. I will have a think about it.

I feel myself relaxing, sleep soon begins to take over. I am happy to be falling asleep with good thoughts in my mind for once, rather than evil. Kayla is the primary reason for the change.

I look forward to waking up now since I have a reason to wake up.

Chapter Thirty-Five

Kayla

"Luca, I need to make a move to get ready for work." I say with a laugh, trying to wriggle out of his tight hold on me.

We came straight to mine when we arrived back. We slept, and then I was woken up by my horny man, and we have spent the last hour naked and fucking. Now he has decided not to let me go.

"Ten more minutes. You have plenty of time." He replies, flashing his dorkiest smile my way.

"You are such a dork! Even if you like to pretend to be some big shot in fancy suits." I tease, prodding his sides.

"Hey! I am a big shot," he replies confidently, followed by a chuckle.

I roll my eyes at him playfully.

"If you say so."

"Stop being a meanie!" he pouts, crossing his arms over his chest.

"Aww, I am only messing, baby boy."

I kiss him softly, and he soon smiles, uncrossing his arms. I can give him ten more minutes. I cuddle into him. I don't want to move. I could happily stay here with him for the rest of the evening. He has become my safe place recently. After what went down with my ex, I honestly thought I wouldn't let anyone close again, especially not someone like Luca, especially after the way he was when we first met. Though, spending all this time with him, I realize there is way more to him than meets the eye. He has a huge heart, but it's a guarded one.

"Can I walk you to work?" he asks, tickling my back.

"You don't need to, love," I reply, looking up at him.

"I know, but I want to…" he trails off.

I nod and smile. I liked it when he walked me to work. We lay in silence for ten minutes until we had to move. I have to shower before work, and I am sure he will join me. I hesitantly get out first, Luca following only seconds later. He slips his arms around me from behind, kissing my bare back and shoulders as we make our way to my bathroom. I switch the shower on, step in, and Luca comes in behind me. I step back against the wall to give Luca room, so we are both under the water. He reaches behind me, grabs the washcloth, and holds it under the water, squeezing shower gel onto it. I expect him to hand it to me, but he doesn't; instead, he starts washing me, starting on my arms and working his way down. I close my eyes, sighing because it feels nice, intimate too.

"Beautiful," he whispers, "every inch of you."

His touch is gentle and enough to make my entire body shiver.

"Thank you." I breathe out.

"Turn around, gorgeous."

I do as he asked, and he continues until he has washed every inch of me. He cleans himself after finishing with me. Once we get out, he slips a towel around me first before getting one for himself.

"You need to eat before you go to work." He says, his tone's firm and with a stern look on his face, "Even if it's only something quick."

"I planned on it. Calm down." I laugh, shaking my head.

"Good, now get your sexy ass to the bedroom to get ready."

"Yes, boss!" I reply, saluting him.

I turn to go, and he swats my ass before I walk away. Luca's hot on my heels. I quickly dry off, put some clothes on and started organizing my bag.

"I will go rustle us something up while you get sorted." He smiles.

He kisses me softly and leaves me to it. I couldn't be assed with work tonight, but I don't have a choice. I'm eager for a couple of days off together. I double check I have everything before heading through. Luca is in my kitchen cooking. I don't know what, but it smells good.

"What are you making?" I question, curiously peering over his shoulder to see, "oh, grilled cheese, yum."

"I know you don't have much time, so I thought grilled cheese and a side salad would be filling enough for now," he says smiling.

I kiss his cheek, "Thanks, love."

"Why do you call me that?" he asks, looking at me with a wondering look in his eyes.

"Habit, I guess. Do you want me to stop calling you that?" I question, nervous in case it was freaking him out.

"No, I don't mind." He smiles, his eyes bright and kisses me softly.

I'm glad it isn't freaking him out. I didn't mean to start calling him that, but once I began to, it became the norm. He parts from my lips, and I prep the salad just in time for him to plate the grilled cheese up.

We settle down at the table and dig straight in. This will keep me going until my break later.

"Do you want to go out for breakfast tomorrow?" Luca asks as we walk hand in hand to the hospital.

"Sure, that would be nice." I beam, I am so happy right now.

We arrive at the hospital, and he pulls me into his chest, planting a tender kiss on my lips. I snake my arms around his neck and kiss back in the same manner. I feel my heart racing in my chest.

"Call me later." He suggests as our lips detach.

"I will when on break." I smile, retaking his lips with mine.

I was not ready to stop kissing him yet. He smirks into the kiss, holding my hips tightly. I moan, feeling myself getting revved up, my cue to pull back. I did, but he kept a hold of me. He strokes my hair and kisses my forehead.

"Luca?" we hear from behind us.

I recognized the voice of one of the Doctors, but how would he know Luca? I feel him tense, as he looks over my shoulder.

"Hello, Dr Flanigan," he whispers, his voice shaky.

"It has been a while. How are you?" Dr Flanigan asked.

"I am better, thank you. How are you?"

I step aside, so I wasn't in between them.

"I am glad to hear that. I am okay, thank you," Dr Flanigan replies.

I look between them; they obviously know each other. Maybe he has treated Luca at one point. I sense an awkwardness on Luca's part. Luca nods, not saying anything else.

"My offer still stands, even three years later. You know where I am if you need to talk about that night or if you need someone to talk to," Dr Flanigan says.

"Thank you, but I will be fine," Luca replies, sadness pooling in his eyes.

Dr Flanigan says goodbye to us and makes his way inside. I glance over at Luca, and his entire body language has changed. The smile has gone from his face; his fingers fidget with the material of his jeans, and his body posture seems tight.

"Luca, are you okay?" I ask worriedly.

"Fine. I need to go. Bye," he replies quickly and rushes off.

I'm left confused and wondering what the hell just happened? I don't think I've ever seen someone change so rapidly. Whatever went down seems personal. I sigh, and run my fingers through my hair. I will talk to him about it later, but I have to get my attention on my work right now. I change into my scrubs and start my shift. I need to try not to get too distracted by what happened with Luca. He may tell me when I ask; he may not.

"Hello," Dr Flanigan said, appearing at my side.

"Hello, again." I smile.

"Have you known Luca long?" he questions.

"Not too long. You?" I wanted to ask why he knew him, but I would never because of the doctor-patient confidentially.

"I met him a few years ago. Is he doing, okay?" he asked with a look of concern on his face.

"He has his good and bad days," I answer. It isn't my place to say any more than that.

We part ways after that, both having a lot of work to do. The emergency room seems quiet for now, but it was still early. I do my rounds, taking the time to chat with the patients, which I enjoy. Sadly, we don't always have the chance to do this if we are overly busy. It's another reason it is more challenging when we are short staffed. We can't have any one-on-one time.

I take a seat at the nurses' station once everyone was seen to. I grab my phone and wrote a text to Luca.

Hey, why did you rush off? Is everything okay? X

I don't know if he will text me back. It's viewing as ready but not replying. I guess he isn't prepared to discuss it. I don't want us to go back steps. I would rather we go forward, especially because of how far we have come. The second I slip my phone back into my pocket, I feel it vibrate. I take it back out and see a text from Luca.

I don't want to talk about it. I will see you tomorrow X
Okay. See you tomorrow X

His walls are going back up, which is the last thing I want. I will let him be, for now. Hopefully, he will answer his phone later when I call. I push it to the back of my head and concentrate on my paperwork.

"Kayla, are you okay? You seem to have something on your mind?" I hear my colleague Dana ask, making me look up.

"Been a strange night..." I trail off.

"Something to do with that cutie you were kissing outside?" she smirks.

"Yes, it's a long story, and I don't want to get into it." If I start telling her the story, we could be here all night.

"Okay, but if you change your mind, you know where I am." She smiles.

"Thank you." I smile back.

I wouldn't take her up on her offer, but I appreciate the thought. She walks away, going to do what she needs and I sit there, waiting until someone needed me. I have a feeling tonight is going to be a long one.

Chapter Thirty-Six

LUCA

I feel terrible because I ignored Kayla's call last night, and cancelled our breakfast plans this morning. Seeing Dr Flanigan just brought everything back. It was the worst time to see him with the third anniversary of Leah's death approaching. My walls have gone back up. I hate myself for it! Of course, none of this is Kayla's fault; she doesn't even know about Leah. I would apologize to Kayla, but I couldn't see her, not today. I don't want to see anyone. All I want to do is get lost in a bottle of Scotch, but that won't solve anything. I chose another option, though, I'm not sure if it will help either.

I am on my way to the cemetery to visit Leah. I had stopped at the flower shop to pick up her favorite flowers, pink lilies. I haven't been by in months; it's time. I pull up in the car, parking it. I sit there for what feels like forever, taking a few deep breaths before finding the courage to move. I lift the flowers from the back seat and slowly make my way to where she is. Leah's parents must have stopped by recently, fresh flowers were already resting against the stone tulips. They always brought tulips. I haven't spoken to or seen them since the funeral. I believe it was too hard for all of us. I will reach out to them one day because I got on great with them, but for now, none of us are ready for it.

I take a seat on the grass, placing the flowers down.

"Hey, beautiful, sorry I haven't been by recently. I haven't forgotten about you, promise. I still think of you every day, miss you every day." I whisper, feeling the tears brim in my eyes.

I can't believe it has been three years already. It still feels like only yesterday. I don't think the pain has eased at all.

"I met someone, Leah, and she is incredible. She is beautiful with a heart of gold and the patience of a saint. She reminds me of you in some ways. But I can't be what she needs. My heart still belongs to you, love, and that isn't fair on her." I whimper, the tears now rolling down my cheeks, a familiar ache in my heart.

Love, something Leah used to call me and the same thing Kayla does too, which I find strange, or maybe it is just a common thing that couples call each other.

"Her name is Kayla, and I am sure you would love her. If I let her in, I am scared, I will start to replace you, and I don't want that. I am not ready for that. I don't ever want to forget about you. I know you will be disappointed in me with the way I have been acting these last few years, and I am sorry sweetheart, but it is the only way I can deal with things."

I am disappointed in myself, and knowing I have let Leah down, everyone down, makes me feel like a worthless piece of crap. I run my fingers through my hair and pull my knees to my chest.

"If you could talk to me, I know you would tell me to be happy, give Kayla a chance, and you would be right." I say with a small smile, "But it isn't that easy. I keep messing up, and I am sure there are only so many times she will forgive me." I add, my voice breaking.

I'm feeling every emotion possible right now. I stay for an hour, talking and sitting. Maybe coming here today wasn't such a good idea.

"I will come back soon, beautiful, I promise. I love you," I say softly and get to my feet.

I wipe my tears away and head back to my car.

"Fuck!" I hiss, punching on my steering wheel.

I lay my head down on it and try to get myself together. I often wonder whether the pain will ever ease. I steady my breathing and sit back up. I check my phone and see a text from Kayla.

I don't know what is going on with you, Luca, but please don't shut me out, not again, not after our last couple of days together X

I hate that I am upsetting Kayla. Yes, I am dealing with a lot, but it is still selfishness on my part because she hasn't asked for any of this. I set my phone aside, not ready to text her back. I need a drink, even if it is only noon. I start the car and drive toward my apartment.

My plan is to go home, lock my door, change into joggers, drink, and switch my phone off for the rest of the day. Work can wait, also. Kayla should be in bed sleeping, so I shouldn't run into her.

I rush inside and go straight to my apartment. I know I shouldn't do this, but it is what I need. I will get back on track tomorrow… I hope. And it's better if I lock myself in and hopefully lessen the temptation of getting something stronger. I have a lonely day/night ahead.

I wake, looking around I realize I passed out on my living room floor. The sun is shining through my blinds. What time is it? I glance at the clock, and see it's eight o'clock in the morning. My head is pounding, and I feel queasy. I shot up, rushing to the bathroom to be sick. I will feel better for it. After I finish, I jump into a quick shower to freshen myself up. I want to catch Kayla coming home from work. I hope she will talk to me after I ignored her.

Once I was organized, I go to wait in the hallway because it would not be as easy for her to avoid me. I slide down the wall to the floor and rest my head against the wall. I close my eyes, stopping my head from spinning. I lose track of time.

"Luca, what are you doing?"

The sound of Kayla's voice makes me look up. She stood with her hand on her hip and her brow raised. I couldn't work out if she was confused or mad. I slowly get to my feet.

"I wanted to see you." I stammer nervously, rubbing the back of my neck and rocking back on my heels slightly.

"What makes you think I want to see you?" she questions, glaring at me.

Mad it is then! I don't blame her. I sigh, stepping closer to her and reaching for her, but she backs away from my touch. **Fuck!** This is worse than I thought.

"I am sorry, angel, I was dealing with some things..." I trail off, my eyes diverting to the ground.

"You are always dealing with things, Luca, and I know it isn't your fault, but I can't be that person you just want around when you are having a good day. This will never work if that is how it is."

There is sadness in her eyes as she speaks, the tone in her voice full of emotion.

"I know, but I told you more than once I need you to be patient with me," I respond, trying to reach for her again, but she refuses me again.

"And I have been Luca, but there is something you aren't telling me! If you can't share what is hurting you the most, how do you expect us to move past it? I need you to be honest with me." She whimpers out, and I can see tears in the corner of her eyes.

I understand where she is coming from, but I will tell her when I am ready and not before it.

"I told you I wasn't ready to talk about it, Kayla! Trying to pressure me into it isn't going to make me tell you any quicker." I snap. I soon regret what I say and how I said it.

"Pressure you? Are you serious? You know what, Luca, I am not in the mood. Do what you want. You always do." She hisses, turning her back to me to open her apartment door.

"Kayla, that was uncalled for. I had no right to snap at you like that," I say softly.

She doesn't respond to me; instead, she let herself in and slammed the door behind her.

"FUCK!" I shout and punch the wall in anger, anger aimed at myself.

My hand throbs, and I see it swelling quickly. It hurt, but I don't care because it doesn't match the ache I have in my heart right now. I've messed things up again, and I honestly don't know if Kayla will ever forgive me this time. I've done worse, but a person can only take so much. Maybe the best thing for me to do is give her some time. I will let her make the first move when she is ready.

I head back into my place, my mood worse than it was yesterday. I take a bag of frozen peas from the freezer and rest them on my hand. I slump down on the sofa. I need to stop fucking everything up, or I will spend the rest of my life alone and miserable, and I will have no one to blame but myself. Once the idea appealed to me a few months ago, but now it doesn't, and Kayla is the reason for that.

I need to get myself together! I've been on a downwards spiral for too long. I know this next week isn't the best time for me to start because I will be a wreck most of next week. I always am at this time of year. I think it's time I see someone. If I continue dealing with things the way I have been, nothing will change. I will lose Kayla for good, and I can't cope with another loss.

I've a lot to think about! I need to get my priorities straight. I never used to be so damn selfish, even after everything I went through when I was young. I can't keep living in the past. It won't change anything.

Chapter Thirty-Seven

KAYLA

Luca has been unreachable for the last four days. Yes, I was mad at him, I still am, but I was ready to talk after a couple of days. Now, I am worried sick. I have tried calling, texting, and knocking on his door, but nothing. I have one option left before I call the police. I scroll through my phone, looking for Holly's number. I find it and hit the call button, anxious for her to answer. The second she answers I feel relief.

"Have you or Spencer heard from Luca?" I ask, panicking.

"Kayla, breathe, tell me what is wrong?" she replies. Worry is evident in the tone of her voice.

"Luca, I haven't seen or spoken to him in four days. We got into a stupid argument, and now I can't reach him. Please tell me one of you have heard from him?" I whimper. I am terrified something happened to him.

"I haven't. Let me get Spencer," she replies.

I hope someone has heard from him. The other end of the phone became silent as Holly goes to get Spencer. I pace my living room, trying not to think the worst.

"Kayla, are you still there?" I hear Spencer's voice come through the speaker.

"Yes. Please tell me you have heard from him, Spencer. I am worried sick about him," I sob, the tears streaming down my face now. I feel sick to my stomach with the thought he isn't okay.

"No, I haven't heard from him either. I am sure he will be fine. This isn't the first time he has done this." He replies. I sense he is trying to be calm for my sake, but I can hear in his voice he is concerned too.

"I have called him multiple times, texted, left voice messages, and knocked on his door. I don't know what else to do. What if he has been hurt? What if something has happened to him, Spencer. I don't know what to do," I respond between sobs.

"What date of the month is it?" he asks.

"The eighteenth, what has that got to do with anything?" I snap. I didn't mean to.

"Shit! I know what's wrong. I have a spare key. I will be there in ten minutes." He replies.

"Spencer, what is going on?"

I need answers; he can't just say something like that and not elaborate on it, that just makes me feel worse.

"I will explain when I get there," he answers and then hangs up.

I rush out into the hallway to wait for Spencer, banging on the door as I do, but there's no answer. I can't even hear any movement inside. I begin pacing again as the tears continue to fall. I know this isn't the first time Luca and I haven't seen each other in a few days, but I usually hear from him.

It feels like forever, even if it has only been ten minutes when I see Spencer approaching me. He looks at me and sees the state I am in.

"Hey now, he will be okay," Spencer says, pulling me in for a hug.

"What is going on?" I ask desperately as we part.

"He hasn't told you about Leah?" he asks, surprised.

"No, who is she?" I question him, confused.

"Leah was Luca's girlfriend; he was going to propose to her. She got killed three years ago, three years ago today, by an idiot who ran a red light. He always disappears at this time of year. He blocks everyone out, locks himself in and drinks stupid amounts. We've tried different ways to distract him over the years, but nothing's ever worked," he says sadly.

I feel my heartbreak for Luca. That explains a lot. That's why he keeps me at bay, why he's hurting, and scared to be with anyone else. I feel horrible for acting the way I did. I can't even imagine how he feels, losing someone like that.

"I didn't know. No wonder his heart is so guarded, and he is scared. He seems to lose the people that mean the most to him."

"He has had a tough life. Kayla, you should be prepared before we go in here. He will be a mess, worse than you've ever seen him. The apartment will be a mess, and he probably hasn't even showered the last few days. It's hard to see, but sadly we haven't yet worked out a way to help him." He sighs, clearly worrying about his best friend.

I nod, and he finally lets us in. I prepare myself the best I can. The place is in darkness; all the blinds and curtains are closed. Spencer switches a light on, and the first thing that comes into view is the empty bottles and can lying around everywhere.

"Luca?" I call out since he is nowhere in sight.

We get further into the apartment, and that's when I see him. He's on the floor, surrounded by empty bottles of Scotch, and I can see he has been sick. I dash over to him, making sure he hasn't choked. I get down on my knees, check his breathing and pulse, both of which were okay.

"Luca, please wake up." I cry, shaking him gently.

He groans but doesn't move. Next thing Spencer comes over, a jug of water in his hand and throws it over the top of him.

"What the fuck," he slurs, sitting up.

He looks around, his eyes finally on me. He seems like a broken man. His eyes are red and puffy, I assume from crying and the drink. His hair's a mess, his stare blank. He smells of puke and alcohol.

"Kayla?" he stammers out.

"Hey, love." I smile, stroking his face.

He closes his eyes and moves into my touch.

"I am so sorry. I never meant the things I said to you. I didn't mean to make you cry or upset you." He sobs.

"It's okay, baby boy. Spencer told me about Leah." I reply gently, "Come here." I add. He comes closer and rests his head in my lap.

"I got you, Luca," I whisper, playing with his hair, and he starts crying.

"I miss her, Kayla, but I need you. I want you, but I am scared I will forget about her, or I can't be everything you need." His voice sounds as broken as he looks.

"Shh, love, don't worry about any of that right now, okay?" I reply, kissing the top of his head.

He has enough going on right now, I don't want him stressing over us. I let him lay there and cry. I look around, spotting cocaine on the table. I sigh. I wish he would stop taking it. Though, I don't think he has touched it since the last time I questioned him about it. Something catches my eyes on the floor, a photo. It was of a beautiful brunette with bright green eyes and a stunning smile.

"Is that Leah in the photo?" I ask, reaching for it.

"Yes, one of the last photos I have of her," he replies sadly.

"She was beautiful." I smile.

He must have truly loved her for him to still be suffering so much pain three years later. You can't put a time limit on grief. Everyone deals with it differently. He takes the picture from me and sets it aside.

"Kayla, can you take him to get showered, and I will clean up?" Spencer asks from behind me.

"I can do that."

I encourage Luca to get up and help him through to the bathroom since he is unsteady on his feet. I switch the shower on to let it heat up.

"Let's get you in the shower, my love." I smile, helping him get his clothes off.

I take my shoes off, assisting him into it, and he sits on the floor of the shower. I take a spot on the floor outside of it. Luca brings his knees to his chest, hugging them. I have never seen someone as vulnerable and hurt as he is now. It's not easy to see. He rests his head on his arms and turns to me.

"Will you give me another chance, angel?" he asks, his voice full of hope.

"Yes, but don't ever scare me like this again, Luca. I thought something bad had happened to you…"

He reaches his hand over, taking mine in his.

"I won't, I promise." He says, bringing my hand to his lips and kissing my knuckles, "I… I am crazy about you, Kayla." He stutters nervously, squeezing my hand.

"And I about you." I smile, reaching over to kiss him softly, not caring about how his lips taste right now. It's only a peck.

I haven't had feelings this strong or soon before. I didn't realize just how much I wanted him, or needed him until after these last few days. I care for him, a lot, and what I feel for him is strong.

"Thank you for not completely giving up on me, even when that is what I deserve." He looks at me, and his eyes seem slightly brighter now, the blank stare no longer on his face, instead, it's a small smile.

"I told you I wouldn't."

I help him to his feet and give him a hand to get washed. I don't mind that the water is soaking me. Once done, I guide him out and slip a towel around him and lead us to his bedroom. He takes a seat on the bed as I get him a pair of joggers. He manages to do it by himself and slips them on, then climbs into bed.

"I will be back soon. When is the last time you ate?" I question.

He shrugs. I will take that as not recently. I will make him something light to eat. Going into the kitchen I see Spencer has cleaned everything up.

"How is he?" he asks, concerned.

"He's sad and tired, but he will be okay. Thank you for coming by to let us in. I will stay here tonight with him, so if you need to go home, that is fine. I will make him something to eat."

Spencer makes sure I'm okay with that, which I am. He tells me to call him if either of us needed anything before he finally leaves. I hope Luca will sleep soon for the remainder of the night because he probably hasn't been getting any of that.

I rustled him up a ham and cheese sandwich, take a bottle of water from the fridge, and re-join him in the bedroom.

"Eat this, please," I suggest, placing it next to him.

"For you, I will try."

I find myself one of his tees, strip out of my wet clothes, and bring it over my head. I climb into bed next to him.

"I've missed you, angel. I'm sorry I scared you," he said, wrapping his free arm around my shoulder, and I snuggle into his side, resting my head on his shoulder.

I nuzzle his neck, his breathing becoming heavier.

"I missed you too." I breathe out. Having him close feels good. It feels like we have been apart longer than four days. I feel a sense of belonging in his arms. He kisses the top of my head.

"I need to sleep. Can I assume you are staying? Please say yes?" he looks at me, waiting for an answer.

"Of course, I am. I am here for as long as you need me." I kiss him. I switch the light off, and we cuddle. He holds me tightly to him.

"Are we going to be okay, Kayla?" he asks anxiously, his fingers tickling the skin of my back.

"Yes, we will be just fine, Luca. We have a lot to talk about, still a lot to learn. We need to be open and honest completely for this to work. Can you do that for me?" I kiss over his chest.

"I will do anything for you, sweetheart."

That is all I need to hear for now. I move up to kiss him goodnight, and we settle down. I hear his breathing become shallow, and he is out like a light in a matter of seconds. He will be physically and mentally drained.

"I got you, my love, I swear," I say quietly and close my eyes, hoping for sleep to take over.

It is only nine o'clock at night, but I haven't slept much recently because of everything that's happened. I am ready for a good night's sleep, too, and tomorrow we can talk things through.

Chapter Thirty-Eight

LUCA

The second my eyes open, the first thing I do is reach over to make sure Kayla is next to me. I was worried last night was nothing but a dream while in my drunken state. I let out a sigh of relief when I realized she's here.

"Kayla." Her name came from my lips in a whisper.

"I'm still right here, my love," she replies.

I roll onto my side, and Kayla does the same, so we are facing each other. She smiles and reaches over to caress my face. A simple touch from her is enough to get my heart racing.

"Morning, angel." I smile back, leaning in to kiss her softly.

"How are you feeling?" she asks, her voice gentle.

"Emotional…" It's the best word to describe the way I am feeling. I have a mixture of emotions running through me—sadness because of the time of year, confusion due to not remembering the last few days, happiness because Kayla is here with me, and that is only the start of my list.

I should have been the one to tell Kayla about Leah, but a part of me is glad that Spencer did, and she stuck around even after everything. It was wrong of me to vanish without a trace for four days. Spencer and Holly know I can be like that at this time of the year, but Kayla didn't, and it was unfair of me to make her worry about me the way I did.

"Do you want to talk about it?" she asks, running her fingers up and down my arm.

"Not right now. I want to talk about us. Everything else can wait until later." I respond, bringing her closer to me, our bodies pressed together.

Yes, we have a lot to discuss, but in this moment, the most important thing is us.

"Are you sure?" she confirms, and I nod, "okay then, we can talk about us."

I know I should start. I am the one who has fucked up more than once, and I need to tell Kayla how I genuinely I feel since I haven't done the best job of showing it. I take a breath. I can feel my heart beating rapidly, and I am nervous. I haven't spoken about my feelings in-depth for a long time.

"My behavior towards you since we met has been all over the place, and for that, I… I am sorry. Now you know why. I hope you understand that it had nothing to do with you. It's all on me. I… I haven't felt anything in such a long time, especially feelings of the romantic kind, and I have forgotten how to express them." I stammer out, my palms beginning to sweat.

"I do understand." Kayla replies, resting her hand on my chest, right where my heart is, "Your heart is beating like crazy, baby boy. Relax, it is me you are talking to." She adds, her voice enough to calm me.

I couldn't help but feel apprehensive with the entire situation. It has never been easy for me to open my heart to anyone, and the last time I did, look what happened? I sometimes wonder if I am some sort of curse or cursed. That sounds ridiculous, but it seems like anytime I let anyone close, they either hurt me in the way my so-called parents did, or I lose them; it happened with Jasper and Leah. I need to stop thinking of my past, now isn't the time.

"I know at times it didn't seem like I gave a damn about you, Kayla, but that couldn't be further from the truth. When we first met, it was purely sexual for me, it was the main reason I initiated myself into your life. And to start with, that was all it was, but the more time I spent with you, got to know you, I realized it was more, my feelings changed, and it scared the hell out of me. I was nowhere near ready to give myself to someone else entirely, but as the days passed, then the weeks, my feelings became harder to fight, and it was because of them I acted like an utter dickhead many times," I say, then force myself to stop to take a breather.

I plan on putting it all out there. Kayla deserves my honesty and openness one hundred percent. Kayla has made it clear she has feelings for me, and hopefully on the same level as mine are. Surely, they are as strong. Why else would she have stuck by me the last few months?

"What I am trying to say is I am crazy for you, Kayla. I am utterly smitten. When you are around, I can be myself, brokenness and all. You never fail to make me smile and laugh, which isn't an easy thing to do. You deserve so much better than me, but I hope you are willing to give us a chance because I am falling for you—hard and fast. I can't promise to be perfect, but I can promise to try my best for you. I want to be the man to look after you, protect you, and love you." I breathe out, my voice breaking, and my hands shaking.

It feels incredible getting all of this off my chest, but it is so nerve racking at the same time. I don't do vulnerable well, and right now, that is what I am, but after last night, and the way Kayla saw me, I guess this is nothing. I take a moment to steady my breathing and wait for her to respond. She is looking at me with a look in her eyes I can't read. I can usually tell what she is thinking but not now, which puts fear in me. What if I have said too much? Suddenly her lips curl into a smile. A smile is a good sign, right?

"Luca, you are what is best for me, what I want. This will not be easy for either of us, but anything worth having isn't easy. I care about you more than you realize. I have never met anyone like you. You are unique, for sure, in the best way. I don't expect you to give me all of you so soon because I know you are still grieving. I just need to know that in time you will be able to give me your heart." She replies, the last words coming out is a sharp, ragged breath.

I believe she's worried in time I won't give her my everything, and I understand. Leah will always have a place in my heart, but I also have room for Kayla.

"Kayla, sweetheart, I'd give you the world if I could. Yes, Leah will always be in my heart, but I know I will eventually love you, and it will be different," I respond honestly, stroking her face.

The last thing I want is Kayla thinking she is going to have to compete with Leah. That isn't the case. Yes, what I had with Leah was incredible, but we had our time, and sadly she got taken away from me, which still kills me every day, but if I ever want things to work with Kayla, I need to let Leah go in some way.

"Please don't take what I said as me trying to replace Leah, because I would never want to do that. All I ask is one day you can learn to love me, and find somewhere in there for me." She whispers, placing her hand over my heart again and looking at me with eyes full of wonder and hope.

I press my lips to her, and she instantly moans, kissing me back, and snakes her fingers into my hair. I grip her hips and hold her tightly to me. The kiss lasts a minute before we part.

"You already have a place in there, angel, and have done since the moment you showed me you gave a damn." I smile. It's the truth; no, it isn't quite love yet, it is getting there, that will take time, though, but she is special to me.

"Be careful with my heart too, okay?" she whispers, running her fingers into my hair.

After everything she went through with her ex, I am sure she is scared to give her heart again. I don't want to add to her pain, I'd rather be the one to take it away from her, to help her heal.

"I promise, beautiful," I answer, capturing her lips with mine.

The kiss is soft, sensual and passionate, and says so many things. It is like everything we discussed is being spoken again in this one kiss. I didn't want it to end, but I had to pull back to catch my breath. I rest my forehead to Kayla's, smiling and holding her face in my hands.

"Does that mean I can officially call you mine?" I smirk.

"Hmm, yes, only I get to do the same," she replies, smirking back.

"I am sure I can deal with that, I guess..." I tease, giving her a dorky smile.

"Hey! If you don't want to, I will find someone who is willing," she says smugly, and shifts away from me.

No, that isn't going to happen. I swiftly stop her, pinning her back to the mattress and climb on top of her, sitting on her so she couldn't move. I take her hands and hold them above her head, restraining them with my hands.

"Nope! You are mine now and only mine. If any other man comes near you, I will not be held responsible for my actions, sweetness. I am protective of what is mine. I don't share." I state firmly and attack her neck with my lips.

She laughs and squirms below me, trying to wriggle out of my grip, but failing.

"Mine!" I moan, biting her neck.

Kayla moans and shudders below me. I will be the first to admit I am a jealous man when it comes to my girl. I don't take lightly when other men look at what is mine. You can call it possessive, but not in a crazy, horrible way.

"Yes, yours." She breaths out, digging her nails into my hands.

"Good, and don't forget it," I respond, swatting her thigh.

"Yes, sir." She pants and rolls her hips up against me, "I think you should claim what is yours right now."

The last part comes out more of a demand. I groan at her words.

"Happily…" I trail off and cover her lips with mine roughly.

Things are different now, and I plan on showing that. I don't plan on rushing anything. I want to take my time with Kayla, and show her I can be gentle and caring, yet still be passionate. We have had moments similar before, but everything has changed since then.

I am ready to show her the other sides of me.

About Author

E.L Shorthouse is a new up and coming author. She has been writing from since she can remember. What started off as song lyrics and silly stories turned to more the older she got. She is a writer on many writing apps, under different pen names where many of her books have been read by millions. E.L shorthouse finally decided to take the leap to self-publish on Amazon in the year 2021, her debut book, a young adult book, which is one of the many genres that she can write.

E.L Shorthouse is not only a writer of young adult books. Her main genres include romance and erotica books. She has many books planned for release over the next year.

E.L Shorthouse is from a small town in the west of Scotland where she was born and raised. She is very proud to be Scottish and enjoys mentioning her home country in her books, some even set in Scotland.

She can be found on Facebook https://www.facebook.com/AuthorELShorthouse

Also By

Seducing My Professor

Two Souls Series

Two Broken Souls

Two Healing Souls

Two Unbreakable Souls (Coming Soon!)

Printed in Great Britain
by Amazon